HOOK, LINE & SINISTER

HOOK, LINE & SINISTER

EDITED BY

T. JEFFERSON PARKER

THE COUNTRYMAN PRESS
WOODSTOCK, VERMONT

Hook, Line & Sinister
ISBN 978-0-88150-866-6
CIP data are available.

Book design by Bob Kosturko
Composition by Jacinta Monniere

Published by The Countryman Press, P.O. Box 748, Woodstock, VT 05091
Distributed by W. W. Norton & Company, Inc., 500 Fifth Avenue, New York, NY 10110
Printed in the United States of America by Versa Press, Peoria, IL

10 9 8 7 6 5 4 3 2 1

CONTENTS

PREFACE · vii

RIVER TEARS—RIDLEY PEARSON · 1

CUTTHROAT—MARK T. SULLIVAN · 39

BLUE ON BLACK—MICHAEL CONNELLY · 65

UNSNAGGABLE—JOHN LESCROART · 76

DARMSTADT—ANDREW WINER · 97

CHERCHEZ LA FEMME—DANA STABENOW · 119

SANDY BROOK—DON WINSLOW · 134

THE NYMPH—MELODIE JOHNSON HOWE · 147

TIGHT LINES—JAMES W. HALL · 155

EVERY DAY IS A GOOD DAY ON THE RIVER—C. J. BOX · 177

DEATH BY HONEY HOLE—VICTORIA HOUSTON · 192

THE BLOOD-DIMMED TIDE—WILL BEALL · 214

DEAD DRIFT—SPRING WARREN · 235

GRANITE HAT—BRIAN M. WIPRUD · 264

MR. BRODY'S TROUT—WILLIAM G. TAPPLY · 276

LUCK—T. JEFFERSON PARKER · 300

CONTRIBUTORS · 321

PREFACE

This book is further proof that anglers love to write and writers love to fish. Much has been said and written about why this is true—some itself true and some of it less so. I think the nub of it is that writers and anglers are happy to trade the known for the unknown. The blank page yields words that were not there; the unpromising water yields fish that were not seen. Mysteries both.

But blank pages and bodies of water are stubborn, private things. The author/angler wants passionately to extract something wild and unseen from them and this is an unpredictable enterprise. It can be joyous and it can be heartbreaking. As is often the case, it's the passion that lights the way.

Here are sixteen short stories by sixteen author/ anglers. The only instructions they were given were to write a mystery that involves fishing. Not all of these authors are mystery writers, but for this volume they all wrote a mystery.

These writers almost uniformly jumped at the chance to contribute. Back to that passion thing. None of us could staunchly resist the opportunity to write about something we truly love to do. However, I will say that often, when I had a question about a story, my phone call or e-mail to a contributor might go unanswered for days. Why? Because my writer was out fishing, of course.

We all had one more incentive to write a story for this book. It's a fund-raiser for two fine groups.

One organization is Project Healing Waters, which takes wounded combat soldiers on fishing trips to help heal body and soul. Healing Waters does some truly wonderful work. It's their way of saying thank you to these men and women.

The other group is Casting for Recovery, which takes women suffering from cancer on fishing excursions in search of restorative hours. They've done some terrific things for women who are fighting valiantly to keep a disease from taking away their passion and their lives.

The authors here will donate all their royalties, equally, to these two groups. And our publishers, The Countryman Press and W. W. Norton, will donate a portion of their proceeds also.

So enjoy the stories. You'll be surprised at what these writers have pulled from blank pages and bodies of water.

Special thanks to Rick Raeber of W. W. Norton and publisher Kermit Hummel of The Countryman Press, in whose fertile imaginations this book began.

Special thanks also to Ridley Pearson, who came up with the title. For that, my friend, you get to lead off.

T. Jefferson Parker

RIVER TEARS

RIDLEY PEARSON

The karst mountains appeared through the gray veil of "fog"—air pollution so thick it reduced visibility to less than a half mile—looking like bishops' caps in a Vatican ceremony. The Li River showed little sign of strong current; the flat-bottomed fishing vessels moved lazily across the surface like sun-drugged water bugs. Or maybe it was simply that Karen and Skip, watching from the observation deck of the riverboat, wanted to ignore the small horsepower outboard motors and see instead the China of a hundred, a thousand years earlier. Maybe they wanted to believe the fog was fog, that time had changed nothing and their marriage remained strong. Vacationing couples not only bought discounted brand-name knockoffs from street vendors, they bought illusion as well. If they'd wanted reality, they would have stayed home.

"I don't blame you," she said, leaning against the rail, then wiping her hands on his jeans, unwilling to soil her own skirt, a colorful thing she'd bought in Provence a month earlier. For all of her wanting to be here, Karen seemed to believe there was an antiseptic way to see the country, the Discovery Channel but without the screen and surround-sound speakers.

"Sure you do," he said. "I thought we weren't going to talk about it. Or were you just waiting for somewhere I couldn't walk away from it? Somewhere you had me trapped."

"We have to talk about it."

"Why? Because some counselor says so? I don't think so."

"Because it's become this thing between us."

"No it hasn't."

"Of course it has."

"Has not."

"Look! We can't even talk about it."

"Because there's nothing to talk about."

"That's not true, and you know it." She was beginning to sound like the counselor herself.

"You want a beer?"

"And why is it every time we try to talk about it, you need to drink?"

"I don't need to drink. I'd like a beer. I imagine there might be one somewhere on this thing. I saw some people eating down below."

"It's simple enough to do."

"Jack off into a petri dish? No thanks. And you know that's not the point. Not my point, anyway. The point is. Well, shit, we've been over this a thousand times."

"But it's a scientific process."

"No, it's biological. If it's going to happen, it's going to happen. If it's not. Well . . . no guarantees, right? You see what you're doing by starting this again? It goes nowhere. Will never go anywhere."

"That's your opinion. My opinion is that we should get—"

"I'm not going to manufacture a baby," he said. "I'm not going to measure, mix, and repeat, or count days or spin sperm or whatever."

"But it's so selfish!"

He found a beer a few minutes later that said ADVANCED TECHNOLOGY on the label, as if brewing hops was something new. It tasted bitter but had more alcohol than American beer, meaning he liked it a lot.

They watched the landscape of limestone spires slip by while their feet vibrated from the shudder of the riverboat's engines, and cormorants dove and disappeared beneath the murky brown water only to reappear thirty seconds and twenty yards later. They listened to the endless chatter of Mandarin and watched as barefoot, dark-skinned children ran along the shore as the river turned to reveal yet another small village of stone buildings with tile roofs.

He had two beers, she a Coke. She took pictures with her iPhone. He checked for BlackBerry reception, surprised to find he was still connected all these miles from Guilin. Was tempted to marvel at that to her, but was afraid she'd dampen his moment, so he kept the thought to himself and put the BlackBerry away, wishing they'd never agreed to the whole around-the-world honeymoon thing. There was no such thing as a delayed honeymoon; the reason you took one quickly after the marriage was to recover from hangovers and spend a lot of time in bed before you learned too much about each other. They were two years past that opportunity; they knew too much and shared too little and the bedroom activities had lasted all of the first three nights on this six-week voyage. Then she'd gotten her period, he'd had some diarrhea, and they'd both lost interest. They read now, or pretended to be involved in television broadcasts in languages neither of them spoke.

They spent that night in Yangshuo at a small hotel out on a single-track road that ran along the river's edge, up a hill so steep and with a driveway so narrow, the taxi drivers tried to drop you off at the bottom. Spent the night in twin beds with a wall-mounted air conditioner wheezing and some yesterday rock-and-roll floating down from the rooftop bar with a name like Margaritaville or some other Jimmy Buffett–influenced title that had nothing to do with China. He spent much of it awake, making breakfast a quiet affair where he drank black tea and avoided the scrambled eggs because he'd seen how chickens lived here and we wanted nothing to do with it.

He drank a beer at ten-thirty under a scorching sun outside a western café while she browsed the stalls on West Street, collecting scarves she'd never wear in Palo Alto. She orbited by his location, drawn like a moth to flame, hoisting yet another bag to indicate her success, and he mugged a smile that they both knew fell short.

The sign read "RIVER TEARS, CORMORANT FISHING, DAY CRUUZ." He'd been facing it through two beers but only read it now as he leaned back to doze before she came back for him and dragged him off to lunch. He crossed the crowded market street and sign-languaged his way through a young woman's Chinglish until he thought he'd made an appointment for nine o'clock that evening. But when they arrived at the boat ramp, those many hours later, the same woman threw her arms in the air and cackled and wailed and left the impression he'd screwed it all up and that the reservation either had been missed or was for a future date—he couldn't figure out which.

He spotted a nearly toothless old man with a hunched back and a fine smile watching him in the yellow light of the quay. He approached the man, dragging a reluctant Karen by the arm. Pointing to the water and then to the birds in the bamboo cage in the front of the skiff and making diving motions with his hand, he won a vigorous nod of assent from this fisherman, who gestured them into his low flat boat. For the first time, Skip discovered the bent bamboo pontoons were in fact PVC plastic. Disappointment seeped through. He thought they were about to shove off when the old man called brightly up the cracked concrete roadway and a pale electric lantern appeared from under a blue-glowing awning, throwing its light onto the thin arm that carried it.

He thought it was a boy at first, perhaps thinking that fishing was boys' sport or maybe that the loose-fitting shorts, torn T-shirt, and thin frame had to belong to a boy. But the shadows fled behind the glow of the lantern and the black hair was pulled back in a long ponytail and a woman grew out of the dark, her shadow dancing to stay with her fast movement.

She climbed onto the boat behind a white smile that caught and reflected light in a way that suggested some other source of energy. No lantern could possibly cause that kind of brightness. And now her eyes came alive as well, and Skip couldn't help but notice the cracked skin on the soles of her feet, the worn flip-flops, couldn't miss the music of her laugh as Karen tried to say hello in Mandarin. Couldn't keep his eyes from the glimpses of skin through the tears in her shirt and wondering if the holes were intentional, whether the shirt had been bought "as is" from one of the stalls on West Street, or given to her by a grateful tourist, or if it had simply been hand washed at river's edge for so

long that it was slowly decaying in the same unstop-
pable way as his marriage.

The old man steered the boat into the dark, heading upstream. They soon left the ambient light of the
city behind. Ten minutes later he cut the motor and the
boat drifted with the current. Skip had thought his eyes
might adjust, but they didn't. It wasn't until the girl
hoisted the lantern, revealing the deep brown of her
skin and another flash of white smile, that he saw anything. And then it was everything—the girl, the restless
birds in the bamboo cages, the gentle ruffle of water
along the hull of the boat.

He watched with keen interest as the girl and her
grandfather (for their closeness had to be explained
somehow) moved in concert to first free a bird, then tie
off its neck, and send it over the side. The cormorant
dove almost immediately and stayed down an impossibly long time. Then, as if receiving some signal
missed by the rest of them, the grandfather took the
lantern from the girl and held it above the water and
the bird surfaced, its throat bulging. The toothless old
man looked to Karen and Skip with heightened excitement in his eyes, his thin, parched lips curving into a
grin as he lifted the dripping cormorant into the boat
and miraculously coaxed a small fish from its sealed-
off throat, like a farmer milking an upside-down cow.
The fish flopped in the bottom of the boat and Karen
recoiled from it like a petulant child, letting out embarrassing whoops and cries as the two locals laughed
out loud and the grandfather dumped the bird over-
board for a second time.

Soon, they had three of the cormorants fishing and
returning to the glow of the lantern. A half dozen small

fish flopped and struggled and died at their feet, while Karen kept her eyes averted and Skip found the movement of the girl of far more interest than the fishing. She displayed the well-practiced, choreographed manner of a dancer, or a laborer trying to minimize effort. He heard music as she moved, cymbals crashing as the neck of her shirt sagged open while she was bending over or as he caught the whites of her eyes aimed at him. Untying a bird's neck. Retying another. Her practiced hands going about it blindly. One bird in the cage; another out. And with each movement the chance of a glance in his direction. A faint and provocative smile.

Karen's complaints continued and she grew more obstreperous with the arrival of each new fish.

"What are they going to do with the poor things?" she whined. "We're just killing them for nothing. It's not like we'll eat them. Stop them, Skip. Tell them we get it. Fascinating! Never mind primitive and abusive. Just tell them to stop."

"We paid to fish. Don't worry, what we leave behind will not go to waste. The irony is we've just paid them to fish for their own dinner. They know damn well we won't take the things with us."

"But it's so barbaric!"

"It's been going on for thousands of years. You are getting a glimpse of history, same as the Great Wall or the terra-cotta warriors. Only this piece of history has been feeding these people for eons, and still is."

"It's awful, what they do to the poor birds."

"They give them every third fish. The birds get what they want—food. The old guy gets what he wants. It's symbiotic. If it didn't work out, the birds would take off. The way of nature." He thought about her feeding him his needs, his providing for her, the blurring of lines, the slow disintegration of the string that bound them together.

"They tie a string to their legs. They couldn't take off if they wanted to."

He hadn't thought she'd looked closely enough to know this. But for all her pretense of abhorrence, Karen didn't miss much.

"And besides, you stopped watching the fishing a half hour ago," she said in an accusing tone.

"The show is in how the two of them do this together. It's not about the bird."

"I noticed for you it's not."

"So, you'd like to go back?" he said.

"Only for about the past hour."

He caught the girl's eyes then, eyes that had remained fleeting and elusive for much of the evening. They were fixed on Karen's pearl bracelet. The string was worth less that twenty U.S. dollars, bought in Shanghai's International Pearl City Market the week before. But the way the girl stared, it might as well have been a million, and had Karen not harped upon his own fixation, he might have asked her to part with it right there and then. But he knew better than to try.

They returned to shore. Skip tried to catch the girl's eye again, but she wasn't playing along. She searched the mud around the edges of her flip-flops, her ponytail dancing like a topknot, and he said goodbye in passable Mandarin, drawing a fleeting glimpse and a giggle from her.

He returned with his wife to the hotel room and undressed her before she reached the bathroom, her initial protestations giving way to his determination, and finally she was wrapping her legs around him and holding him around the neck as her backside slapped the wall and the roughness of his unshaved face raised red on her neck. She bit back her cries to mere whimpers, denying him any satisfaction of virtuosity as together they slumped to the wooden floor and lay in a tangle of sweat and scents. She drew patterns on his upper arms while he kissed the salt from her chest.

"Well," she said, "now that that's done, do you think we can get ready for bed? I need a shower now, and you know how I hate showering before bed. I hate it when my hair's wet."

"You don't need to do that, you know," he said, watching her bare ass as she removed her makeup at the mirror. "Make a point of ruining the moment just to make it seem like I was the only one who enjoyed it. You're allowed to enjoy it."

"You know how I feel."

"That it can't just be for pleasure, that it's about procreation? Oh, yes."

"I didn't say that. Not exactly like that."

"Close enough."

"The child part, yes."

"It's okay to feel good. It's okay to want it, to *need* it, even. Men and women."

"Men more."

"Probably. I'll give you that, but that's just because we're more honest."

"As if."

"It's true."

"When it comes to sex, nothing you say is true: you'll say anything to get more."

"That's true as well."

She bent over the sink slightly to get a closer view of herself in the mirror, revealing more of her dark, tawny thatch and sending a pulse of desire through him. She would rebuff him if he tried. Once was always enough for her—she would point out that the semen count in anything after that offered a diminished percentage of a chance for impregnation. She had made the most sanctified part of their union a science, and in doing so had practically emasculated him.

He wished he still smoked. He wanted to climb onto the bed naked and smoke a cigarette and watch the coils of smoke get caught by the ceiling fan.

The shower ran and she came out with a towel on her head, complaining about the water pressure and the temperature of the water and how the hotel didn't provide shower caps. He asked her to lie down with him, meaning she should do so naked, and she put on a nightgown, her back turned to him, and slipped under the sheet. She put her pillow under her bottom, raising it to hold in his sperm, and slept without a pillow under her head despite the discomfort.

The following morning Karen was ill or just bored with him, or afraid he might try for morning sex. She claimed infirmity, and he went out in search of coffee and an *International Herald Tribune,* if he could find one, which he could not. He spent an hour at a café, drinking horrible coffee, watching West Street wake up ever so slowly. Nothing much would open until after ten A.M. Some kids ran around chasing each other, and he marveled that there was no end to the reminder of their failure to produce a child.

He returned a few minutes past nine with a Chinese

attempt at a Western donut, twisted bread with some sugar on it. He had just shut and locked the door when she threw back the covers. She was naked, her bottom on *two* pillows, and she touched herself, which she knew he liked.

"Make love to me," she said.

"Jesus."

She continued to ply herself. "You'd like that, wouldn't you?"

"Whoever you are," he said, pulling off his T-shirt, "what have you done with my wife?"

"I think it was morning sickness," she said.

"No way . . ."

"It passed. I feel better now. I feel fine. I feel . . . *ready*."

He knew what this was: she was just pulling up to the pump at the filling station. But they would both benefit from it, so he saw no harm. In truth, he couldn't stop himself; she knew him too well. For the first time in months the act felt halfway to normal, less about making a baby for her than finishing what she'd started and they celebrated together in a contraction of muscle and clenched jaws and wicked smiles. He lay beside her, buzzing from the coffee.

"I want to stay here awhile," she said. "Not in bed, although that too. I mean here: Yangshuo."

"What? Why?" He didn't see her wanting to be anywhere. Lately she hadn't seemed happy anywhere.

"There's something about this place. The river. The attempt at some Western restaurants. The catering to us. And I don't want to travel when I'm feeling like this."

"It could be the crud, Karen. It could be you ate something bad. It doesn't mean—"

"It means whatever I want it to mean," she snapped. "I want to give it a chance. Okay? It's a nice hotel. I can hang out here. Take it easy. Stop running around. Stop running. Maybe it happens, maybe it doesn't, but we'll know in a few weeks."

"Weeks?"

"Fifteen days. Why not? What's wrong with being here? Can't we stop moving for five minutes?"

"Of course. But I mean: here? There's really nothing here but the mountains and the river."

"You can rent bikes. You love to bike."

"They're single-gear street bikes, Karen. They're not *bikes*."

"I'll bet you can find one."

"And you're just going to lay around in bed?"

"You make it sound decadent. Not like that. I'm taking it easy. I'm looking after myself. That's what you want, right? Go fishing again, if you liked it so much."

He hadn't wanted a cigarette so badly in years. He stood at the window naked, looking out at the sharp conical mountains unlike any others, the swell of green and the gray mist of air pollution. "Well, at least it's some of the most beautiful smog in the world," he said.

She laughed. It had been a while since he'd heard that particular laugh, and he thought she was putting far too much onto her feeling sick, and he feared the crash that would come in the days or weeks to follow. She had grown self-destructive in her determination.

"When I feel up to it, I can shop. It's great shopping here. We can explore the restaurants. You have to admit, there's more choice here than about anyplace we've been in the country."

"In the countryside, yes. That's true."

"So let's stay until we're so bored we want to move on. What's wrong with that?"

She had pulled the sheet over her, her pelvis still hoisted so that her chin pressed down onto her chest.

"Since when do I ever say no to you?" he said.

"Thank you!" She sounded about twelve years old.

By the following day, he'd convinced himself she might be pregnant after all. Either that, or she was a manifest example of mind over matter, the power of the brain over the body, because she began sleeping impossible amounts. Like a switch had been thrown. An hour's nap after breakfast. Two, after lunch. And still tired by evening. He hoped she wasn't seriously ill, even broached the subject, but she rebuked him, claiming she'd never felt better. This, despite several bouts of the dry heaves.

He placated himself with walks up West Street and people watching from the cafés. He began to recognize vendors, and they, him. By the third day he was bored to tears and talked himself into another evening cormorant adventure, seeking out the same small boat with the old man and the girl. They fished for an hour and a half, he rarely taking his eyes off the young beauty, enchanted by her economy of motion, her stunning gracefulness in everything she did, the joy with which she went about her work, the love and generosity she displayed toward the old man and, to a lesser degree, even to him. He left them the fish and over-tipped them again. And like before, he hoped to make some meaningful contact with her once to shore but yet again found her uninterested, content to tidy up the

boat while her grandfather dealt with the *Meiguórén*—
the American.

He returned the next night, and the next, beginning
to sense his obsession with her but content to deny it
by convincing himself he might write a magazine article on the ancient art of nighttime fishing with a bird.
He brought Karen's camera and took seventy shots—
mostly of the girl.

Happily, Karen showed no signs of fever. Perhaps
it was pregnancy after all. On the fourth day she got
out of bed and spent a part of the afternoon shopping,
moving stall to stall like an old lady, so careful with
herself she became the focus of concern and attention
of many of the thoughtful merchants. He tagged along,
embarrassed by her but vaguely tolerant, seeing once
again the effects and extent of her determination to
produce a child.

That evening, following dinner, with Karen heading upstairs to turn in early, Skip found himself walking West Street amid the dim lights, the smell of
cigarette smoke, and the cacophony of Chinese voices.
His legs steered him to the quay where the cormorant
fishers hawked their wares to interested tourists. He
waited there in an outdoor café, drinking Chinese beer
and watching bugs dance on a fluorescent tube light.

At nine-thirty the girl and her grandfather pulled
their flat-bottomed boat up the concrete and tied it off
to an iron ring that had to be a hundred years old. As
she walked back into town, Skip followed.

He kept at a distance, admiring her and feeling
somewhat guilty for his stealth and for his keen interest. She waved hello to merchants on West Street,
bought herself a candied fruit on a wood stick, and

nibbled at it as she continued.

Five minutes later she entered a very narrow dark alley alongside an upscale massage parlor, and he watched her silhouette disappear through a side door. When, five minutes later, she hadn't reappeared, he found he wanted a massage.

He entered through the front and read from a list of offerings on a blackboard: Chinese massage, body oil massage, cupping, foot massage. He was amazed by the prices—a sixty-minute massage ran less than ten dollars.

He asked for a tour and passed a room that held the masseuses, and spotted her without her looking over to see him. He asked the receptionist about her and, when she was identified as "number five," he requested her and an hour of Chinese massage.

He was led up a narrow set of stairs to a small, overly warm room with quiet Chinese music playing through a boom box in the corner. He was left to change into a pair of cotton pajamas: shorts and shirt. He stood waiting.

A knock came at the door. He answered hello in Mandarin. He feigned surprise as the cormorant girl's eyes went wide and a self-conscious smile crossed her face.

For a moment she allowed herself to look both excited and terrified. Then she adopted a more professional demeanor. He hoped his surprise looked genuine. If not, she gave nothing away.

She made up the table with a fresh sheet and a folded towel at the nose hole and motioned for him to lie down. And from the first touch a kind of electricity penetrated him, moved between them. She seemed to sense it as well, working reluctantly at first, perhaps even considering asking someone else to take him for her. But she stayed, and the longer she worked, the more incredible—her hands finding his tension, her beige uniform brushing his arms as she leaned over, touching his face as she craned to work his lower back. He told her in his limited way how good it felt, what a fine job she was doing. She thanked him in a professional voice. Giggled more than once at his compliments. Her hands went beyond soothing him. She drilled down deeper the longer she worked, releasing pain and mingling it with pleasure and unlocking him in a way he'd never experienced. There was nothing sexual whatsoever in her methods. Sensual beyond limits, but not sexual. After a half hour he wished he'd bought two hours. She worked down the backs of his legs, dealt briefly with his feet, and then asked him to roll over. She worked his scalp and face and he opened his eyes to stare up at her, and she gently eased his eyelids shut behind a smile.

When it was over, he asked her about her schedule and she reacted demurely, averting her eyes, but he could tell she was secretly pleased. If he got it right, and he thought he did, she worked seven days a week until six P.M., and then in the boat with her grandfather until late at night. She returned to the massage parlor from ten to midnight if fishing was slow. She did not go by name but by number: *five*. He could ask at the desk for her.

He returned late afternoon and requested her, but she was busy with a customer. Came back at five but was told she'd left for the day.

They went fishing that night, and all he could think of was the way her hands had made him feel, how he wanted her to touch him again, to pull all the tension out of him to where he felt free of Karen and her drama. They finished at nine-thirty, and he used sign language to inquire if she would return to the massage parlor, and she nodded sheepishly. He thought on the way there that she'd agreed only because he'd asked, that had he not asked, she might have gone home with the old man. At her suggestion, he gave her ten minutes and then he entered the establishment and requested her and was shown up to a different room. He changed into the pajamas.

She entered and turned a small wooden peg he hadn't noticed before, turned it to lock the door. Latticework shielded the glass, and she hung a towel over it like a shade, dimming the room to a twilight dusk.

She made up the table and placed him face down and began to work out the same kinks, but this time with the knowledge of his first visit. She deciphered him, quickly finding his tight spots. Moved freely around the table, working from both sides. At one point his elbow brushed her leg, and then as she moved, briefly came between her legs, the warmth of her stinging him. She stayed there a few seconds longer than she should have, long enough for them both to be aware of the contact. Then she broke it off and continued to his buttocks, and down his legs, melting him into the table. She tugged at the elastic of the pajama bottoms and pulled them down a few inches and carefully worked at the base of his spine. He moaned his appreciation and she giggled in that musical way of hers. A minute later, as she switched sides of the table, he reached out and gently took her forearm, stopping her.

They met eyes and she shook her head no and he motioned to the locked door and pulled once on her arm, encouraging her to join him. She looked to the door, back to him, and in her awkward English said, "Roll over please."

As he sat up to roll over she pulled off his pajama top and he wondered if he was in for an oil massage. But then she pulled off her uniform top and bottom, her back to him, and slipped out of an old bra and a frayed, gray pair of tiny underwear, and climbed atop him onto the table.

He lost track of how they came together. It was as if at some point they melded, melted into each other, and she rode him to a dizzying climax, his hands on her waist, hers stimulating his chest, his head lifted and kissing her wrists. She folded and collapsed down onto him, her small breasts nut-hard. He tucked her head into his shoulder, trembling, and he stroked her back, attempting to soothe her.

"Wrong," she said, the first English she spoke that he absolutely understood on her first try.

"No. Perfect," he said.

"Wrong," she repeated. Though she didn't let him go, clinging to him like a child.

He'd never lost track of time in exactly this same way, the days and nights a mixture of massages and night-time fishing expeditions. The grandfather had found his way out of the picture, so that he and Qín—pro-nounced "chin"—set the sampan adrift in the Li River, bats darting overhead, cormorants testing their bondage, and copulated in the extraordinary positions dictated by the limitations of the vessel. Her occasional squeals and giggles bounced off the limestone, reverberating through him to where they would echo long afterward in the quiet of his hotel room, as he stared at the ceiling while Karen gently snored alongside him.

It couldn't have been better for him. Karen absorbed—obsessed was more like it—with her pregnancy, wanting nothing to do with his penetrating her, with no apparent need or desire for sex. On a few occasions she "took care of him," as she so elegantly and romantically put it, manipulating him mechanically, lovelessly, like pumping up a flat tire. She spent her days confining herself to bed, or daring to take a slow stroll down West Street to meet him for lunch, where she would eat nothing more than overcooked chicken and plain rice. Beyond that she left him on his own, rarely asking questions, more interested in his asking her about the changes in her body and what she was experiencing. She would stretch a simple answer into minutes, giving him far more details of her physical condition than he might have wanted. As far as he could tell, pregnancy was a nightmare of growing breasts, constipation, and nausea, and yet it seemed the happiest time of her life.

More than once he suggested that they leave, never meaning a word and carefully timing the offer, knowing her response. Qín tutored him in Mandarin, though not the vocabulary of a typical beginning student. During massage she would school him on the parts of the body, male and female. He proved himself a willing student. Even an overachiever.

Six weeks passed, Karen now insistent they shouldn't consider air travel until after the first trimester. Skip went along, outwardly reluctant to "drag it out" but secretly thrilled. As she napped one day, he borrowed her hairbrush at the hotel's vanity mirror and spotted the pearl bracelet Karen had worn the first night they'd gone cormorant fishing. It peered out from beneath a tangle of necklaces and earrings in the crush of the box's red plush lining. He hesitated only briefly, sweeping the bracelet off the table and into his pocket with the deftness of a magician. He paused there, looking at himself in the mirror, wondering what had become of him, but deciding whatever it was, it was all for the good. He'd never been so perfectly content.

Qín was about to pull her shirt off in the river's darkness late that evening. They hadn't seen each other in several days—he'd been fishing with the grandfather to keep up appearances—when he stopped her. In choppy, poorly pronounced Mandarin he attempted to say, "Me, for you," and he opened his hand, revealing the bracelet. She allowed her shirt to fall back into place, looking in the glow of a single lantern between the luminous pearls and his excited face.

She shook her head and averted her gaze, her chin over her shoulder.

"*Qing,*" he said. *Please.*

Again she refused, her chin brushing her shoulder.

But he took her arm and pulled it to him, uncurled her clenched fingers, and deposited the bracelet into the upturned palm. So small and delicate despite the calluses. Shadows broke across her face, changing with the light and the movement of the sampan, and he thought he saw a tear. She came off her bench and into his arms and kissed him so hard it almost hurt, tore after him hungrily, in a way they hadn't known in many weeks, the act born of her choreography, her desire to pleasure and please him. She delayed him, extended their malfeasance until he found himself repeating, *"Qing, qing!"* to the rhythm of the slap of water against the thin hull and the hoarseness of her breathing. He looked up to see the cormorants in the cage, agitated and shuffling side to side, their black, beady eyes seeming to see right through him.

"Oh, God," he finally gasped, and though she didn't know the words she understood the language.

"Hen hao," Qín whispered, her lips wet on his ear. *Very good.*

Later, she poled them back, forgoing the small outboard engine, standing at the stern, working a long pole, her eyes only on him as he sat on a bench looking back at her, the moon peering through the gray of the smog and the landscape of massive cone-shaped mountains.

The next day she wasn't at the massage parlor, a first, and that night she didn't show up at her grandfather's sampan. The two men fished together in total silence. The birds brought up only a few fish—the worst harvest yet—and the old man looked at the dead fish in the bottom of his boat with concern bordering on disgust, and back at Skip and back at the fish.

Skip headed directly to the parlor and asked after "number five." He was met with vacant looks and the offer of another girl. In his anger he turned over a display that held tourist pamphlets, spilling its contents. Then, embarrassed, he bent to pick it all up and was pulled off by the women, who proved themselves far too forgiving.

He walked West Street and stopped at the tiny shops and tried to communicate with the merchants as to Qín's whereabouts. Greeted with smiles and offers to buy everything from knockoff sunglasses to Tibetan incense, he drank himself into a stupor in the shadows, watching the parade of tourists with disdain.

The day after, she wasn't at work again. He widened his search, going to a bench where Qín liked to sit and watch the old ladies make sandals of straw and burlap. He sat there alone, wondering what could have called her away so suddenly, worried that he meant so little to her that she hadn't bothered to say goodbye. And if not a trip out of town, then what? His mind went half-crazy with possibility, none of it good.

That night her seat remained vacant in the small boat. Skip's mood had turned dark and gloomy. He hadn't eaten dinner. The three beers he'd managed dragged him down into the depths of despair, and he could see in the grandfather's eye a betrayal of suspicion and anger—blame. Inside those eyes he could see everything he'd done—*they'd* done—and for the first time it all seemed so wrong.

At ten o'clock that night, as the old man was beginning to pack it in, a cheer arose from a nearby boat. There was wild talking and hooting, and the calls out across the water sounded to Skip like celebration.

The old man shot Skip a look that stopped his blood cold, started the small engine, and motored straight for the noisy boat, by which time several others had done the same. They pulled alongside, held there by the arms of two ten-year-old Chinese boys and a pair of Australian tourists.

"You won't believe it!" one of the Australians called to Skip gleefully. "Our mate tried to squeeze a fish out of the dumb bird's neck, but it weren't no fish, was it, mate?"

The old man proffered the lantern, extending it toward the wizened forty-year-old skipper of the adjacent plastic-bamboo skiff.

In the fisherman's outstretched palm was a small but delicate white pearl bracelet.

Skip spent undue amounts of time looking over the tables of trinkets intended for the cruise boat tourists. The booths, a commercial gauntlet of long wooden tables beneath rain tarps and sun tarps, were connected one to the other, stretching for a quarter mile up a narrow, almost impassible street where the boats dropped off passengers. He moved between the "jade" bracelets, the stone chops, the shirts, hand fans, and woven hats as if he cared, one eye stealing glimpses at the two police boats dragging the river.

When the sound of shouting voices carried up the rise, reaching his ears, it blotted out all other sound. There was no negotiating, no hawking, no American voices *ooh*ing and *ahh*ing over the goods. Only the sharp cry of a human voice, like a hawk gloating after a strike, a snake dangling from its talons.

Skip maneuvered to the rear of one booth, pulled back a tarp, and stepped behind the booth, into a thick tangle of foliage. Parting the branches, he got a clear look at the excitement below as several uniformed officers took hold of a taut line at the back of one of the two boats and began hauling in their catch. This was not the first time. They'd been pulling up junk for the past two hours, but something warned Skip that this was different, and he found he had to look.

Ten yards behind the drifting boat rose a swirl of darker brown water, and from within that coil of darkness, the lighter tan of human skin. A woman's bare backside, her legs plied open in a frozen V by bloating and rigor mortis. The small twig Skip had been clutching snapped in his grip. His stomach cramped and he doubled over as the men drew the body to the boat like a charter captain landing a sailfish.

He stepped forward and slid down the steep embankment, out of control as he skied through the loose dirt and rock to the quay below. He moved toward town, bushwhacking his way along an overgrown flood wall, as the morbid retrieval continued to his left: the men bending to take hold of her and haul her into the back of the boat, the body he'd prized—cherished—now exposed graphically, tragically, as ugly in death as it had been beautiful in life. He didn't recognize the body, couldn't make out the face. But he knew.

He stopped, retching again. This time his meal came up and he spit bile into the bushes. When he looked up, he caught sight of the grandfather, just below him, his skiff pulled to shore. The old man was looking right at him. He glanced back to the sight on the river, to Skip, and then shook his head.

Skip found himself staggering up the village streets, having little memory of the past several minutes. He would stop, dry-heave, and then pull himself up and continue toward the hotel. The ten-minute walk took him twenty. He was red-faced and sweating profusely by the time he reached the lobby, having drawn scores of curious looks along the way.

He burst into the room and woke her from one of her endless pregnancy naps beneath the lazy spin of a ceiling fan and the mechanical *whoosh* of the wall-mounted air conditioner. She threw a one-eyed look at him.

"What is it?" she croaked out as he crossed the room.

"Hot," he said. "Not feeling well."

"I can see that much. Have you been crying?"

Had he?

She didn't roll over. With any luck she'd gone back to sleep.

He stripped off his clothes, the shower already running. She lumbered into the small bathroom and sat down on the toilet and peed, with her nightgown gathered into her lap.

He stepped into the water and pulled the shower curtain, wanting to be alone. Wanting to be far away from here.

"What's going on?" he heard her say. He used the sound of the shower to avoid giving an answer. The water pounded the crown of his head as it constantly shifted from hot to cold and back again. He tried to steady it but found himself either in flames or ice water. She flushed the toilet and the stream went nearly to pure steam and he jumped back out of the way, got caught in the shower curtain, and nearly dragged it down.

"Oops," she said, realizing her mistake, and then apologized.

The shower curtain raked back and Karen was standing there naked, her nightgown hanging on the door hook behind her.

"You mind?" she asked, not awaiting an answer. "Maybe I can make it fun for you," she said, pressing herself up against his back and reaching around him with both hands. She pushed him forward into and through the now tolerable stream of water, already working up a lather and using it to oil him, anticipating his response. He wanted to stop her. To turn and strike her. Throw her out of his refuge. But he had nothing to fight with. Weighed down under a mental paralysis, he stood there and let her do what she was so intent to do. Felt her breathing deepen against his back, felt her right hand become busy between them while her left stayed in front on him. And slowly they sank together to where she was craned forward onto her spread knees and he was left holding onto a built-in soap dish for balance.

"Oh, my," she said, releasing her teeth from the base of his neck, kissing her way up to his ear. "Didn't expect that. Phew-eee . . ." She sat back, her buttocks wet-slapping the tile, and pulled him down and wrapped her legs around him and they drowned in the shower stream together, both catching their breath. "See?" she said, kissing his back again. "We can find ways."

He thought he might throw up again. Wrestled his way out of the tangled grip she had on him and climbed out of the shower.

"You just got in!" she said, her voice churlish. "Now you're making this embarrassing. I thought you'd *like* that."

He couldn't get a word out. He buried his face in the slightly sour-smelling towel and wondered how far away he could get however quickly.

"That's where you're supposed to tell me how much you did like it," she said. "Skip? Did you hear me? I did that for you, you know? That was 'cause you always want it and are always complaining I don't give it. And so now I gave it and you're supposed to acknowledge that. That's the way it works. Skip?"

She raked back the shower curtain, the rings crying against the rod. Saw a crumpled wet towel on the floor and the bathroom door pulled shut.

"SKIP?"

He kept to the hotel that night, pushing food around his dinner plate, his appetite gone. Found a chair in the breakfast room where he hid behind an English-language newspaper while the eight-year-old daughter of a hotel guest watched a pirated copy of *Madagascar* on a tube television to the left of a toaster held together with melted strapping tape.

Madagascar long over, he waited well into the night before returning to their room, confident of finding her deep in sleep, which he did. But not deep enough. As he stretched out, she murmured and rolled over and threw a leg across him and held to him, and he hated himself in ways he didn't think possible. Considered weighing his pockets down with stones and following Qín into the river, the first time he'd given any thought whatsoever to how she'd died. Her being found naked meant nothing. He knew clothing often came off drowning victims. So he assumed she'd slipped and had gone over the side of her grandfather's boat. The explanation might have worked for him, except that he thought the only time she didn't go out with her grandfather was when she went out alone with him—and that was always late at night. It might have happened while on one of the river-crossing ferries—though it was hard to see how anyone would have missed that. He knew beyond any doubt that for both the grandfather and him, the first suggestion of her drowning had been the discovery of the bracelet. The grandfather's look was one he would never forget.

A morning paper was delivered on the coffee tray. And there, in grainy black and white, Skip saw a photograph of the body being fished from the river, and alongside, perfectly clear, a sidebar photo of the pearl bracelet recovered by the cormorant.

Police seek questions into death of local woman, read the photo's caption.

Karen enjoyed her morning paper. The edition was an undivided, single section.

"I'll split it with you," he said, pulling out a chunk of center pages and handing them to her. These were the restaurant and shopping pages that she liked anyway. He turned the paper inside-out and folded the front page to hide the photo of the bracelet. She'd finally noticed it was missing a few days earlier, had wanted to blame the hotel's housekeeping staff, a notion he'd challenged since she had a routine of misplacing valuables, only to have them surface later.

He waited five minutes before spilling his coffee onto the tray, soaking his section of the paper, and then balling it up and throwing it out.

"Oh, drat!" she'd said. "I'd wanted to read that."

"I'll get you another copy," he offered.

But he never did.

"It's time we go," he said that evening. They were eating together in the small hotel dining room, a space that held six tables and a TV with a DVD player attached.

She looked up from her plate, mindful of his moods. "I've had no complications. Things are going well for the first time ever. Why rock the boat?"

Had she put added emphasis on that last bit? he wondered. Had she cocked her head purposefully? The chopsticks slipped out of his clammy hands. She was the clumsy one when it came to chopsticks. She eyed him curiously.

"Everything all right?" she asked.

"I'm bored," he said.

"What happened to newfound love?"

He felt his breath catch.

"Chinese checkers," she said.

"Ahh! Yes, well, I'll miss that."

"We're almost through it now. It's only going to get better, you'll see. But please—another few weeks. A month at the outside."

He was shaking his head.

"It's critical to make it past at least the ninth week. Twelve is better. Please?"

"I've got to get back."

"If it's money, I can ask Daddy. Do you have *any* idea how excited they are?"

"You are *not* going to ask Daddy for money. I mean if it's your personal money, fine. But not to pay the bills. Not to cover the hotel."

"It costs nothing to stay here."

"We're going back," he announced. "We'll take it easy, I promise. We'll fly business class. We'll be pampered. I'll pamper you."

"Why are you being like this?"

He mugged.

"You don't want this baby," she said, pushing her plate forward.

"Karen, stop it."

"Do you care at all?"

"That's ridiculous, and you know it."

"Do I?"

"You'd better know it. We're going to have this child and many more." He tried for her hand and caught it just as she pulled away. "Count on it."

Her face softened. "Two weeks," she said. "Please." She pulled herself out of her chair as if she were nine months pregnant. She didn't show yet.

"No," he said. "Tomorrow. The day after. As soon as I can arrange it."

"Then you're going alone."

"I will if that's what you want, but your mother won't love it when I get off the plane alone."

Her face tightened. He was pretty sure she could make herself cry at will. She'd used it effectively for years and only on this trip had he cottoned on to her secret.

"I'll do all the packing," he said.

"As if that was ever in question," she said, turning her back on him and beating him out of the room.

The hotel room phone rang thirty minutes after their return from dinner, at eight-thirty P.M. Skip had started packing. Karen had positioned herself on the bed with her knees up, pretending to read a book, but they both knew she was watching him scornfully and trying to compose a response. They both jumped at the sound. Skip had forgotten the room even had a phone. But it was by the bed and she answered. Her forehead wrinkled, she said softly, "Okay. No, no. We'll be right there." She hung up.

"The police are in the lobby," she told him. "They have a guide as a translator. That was the guide. They want to talk to me."

"Police?" Skip said. "You?"

"I know," she said, swinging her legs off the bed. "What's with that?" She stood and approached the mirror and fussed with her face. "Tell me you did not try to get a black-market exchange rate or something."

"No. Doesn't even exist."

"Pot? You didn't buy pot or something?"

"I haven't smoked pot since college."

"Our visas?"

"Must be something like that," he said, remaining at the open wardrobe.

She approached the room door. "Well?"

He turned.

"Coming?" she said.

"I thought you said they wanted to talk to you."

"And so what, you're going to stay here and keep packing, I suppose?"

"You want me to come with you?"

"Jeez, Skip. You think?"

"Okay, okay."

He quickly washed and dried his hands. She followed all this activity with curiosity and impatience. "What are you doing?"

"Washing my hands."

"I got that. But why?"

"I don't know. I just wanted to." He dried them again on the legs of his pants. He couldn't keep them from sweating.

She waited for him to open the door for her and then lead the way out. Skip shut the door, once again dragging his right palm up his pant leg.

The two policemen wore blue uniforms and unflappable, severe expressions; they carried their caps tucked under their left arms as they shook hands with the couple. The translator, a boyish-looking man no older than thirty who was wearing an ill-fitting white shirt, worked through some choppy English.

They sat in the uncomfortable lobby chairs at a marble coffee table. Both policemen smoked, flicking ashes in the general direction of a weathered ashtray.

The policeman facing them and sitting to their right did all the talking. The translator waited and then directed his words at Karen.

"Surely you are aware of the recent drowning of a local girl," the policeman said.

Karen sat up straighter. She looked at her husband briefly, then the policeman.

"I am not. Was not." She corrected herself. "Skip?"

He kept his attention on the policeman. "Yes," he said. "I'd heard about it."

"Most unfortunate," the translator translated. "We are here in this regard. We do not wish to trouble you in this unfortunate incident."

"No trouble," she said. "But I don't understand. I'm afraid I don't understand why you *are* here. What has this got to do with me?"

"We wish only to answer—*ask*"—the translator corrected himself—"a few questions so as to . . . carry off our inquiry—*the* inquiry. It's a simple enough matter. But the family belonging to the girl requests . . . deserves . . . we answer . . . *explain* . . . their daughter's death to the best of our abilities."

"No parent should survive a child," the policeman explained.

"No . . . ," Karen said in a near whisper. She touched her belly and looked again at her husband.

"How did you know about this?" she whispered.

"It was in the paper, I think," he said.

"Specifically, our investigation had led us to question a single item . . ." The lead officer reached into one pocket and then tried its opposite. Skip did not flinch; his eyes did not leave off following the movement of the man's hand. He took out a box of cigarettes, placed one between his lips, and lit it, looking squarely at Skip through the smoke.

As he spoke, the secondhand smoke blew in Karen's direction, and Skip could see that it was everything she could do not to fan it away.

Skip wanted one of those cigarettes badly.

"What was left out of the newspaper article for the sake of the family . . . for the family's sake . . . was that the young girl was pregnant. About four weeks pregnant." He looked between the husband and wife. "It is believed this may have played a factor in her death."

"She killed herself?" Karen spit out, coughing as she finished.

The cop pulled his cigarette to the side out of courtesy, but then took another drag and blew smoke up and in the direction of a ceiling fan.

"The cause of death is drowning," the officer said. "But as I was saying . . ." He held out a hand to his partner. The other man reached into the pocket of his uniform coat and pulled out a plastic bag. As he laid it down, Karen gasped.

A pearl bracelet.

"One of the local market girls remembered you wearing a similar bracelet," the policeman said.

"Well . . . yes," Karen said, scooping up the bag.

Skip felt cold as stone, knew his face must be bloodless, his lips near blue.

Karen caught his reaction. She looked back at the policeman, then addressed her husband. "Look, honey . . . you were right . . . not stolen after all."

"Stolen?" the cop asked, glancing at his partner.

And Karen at hers.

Skip met eyes with her. His were dead and lifeless and resigned.

"Remember, honey?" She studied the bag more closely, and Skip felt it was all intentional, that she'd slipped into an act. Years ago he'd seen her behave this way at social engagements, able to turn on a different person than the Karen who'd entered the party. He'd always admired that ability of hers, but over the years it had faded into her dissatisfaction. She'd become unhappy and had seemed to want everyone to see it in her—the childless mother; the barren woman. God, how he'd hated her for it.

"It's yours?" the policeman asked. But his eyes remained on Skip.

"It most certainly is."

Skip shuddered. He'd prayed she'd have the good sense to disown it. But it was done now. She'd seen her opportunity and she'd taken it.

"It's so obvious," she said, looking at her husband.

For a moment there was only the coil of smoke rising into the wash of the fan overhead. That, and the sound of a cash machine at the reception desk, counting a stack of currency.

"I thought I'd lost it in the room, you see?" she said, addressing the officer. "But my husband . . . he defended the hotel staff, saying they would never steal from me."

The translator relayed this to the two officers. "And of course he was right! We'd gone fishing . . . cormorant fishing . . . on one of our first nights here."

"Yes. We understand your husband has gone many, many times since."

"He loves fishing," she said, reaching over and touching Skip's cool hand. "Don't you, sweetheart?"

"I do." He addressed the officer. "I'm writing a magazine article on cormorant fishing."

"Always with the same boat," the officer replied. "Your evening fishing."

"We struck a bargain," Skip said.

"I must have lost it that first night we went," Karen said. "The bracelet," she said clearly for the sake of the translator. "The girl must have found it."

"Your husband would have seen her wearing it, I would think," the officer said. To Skip he said, "Did you see the young girl wearing your wife's bracelet?"

"I don't recall it," Skip said. "But they're everywhere, you know, those bracelets."

"Not here they aren't," the officer replied. "Shanghai, perhaps. Beijing." He said both place names with distaste. "More common there, maybe. Where did you travel before coming here? What cities?"

"The point is," Karen said, "you found it for me. I'm happy you did. I'm extremely grateful. It's only a trinket, I know, but I'm quite fond of it. I'm pleased to have it back."

"Did you know the girl?" the policeman asked Skip.

"I fished with her and her grandfather. But there's the language barrier, you know?" He motioned to the translator. "We couldn't really communicate."

"And were you aware she worked at a massage parlor here in Yangshuo?"

"Absolutely. I frequented the place."

He didn't think Karen breathed for a moment. She looked transfixed. Skip kept his attention on the policeman, not the translator. Not his wife.

"She was very good," Skip said.

"Excellent, I'm told," the officer said.

"We're grateful for the return of the bracelet," Skip said.

"Are you returning it?" Karen asked, hopefully. "It's okay if you can't."

The policeman studied the plastic bag. He looked at Skip, then Karen. "We are pleased to return your property; clearly, the girl's death was an unfortunate accident. The river claims many lives, I'm sorry to say."

The two didn't just leave. They stayed for a cup of tea and another cigarette each and tried to make small talk. It was a difficult few minutes for all involved and mercifully they finally left, and Skip and Karen went up to their room.

She began packing the moment she entered. She didn't speak a word to him for the remainder of the night, a long night during which she packed all her belongings but a single change of clothing and her toiletries.

Karen awoke to an alarm clock the next morning. The first alarm clock they'd used since their arrival. She showered and applied her makeup and dressed silently. Packed the remainder of her belongings and left the room with a roller bag and her purse.

Skip heard the purr of the taxi arrive and depart and knew he would never see her again.

On the dresser was the small white pearl bracelet, still in the evidence bag.

The dark water swirled and coiled around the nearly silent effort of the fisherman poling the flat-bottomed boat out of the shallows. Skip sat on the rear bench, watching the cormorants impatient in their bamboo cage, the lantern light jumping and shifting with the motion of the boat.

He waited a good fifteen minutes. Waited until he sensed the man was done with propelling the small boat and moving into the fishing stage.

Skip moved to the side, to avoid the drip from the end of the long pole used to punt. He reached into the pocket of his coat, feeling the small beads of the bracelet, feeling relief.

He slipped the bracelet out and hung his hand over the side, ready to release it, to return it to her.

And just then the *swish* of water caught his ear and the play of a golden light caught his shoulder—lantern light. He followed that light to another flat-bottomed boat coming up from behind them, the caged birds at the very front, steadied by a delicate hand. His eye followed that delicate hand to a shoulder and up to the face. She couldn't have been more than sixteen or seventeen but was as beautiful a girl as he'd ever seen, and her smile, as she caught him staring, seemed to glow in the lantern light. He hung his head, hiding his own grin.

Then he returned and slipped the bracelet back into his pocket, patted it from the outside, ensuring it was back where it belonged.

"Let's get fishing," he told the fisherman in passable Mandarin.

The man smiled his toothless smile and nodded excitedly.

The girl giggled as her boat passed by.

CUTTHROAT

MARK T. SULLIVAN

The fires came early to Southwest Montana. By the tenth of August timber complexes were burning in the Beartooth, the Bob Marshall, and in the Helena National Forest near my home.

Which is partially why I was on edge as I drove our pickup back from Billings around one that afternoon. The air in the Yellowstone River Valley was so smoky I could not see the Crazy Mountains as I passed Big Timber. Ash spit against my windshield, making me recall a hellish vision from the night before.

My husband, Tom, and our daughters and I spent hours watering our house as the fire swirled two ridges away. We were witness to a phenomenon known as the dancing ladies, where hot winds blow uphill into a fire feeding on tinder-dry pines. The result was a chain-reaction explosion as entire trees ignited and burned so fast that huge plumes of fire ballet-leaped from tree to tree.

The winds had shifted around midnight, and the fire stopped marching in our direction. But Tom called as I was leaving Billings to say that he thought we should evacuate because the winds were picking up. I told him to wait until I got there.

The rest of my irritation came from the fact that I'd been forced to leave my threatened home at five-thirty that morning to testify in a murder trial in Billings. But when I got to court, the defense attorney asked for a delay. Request granted. Seven hours of driving for nothing. Such is judicial life in Montana.

My cell phone rang. I snatched it up. "Lee Ann Duffy," I said.

It was my boss, Dick Adler, my supervisor in the Montana State Attorney General's Division of Criminal Investigation. He said a fisherman's body had washed up on the banks of the Yellowstone River between Emigrant and Pray. His name was Edward Campbell. Campbell used to run one of the Wall Street fiascos, jumped ship before the crash, and skated with twenty million in bonuses. He'd been getting death threats. Adler wanted me there. I told him I had a house on fire and to send someone else. Adler said the situation was not negotiable.

"Who called us in?" I asked.

"Park County sheriff and Livingston police," Adler said.

Under Montana law, investigators like me have to be invited into any active case. It's a useful law. Because of it we rarely encounter jurisdictional turf battles. The only way we're involved is if local law enforcement wants us.

Forty minutes later, I left Montana State Highway 89 and drove down a long gravel driveway toward police cruisers and an ambulance parked to one side of a log McMansion on the west bank of the Yellowstone between Emigrant and Pray.

I got out of the car, wishing I'd brought a change of clothes. The suit I'd worn for court was stifling in the smoky air. Luckily, I'd brought a pair of running shoes to replace my black dress flats. The sun shone weirdly through the smoke, reminding me of the fire dancing near my house the night before.

"Duffy?" a male voice called.

I spotted Bill Dexter, chief of police in Livingston, and Harry Marks, the sheriff of Park County. Dexter was an intense man roughly my age, thirty-five, with a cow roper's lean body, and Marks was shorter, squatter, with big forearms.

They brought me up to speed as they led me toward the crime scene. Both men knew Edward Campbell. He'd made it a point to stop by their offices to introduce himself shortly after he'd moved out from Connecticut in late March. He said that he'd received death threats and that he feared someone would track him down in Montana. They said they had copies of the e-mails.

I ducked under the tape to find a short, ginger-haired woman named Chris Lunt, a medical examiner who works for my division, kneeling by the body.

The body was half in, half out of the water, and face down on a slip of rocky beach. He wore light tan chest waders with no belt, wading boots, a blue long-sleeved shirt, and a dark green fishing vest.

"Hey Chris," I said. "How'd you get here so fast?"

Lunt said, "I was visiting my aunt in Bozeman."

"And?"

Lunt gestured at the body. "From the temperature of his legs and the minimal bloating you see around his face, I'd say he's been in the water fifteen hours tops."

"You can't get it tighter than that?" I asked.

"He's been half in, half out of the water since before dawn," Lunt said. "Air temp's pushing ninety right now. It throws off everything."

"What else?"

Lunt shrugged. "I'm going to want to see the rest of the body before I make the call, but I'd say from first glance he's a drowner. Wasn't wearing a belt on his waders. I figure he got out deep, slipped maybe, the waders filled, and he was gone."

While Lunt finished her in situ examination and cleared the body to be bagged and moved to the morgue in Livingston, I asked Sheriff Marks to mobilize his men and look for Campbell's car, while I took a trip to his house in Tom Miner Basin.

The drive took fifteen minutes. Campbell's house stood on a knoll facing southwest, looking high into the drainages that drop out of Yellowstone Park. It's big country, the kind you could get lost in, and Campbell's house seemed a response to that vastness, a fortress of huge logs and towering sheets of glass, the kind of place that someone with a monstrous ego builds to tell himself how special he really is.

I went in using the security code Chief Dexter had given me. The interior looked like a photo shoot for L.L. Bean. It struck me as a man's place that had been designed and decorated by a woman, if that makes any sense.

In any case, it did to me at first glance, but I was soon in doubt. There were pictures on tables of Campbell with two children, a boy and a girl. In one they were skiing. In another they were hiking. In a third, they swam in the Yellowstone River wearing life preservers. No woman.

Divorced or dead? I chose divorced. Most widowers keep pictures of their late wives around unless they've remarried.

About that time I noticed that the message light on Campbell's answering machine was blinking. The first message was from Erika, Campbell's daughter, around three in the afternoon, worried about all the fires she'd seen on the news. The second was from a local mason, threatening Campbell with a lien on his house because Campbell was three months past due paying for the chimney work. The third was from Erika again around four the previous afternoon. The fifth and the sixth calls came from a sheet metal roofer and a painter, threatening Campbell with liens if he did not pay his bills, which were sixty days past due.

The seventh message was from Campbell's soon-to-be ex-wife, Alicia, and consisted of several inventive expletives hurled at the former hedge-fund whiz kid, followed by a threat to seek an injunction barring him from talking to his children unless he paid up the support money. The last call had come in just a few minutes before from Yellowstone Angler, a fly shop in Livingston.

"Ned?" came a deep, excited voice. "Pick up. It's Rod Zullo. You won't believe the fish that Jeb Timmons caught. It could be the world-record cutbow from a river. Thirty-six and a half inches. Thirty pounds. From the upper Yellowstone, Ned! They're down here taking pictures. FWP's coming to certify the weight. Call me."

I stood there, semi-stunned. *A thirty-pound fish. Out of the upper Yellowstone?*

I flipped open my cell phone. My husband answered in a hurried tone.

"*We're packing,*" Tom said.

"How close is it?" I asked, fearing the worst.

"*Wind's swirling,*" Tom said. "*Lots of sparks in the air.*"

I had to sit down in one of Campbell's leather chairs, my eyes suddenly burning. "I can't believe I can't come home."

"*By the time you get here, we'll be gone,*" Tom said.

My husband's a fly-fishing fanatic, so I told him about the fish.

The anxiety in Tom's voice disappeared. "*Holy shit! Thirty pounds? That could be a world record!*" He paused. "*Do me a favor?*"

"Anything," I said.

"*Go to that fly shop and take a picture,*" Tom said.

"I'm kind of on duty," I said.

"*Oh, hell, it will be all over the Internet. Who did you say caught it?*"

"I didn't say. But it was Jeb Timmons."

"*Timmons?*" Tom said, surprised. "*That's gotta be the high point of his life.*"

"If you don't count the Hollywood starlets, the Pulitzer, and the Oscar."

"*You're right. But, Jesus, thirty pounds? Your dad's gonna birth a calf.*"

"I gotta go."

"*Love you.*"

"Love you too," I said, and hung up.

I got back in the truck and drove out dialing the number of Campbell's ex-wife. Of all the things I do, this is the task I hate the most, especially by phone.

She answered on the second ring. "*Alicia Campbell,*" she said brightly, with none of the damning tone of the message she'd left the night before.

I identified myself and told her.

"Dead?" she cried softly. *"Ned?"*

"Yes, ma'am," I said. "I'm afraid so."

I heard choking before she whispered hoarsely, *"Oh, my God. I left a horrible message last night."* She broke off into weeping.

Once I was able to soothe her, she told me that Campbell had walked away with a hefty bonus the year before, but lost a lot of it in the crash he'd helped cause, and spent too much of what remained on the cabin in Tom Miner.

"He was behind on paying contractors," I said.

"He was behind on paying everyone," Alicia Campbell said, sniffling. *"But he was just avoiding it by fly-fishing, the same way he avoided our marriage disintegrating by fly-fishing. It's all he does, just stands there in a river and . . ."* She broke down again. *"I'm sorry. I've got to go tell my daughter and son."*

"I understand," I said. "Just one more question. Did he have life insurance?"

"Life . . . yes," she said. *"He bought it years ago."*

"The payoff?" I asked.

There was a pause before she said, *"Five million."*

My eyebrows shot up. "Lot of money."

The line was static for a moment before she said, *"It won't bring him back."*

I let it go, gave her my contact information, and hung up just as I was coming to George Anderson's Yellowstone Angler fly shop. The parking lot was jammed with trucks, including a tan one with the MONTANA FISH, PARKS & WILDLIFE emblem on the door panels. I checked my watch. Lunt wasn't going to start the autopsy for thirty-five minutes and the morgue was just down the road. I pulled in.

Tom and my dad mostly fish the upper Missouri, but the Yellowstone is a close second, which means I had been to that fly shop before on various trips. When I went inside, thirty or forty people were straining to get a look at the game warden, who was putting a tape measure to an ungodly huge fish.

The cutthroat-rainbow hybrid looked more suited to salt water than fresh, like a tuna. The caudal fin was more like a beaver's tail. The fish was lobster red beneath the jaw and across the gill plates. Its nose was shaped like a salmon buck's beak and gleamed like mercury. The rest of the body was speckled pewter and splashed with shades of pastel rose from one end to the other.

"Thirty-six inches and a quarter," the warden called out.

"That breaks the state record!" yelled a short brown-haired man whom I recognized as George Anderson, the shop owner.

A roar went up from the crowd. Behind the warden, who together with another man was now lifting the giant trout onto a scale, three men, including a reasonably famous actor, were pounding on the back of a burly guy in his sixties, who was clutching a half-empty Corona that he'd raised overhead in victory.

I knew Jeb Timmons from his pictures on the back of his books. He was one of those men who, depending on the light and the angle of his face, looked either butt-ugly or coarsely charismatic, with dark, receding hair, thick brows, gray eyes, pouched cheeks, and a cleft chin. But it was the ear that caught your eye, the left one, which was barely the bottom half of an ear and ended in a scarred, discolored ridge.

I knew the story because Tom had all of Timmons's books, the novels, the novellas, and the poetry. Timmons lost the upper ear in a knife fight in a brothel in Juárez. Or so he claimed. In any case, Timmons was one of Tom's favorite writers.

My husband writes thrillers and mysteries and is quite good at it. But Timmons was not a commercial writer. Timmons, Tom liked to say, wrote for the ages. His voice was unlike any I'd ever read, with the ability to assume God's perspective as easily as a bear's or a frightened boy's.

Timmons's sentences were each like a cannon blast, one after another, destroying every preconception you might have had about his stories, which were at once powerful and funny and moving. He was also the best writer about fly-fishing I've ever read, able to draw you in effortlessly to the subtle dance of it.

But Timmons had won the Pulitzer for poetry, not prose. He won his Oscar for the adaptation of his third novel, *Headwaters,* the story of an Irish boy brought to Montana by his grieving father in 1909 after watching his wife succumb to tuberculosis. The father is an absinthe addict and has hallucinations in which he encounters angels in the streets of Dublin, telling him to go to the American wilderness in order to cleanse himself and his son from grief.

They end up heading into the wilderness as spring's coming on, completely ill-prepared, and the father drinking whiskey. Third day in, a grizzly appears in their camp and kills the father and starts eating him before the boy wounds the bear with his dad's rifle. The rest of the story is the bear hunting the boy as he tries to find his way out of the wilderness. Like Tom says, a writer for the ages.

"Thirty pounds, eight ounces!" the warden yelled.

"World-record cutbow from a river!" George Anderson bellowed.

The place went nuts. Timmons pranced like a boxer after a win.

"Tell us how you caught it, Jeb!" someone yelled.

Timmons raised his empty bottle and roared, "You get me another beer while we get this fish on ice and I will. I'll tell you all how I caught it."

Quickly all hands assembled and the monster trout was safely inside a cooler on ice. The man who'd helped the warden with the fish walked by, stripping off thin latex gloves. He wore a nameplate that said ROD ZULLO.

"Excuse me," I said, showing him my identification. "Can I talk to you?"

"'Bout what?" Zullo asked.

"You called Edward Campbell this morning?" I said.

Zullo nodded uneasily. "Yeah. So?"

"He's dead," I said. "He washed up on the bank between Emigrant and Pray this morning in his fly-fishing gear. No wader belt."

Zullo looked like he'd taken a bat across the chin. "Ned? Oh, my God."

I led Zullo outside, where he told me that Campbell took up fly-fishing the fall before, but he was serious about it, coming to casting classes offered by the store, hiring guides like Zullo to fish with him. He'd even started to tie his own flies.

"Jesus, he was just in here yesterday around noon to show me a fly he'd invented, a variation of a blue-winged olive tied on a size-eight shank with this funny little sparkle ribbon he'd wound around the body."

"Kind of big for a blue-winged olive," I said.

His face fell. "That was the last thing I said to him. I warned him about that belt. It was the first thing I taught him. He was probably in a hurry, and . . . Jesus."

We chatted a few minutes before I headed for my truck. Before I slammed the door shut, I heard Timmons's booming voice: "My hip was killing me, and no amount of Bordeaux and codeine was stopping it, so I got up this morning about five to fish."

Chris Lunt was waiting for me in the basement of one of the local funeral homes. She had Campbell's body up on the stainless table and had already removed his clothes. His body was heavily bruised. One of his legs was broken.

"This happen in the water?" I asked.

"In the rapids," said Sheriff Marks, who was just entering. "We found Campbell's truck parked at Corwin Springs, right above Yankee Jim Canyon."

"They find his wader belt?"

The sheriff shrugged. "Does it matter?"

"It would be nice to know he just forgot it."

"Lee Ann," Lunt said. "You should see this."

Lunt had rolled Campbell over on his belly. She was hunched over a magnifying glass suspended from the ceiling on an arm, looking down at a swollen mass at the back of the corpse's head.

"It kill him?" I asked.

She pointed to fluid seeping from Campbell's nose and mouth. "He's got a lot of river water in there, which means he was breathing when he went in river. He definitely drowned. He probably hit his head on a rock as he was dying or just after."

While Lunt peeled off Campbell's skin so she could examine the skull, I went over to his clothes. I put on gloves and started going through the fly vest, finding what you'd expect: gink, tippet, sinkers, strike indicator, and three big fly boxes. I opened them, scanning the patterns, which ranged from salmon flies and golden stones to the tiniest midge. Dead center of the last and largest box were two ridiculously large blue-winged olive flies, with room for a third.

I picked one out and studied it. Campbell wasn't a bad tier. It's just that the whole idea of a blue-winged olive this large was akin to a flat-chested gal opting for a pair of size-forty double-Ds at the local plastic surgeon's office. The falseness of the lure in either case was likely to be a turnoff. Well, maybe not to men. But certainly to any fish in the Yellowstone.

I shut the case just as Lunt said, "Okay, it did crack his skull."

I came over. Lunt pointed to the base of his skull, which was slightly concave.

"A blow like this almost certainly injured his spinal cord. I doubt anyone hit there before going in the water would have been able to breathe at all."

Part of me wanted to let it go right there, call Campbell's death a drowning, and race back to Helena to help Tom save the house. But something told me to keep the investigation alive. At lease until I tied up loose ends.

"Dissect the brain and the cord," I said. "Make sure."

I went back to the fishing vest to see if there was anything I'd missed. Sure enough, I found a cell phone inside a neoprene sleeve inside two Ziploc bags.

"Now that doesn't add up," I said. "The guy triple-wraps his cell phone but doesn't wear his wader belt."

Marks shrugged. "It's probably in his truck."

"It still at Corwin Springs?"

"Far as I know."

On the way to Corwin Springs, I called Tom. He said the drainage where we live had been evacuated. All we could do now was pray, which is what I did. I pulled off the highway, bowed my head, and begged God to spare our house.

I finally got to the Corwin Springs fishing access about seven that evening. The light through the smoky haze was slanted, and shadowy. The river turned golden in that light and rushed north toward the mouth of Yankee Jim Canyon. I could hear the roar of whitewater when I got out next to Campbell's Suburban.

There was only one other car in the dusty parking lot, which surprised me. Corwin's usually a popular spot. But the air was so fouled and hot that few anglers or rafters seemed to want any part of the upper Yellowstone.

I jimmied the Suburban's door and used snips to cut the alarm wires after barely three wails. I searched the car. No wader belt.

An older man tramped out of the willows, carrying a fly rod.

"Any luck?" I called, shutting the door of the Suburban.

He eyed me suspiciously. "They patrol here for people who break into cars."

I showed him my badge and identification. His name was Alan Hayes, a computer science professor from MIT out on his annual angling holiday.

"You here yesterday?" I asked.

He nodded. "Late in the day."

I described Campbell and asked if he'd seen him. Hayes laughed. "You couldn't miss him. He wasn't a very good caster, more like a thrasher, and he was using this enormous blue-winged olive and hucking the thing into the pool right above Yankee Jim. I tried to tell him he wasn't going to catch a damned thing on that fly. But he was determined. Why?"

I told him.

"Is that right?" Hayes said, shaking his head. "He was alive this time last night. Must have fallen in and gone down the chute?"

"That's what it looks like," I said. "You see anyone else?"

"No."

"One more question," I said. "Was he wearing a wader belt?"

Hayes squinted before nodding. "He was. A brown one."

I thanked him and decided to have a look at the large deep pool that butts up against the steep spillway of Yankee Jim Canyon. I tried to imagine how Campbell had fished it, where he'd laid his line and mended to true his drift.

The only safe place that I could see to cast was in the river, along the bank up against the willows about forty yards back from the canyon mouth. I climbed over rocks into the water, almost laughing at the idea that someone would see me here in my skirt and blouse, mid-thigh-deep in the water. It was the best sensation I'd had all day.

I stood there, enjoying the cool water and gazing down the shadowy bank toward the rock walls and the whitewater starting to churn between them. This was a fool's game. No way Campbell was ever going to catch a fish from this position using one of those porno flies he'd tied.

I tried to imagine Campbell on the steep bank closer to the canyon, casting into whitewater, but couldn't figure out how he'd have kept his balance. Then the light changed ever so slightly, altering the shadows beneath the willows. Ahead of me about fifteen feet, hanging from a low limb, was a brown chest wader belt.

It was well past eight when I got out of there, having photographed the placement of the belt before putting it in an evidence bag. Dusk was coming on when I reached the valley floor. The truck was immediately blasted by a gust of wind. I startled, tightened my hold on the wheel, ducked to look toward Livingston, and saw one of the best sights of my life. Thunderclouds were turning the sky black.

My cell phone rang.

"*It's raining!*" Tom yelled. "*Pouring! And hailstones as big as golf balls!*"

I started crying and had to pull over.

"*Honey, this is a good thing,*" Tom said.

"I know," I said, sniffling and smiling. "I know."

"*You coming home soon?*" he asked.

"Maybe tomorrow," I said.

"*Call me before you go to bed,*" he said, and I promised I would.

Chris Lunt called a few minutes later. Campbell's

spine was only mildly traumatized. He could have taken the shot and gone in the water alive.

Lightning cracked and rain pelted my windshield as I drove into Livingston. I got a room at the Murray Hotel because they've got great pillows and because the film director Sam Peckinpah used to live there, get drunk, and shoot holes in the walls. Who wants a Super 8 when you can get all that?

I found a store still open that sold me a pair of Wranglers, a short-sleeved shirt that featured a leaping rainbow trout, and a pair of white socks, and then went back to my room, showered, and changed. The rain was still falling when I left the hotel and ran around the block, past the Owl Lounge to the Stockman's Bar. I ate a twelve-ounce strip and a cold Moose Drool Ale that put me in a happy girl state of mind as I headed back to the Murray.

The rain had dwindled by then, but I could hear more thunderclaps coming. I passed back by the Owl Lounge, a favorite of the celebrities that call the Paradise Valley their second or third home. Tom usually insists on stopping in for at least one beer at the Owl, and I figured I'd better not change routine.

Inside, the band was between sets, and the special was the dollar beer bin—everything's a buck. I plunged my arm in the tub, came up a cold Rainier in the bottle, and paid before I heard the unmistakable growl of Jeb Timmons.

"So I couldn't sleep because of the goddamned hip, so I got up and decided to go fishing about five," he was saying, and I moved to see a knot of people gathered around Timmons, who sat on a stool at the bar.

His friend, the famous actor, was sitting beside him, looking like he'd gone six or seven rounds with Johnny Walker.

I edged closer, hearing Timmons say, "I got out at one of my favorite pools."

"What pool?" a man with thick glasses asked.

"I wouldn't tell my own mother that secret," Timmons brayed.

The crowd laughed. Timmons drank some wine and then rubbed at the stump of his ear. "So like I was saying, I get there and dawn's just coming on, and I'm thinking this is a good time to pull a streamer along the bottom, hoping for a big brown to think it was a crawfish. I shit you not, on the third cast, I'm pulling and pulling and *wham!* I felt like I'd harpooned Ahab's goddamned whitefish."

He paused, looking at the people gathered around him for their reaction, and I got the feeling he was already practiced at delivering this story.

The same man with thick glasses said, "You used a crayfish pattern?"

Timmons said, "Whadya expect, a leech?"

The crowd busted into laughter again, and I found myself wanting to get closer, to hear every bit of it so I could repeat it to Tom later in my room.

Timmons said, "I would have much rather caught him on a dry, seeing a big bastard like that blast out of the water and smash my fly. But that's simply not the way it happened. I went fishing for a scavenger and I caught one."

He turned to the crowd before continuing. "But there I was, holding a six weight when he strikes, and I let him have it a second, feeling his head shaking on the line, before I jerked straight back, like cocking a pool cue, and set the hook.

"The reel spun so fast that when I tried to palm it, I got burned. He was well into the backing by the time I got the drag cranked. And then it was a fight, let me tell you, the fight of my goddamned life."

Timmons paused for effect, then launched into a remarkable description of a fifty-minute fight with the fish, from one side of the Yellowstone to the other, upstream and down. At one point the fish charged him and went by at less than a foot. But Timmons knew that the fish was trying to dislodge the hook, and he ran in the opposite direction, holding his rod high overhead to take out the slack. The fish took him into a deep pool, and Timmons swam downstream after him. He finally landed the fish on a sandbar a quarter mile from where he'd first hooked up.

"Goddamned greatest moment of my life," Timmons said.

Everyone started clapping except the guy with the glasses. I smiled, thinking how intuitive my husband is sometimes before the clapping ebbed.

"Why didn't you release it?" the guy with the glasses asked.

Timmons looked at him as if he were a strange species. "Maybe I'm just less evolved. Maybe I still have some of that caveman in my blood that makes me want to bring home the mastodon. I don't know. But I can tell you, I did not hesitate to lift that big sonofabitch up with my fingers in his gills."

"Jackass," the guy with the glasses said, and walked away.

Timmons chuckled. "Life, art, fishin', there's a

fucking critic at every turn. And if you'll excuse me, my friends, I must visit the outhouse."

He got up off his stool and came toward me, staring at my breasts, with a smirk on his lips. "Mine's bigger," he said, gesturing at the jumping trout.

"So I heard," I said. "Got a second to chat, Mr. Timmons?"

He said in a conspiratorial tone, "I'll be back, sweet thing."

I said nothing, just watched him go, and waited until he weaved his way back. He was drunk but holding it well. "What's your name, sweet thing?" he asked.

"Lee Ann Duffy. I'm a special investigator for the state attorney general.

That seemed to sober him. "What are you investigating?"

"A drowning," I said. "A guy named Edward Campbell. He built a house up Tom Miner Basin last year."

"Probably a goddamned castle," he said, before shrugging. "Don't know him."

"Where'd you catch the fish?" I asked.

"I wouldn't tell my mother that one."

"I'm not your mother," I said. "Above Yankee Jim?"

He studied me a second and then shook his head, "A good guess, but no, it was at the other end as a matter of fact, right there when the river spills out the bottom of the canyon, a deep hole as cold as you'll find, super-aerated and filled with all sorts of nymphs, crayfish, and leeches."

It all made perfect sense and I found myself wanting to tell Timmons about Tom. The two had never met.

"My husband's a writer and fisherman," I said. "We both love your books."

"Thanks. Who's your husband?"

"Tom Duffy," I said. "He writes thrillers and mysteries."

His eyebrows rose and fell. "I don't read pulp."

I said, "Not so nice to have met you, Mr. Timmons."

"Where you going, Detective Duffy?" he asked. "The night is young."

"Special Investigator Duffy," I said coolly. "And this day's already too old."

Back in my room at the Murray Hotel, lying on perfect pillows, I finished telling Tom the entire story of Timmons catching the fish, but left out the part where I mentioned that my husband was a writer and Timmons had put him down.

"Guy's a fishing artist," Tom said. "Swimming after a fish. Who does that?"

"Brad Pitt," I said, referring to his great scene in *A River Runs Through It.*

"It's still an amazing story, one I'm sure we'll be reading about."

"I think I'm going to take a break from Timmons."

"Why's that?"

"Let's say he was less interesting in person than I thought he would be."

We hung up and I was about to turn off the light when I noticed Campbell's cell phone in the evidence bag on the dresser. I'd meant to check his messages. Call me Ms. OCD, but I just couldn't sleep without checking.

I tried to get into his message box but didn't have the password. I scrolled through text messages and found several from his kids. On a whim, I toggled my way to his pictures file and opened the first on the list.

The shot had been taken in low light, and it took me several moments to realize what I was looking at. My hands started shaking, and I told myself to calm down, to figure out how to handle the situation.

In the end, I Googled up an address and drove across town to the home of Rod Zullo, the guide at Yellowstone Anglers who seemed to be the only person who had anything good to say about Campbell. He was awake, watching Letterman. When I told him what I was looking for, he told me he'd need to make a phone call.

I left his house five minutes later, with Zullo following in his truck, and drove back into town across the train tracks and down a dirt road to the studio and home of Sean Lawlor, a famous taxidermist who specializes in fish. A portly guy in his forties, Lawlor was waiting for us when we got there.

He took us into his studio and opened the cooler that held the monster cutbow. I crouched, lifted the gill plate, and shone a light inside. The gills were damaged from the death grip Timmons had used. I asked Zullo and Lawlor to flip the fish. The gills on this side looked damaged as well, but not nearly as broken up as on the other side. It was more like a groove had been worn in the gills. I used a magnifying glass and saw a tiny thread of fiber caught in the gill. I used tweezers to pluck it out and put it in an evidence bag.

"What is it?" Zullo asked.

"I'm not sure," I said, though I was.

"Think we can get his mouth open?" I asked.

Lawlor gently pried open the trout's jaw. I flashed the light around the mouth, looking for a tear or a hole of some sort. There was one, along the left jaw, which disappointed me. I used a pencil to push down the flesh at the brink of the esophagus. Sticking up out of the tube that led to the stomach, I saw the tip of a strand of translucent filament.

"I'm going to need to gut this fish," I said.

Lawlor looked horrified. "This has to be skinned in the morning."

"I'll make one cut, two inches long," I promised, and then inserted the blade of a penknife into the belly of the fish. I sliced open the stomach and had to push aside a small frog and some other undigested food to find what I was looking for.

I held it up for Zullo to see.

"That sonofabitch," Zullo said.

I entered the Owl Lounge at a quarter to one in the morning. As I expected, Jeb Timmons was still holding court, retelling the story of his record-breaking catch to a new knot of admirers. His friend, the famous actor, was passed out on the bar.

Timmons had just delivered the line about feeling like he'd just harpooned Ahab's whitefish when he spotted me watching him. He winked. I hate it when men wink at me.

Someone asked where he caught it, and Timmons replied the same way he had earlier in the evening. I called out, "What if your mother caught that fish?"

Timmons appeared confused. "My mother doesn't fish."

That drew a laugh, but several people stepped back to give me room. "But if she did, and she caught that fish," I said, "would you kill her for it?"

Timmons stared at me from deep inside his wine-addled brain before saying, "Her husband's one of those mystery guys who call themselves novelists. God only knows where this is coming from."

"Actually I'm with the State Attorney General's Office and I'm here investigating a homicide," I announced.

Timmons's lips pursed. "Thought you said it was a drowning."

"Homicide by drowning. Where were you fishing last night?"

He rubbed at his stumpy ear before he replied. "I told you."

"Anyone see you there?"

He shrugged. "When I fish, I'm usually not looking to be social."

"What's the first thing you did after landing that fish this morning?"

"What?" Timmons said, scratching at the ear again. "I don't know. I sat down on the sandbar and just sat there looking at it. Kind of in shock, I'd guess."

"You know what most people would have done in your situation?"

"Case you didn't notice, I'm not most people," he said, hardening.

"Most people would have whipped out a camera or a cell phone and taken a picture of the fish and sent it to everyone they knew."

Timmons smiled. "That was the second thing I did. Six oh five this morning."

"Memorized the time. Know what I found in the right gill of your fish?"

His head pulled back. "You examined my fish without my permission?"

"A strand of nylon from a stringer, you know, the kind of nylon rope kids slide into the gills of a fish before putting it in the water so they can keep it alive?"

"Could have come downstream and got lodged in his gill."

"Want to know what I found in your fish's stomach?"

He glared at me. "You cut my fish?"

"Small incision," I said, before holding up a small evidence bag that contained a ridiculously large blue-winged olive fly with a twist of silver through its belly.

Timmons's face reddened. "That's the worst excuse for a fly I've ever seen."

"It was a fly that Edward Campbell tied," I said. "It's what he used above Yankee Jim. The fly that brought up the beast. That fish wasn't caught on a crawfish pattern, and you didn't catch it. Campbell caught it, a raw amateur, on a dry fly."

"Bullshit!" Timmons snapped. "I caught that fish this morning on a streamer below Yankee Jim. I have no idea how that fly got in its stomach. Maybe, maybe, this Campbell guy hooked up and it shook it off. I don't know. I'm going home."

"No, you're not, Mr. Timmons," I said, reaching into my pocket for Campbell's cell phone. "Because Campbell did what any fisherman would do if he ever landed a fish like that—he immediately took a picture. It's not a great picture, but I'm betting it's going to put you in jail for the rest of your life."

For once Timmons had nothing to say. He just stared at the picture.

I said, "So the way I figure it, you were fishing up around Corwin Springs late yesterday evening, and you saw Campbell thrashing the water with that absurd fly before that absurdly huge cutbow decided to smash it, coming up like a shark. Then you watched Campbell, a rank amateur, fight the fish and land it. And you couldn't believe how big it was when you got over there to him."

Timmons seemed to be staring off into space.

"What made you pick up the rock that you hit him with?" I asked.

Timmons's eyes unglazed and he looked at me as if I were an imbecile before saying, "He was going to let it go. Can you imagine that? The biggest goddamned cutbow ever and he was going to release it."

He gazed around at his crowd, which was edging back from him, leaving just me facing him and his passed-out actor friend. "I mean, right?"

"Right to hit him from behind?" I asked angrily. "Right to take off his wader belt and push him into the water alive? Still breathing?"

Timmons had that faraway look again, the same sort of gaze my husband gets when he's in the heat of writing one of his books. "He was still breathing?"

"He was," I said. "And then you put a stringer line through that fish's gills and anchored that rope enough to hold the fish all night, barely alive, before you took it downstream and killed it with the death grip and took your pictures as your alibi."

Timmons jumped off his chair and tried to attack me. Sheriff Marks and Chief Dexter, who'd come in behind me, jumped out and grabbed him.

"Jeb Timmons," I said, as they wrestled him into handcuffs, "you are under arrest for the premeditated murder of Edward—"

"Screw you, bitch!" he shouted. "You think this is going to change things? I'm still a great writer. And your husband's still a hack. That won't change."

I stepped up to him, so close I could smell the sour wine on his breath. "Mr. Timmons, by tomorrow morning your Pulitzer and your Oscar will be forgotten. You'll be nothing more than the hack fisherman who killed an innocent man so he could claim a trophy as his own. That's all anyone's going to remember about you."

Dexter and Marks dragged Timmons out of the Owl. I looked at the bartender, who was in shock. I pointed to the famous actor passed out on the bar.

"Make sure he gets home," I said.

The bartender nodded.

I went outside into the August Livingston night. The rain had stopped and the air smelled like someone had just doused a campfire.

I could not have imagined anything better.

BLUE ON BLACK

MICHAEL CONNELLY

Bosch had left her alone in the room for almost an hour. It was time. He knocked once on the door and entered. Rachel Walling looked up from the table. She had the photos spread out across it so she could view them all at once.

He moved into the room and sat down across from her.

"It looks like you like the photos," he said.

"There isn't much else here," she said.

She waved her hand dismissively at the record of his work on the case. He nodded. She was right. He didn't have jack.

"You see anything? You said you could only give me an hour. I don't want to—"

"But you knew I would start to look at the photos and I'd get caught up in it. That's why you called me, Harry."

"No, I called you because I'm desperate. I know this is the guy. I can put him in close proximity to both women. He was following them. He's got the history and profile—the guy's an apex predator. But after that, I've got nothing. So what have you got, Rachel? Can you help me or not?"

She dropped her eyes from Bosch's without answering. She returned the focus to the photos. Denninger's prior mug shots and prison ID shots from the rape conviction. Denninger posed with a number of prize fish he'd caught in Santa Monica Bay. Denninger on his boat. On the Avalon Pier on Catalina. Photos of his home, inside and out.

"He likes to fish," she finally said.

"Yeah. That and poker. He told us those are his hobbies."

"Does he own this boat?"

"Uh-huh. He keeps it down in Marina del Rey on a trailer lot. We were thinking he probably used the boat to dump the bodies. Because we sure haven't found anything in his house or pickup. Nothing on land."

"And you searched the boat."

"Yeah, we searched it. And got nothing. We took it to the police garage and put it in the blackout room. Lumed the whole thing and it glowed like Christmas. Blood everywhere, but it was all fish blood. Not a drop of human blood, not even his own."

She nodded and picked up the photo taken off the ATM video that showed the first missing woman, Olivia Martz, making a withdrawal. It was taken through a fisheye lens, designed to capture the entire environment around the ATM. Denninger was behind her and to the right, probably never thinking he would be on the film.

"So," Walling said. "You have his prior record as a sexual predator and then the two videos. The parking garage video puts him in the Grove at the same time Allison Beaumont was there on the day she disappeared, and likewise you have the ATM video of Olivia Martz making a withdrawal that puts him right behind her at the Third Street Promenade. Together this got you probable cause for search warrants, and the searches turned up nothing."

Bosch nodded in defeat.

"That's about the size of it."

"Are you watching Denninger?"

"We have a loose tail on him for now. But that won't last forever. There's no overtime left in the budget. That's why I called you."

"You should have called Behavioral. You'd get the whole package from them."

"Yeah, in about six months. How many more girls might go missing by then? Look, Rachel, I know this isn't your beat anymore, but you're good at it and you're fast. That's why I called you. Now is there anything in all of that that can help me? Your lunch hour's over."

She glanced at her watch to confirm the time and picked up one of the photos. It was the one of Denninger on his boat, holding up a fish with both hands. The seas were choppy in the background and the spine of an island rose in the distance. Catalina, probably.

"When I was in Behavioral, a significant number of the predators we encountered had hobbies like hunting or fishing. The percentage was higher than the percentage in the general population. It wasn't anything we could really quantify, but it was there. It has to do with the personality. The tracking and baiting. And, of course, the killing. I noticed that between the two personalities that the fishermen committed crimes that had more finesse, took more thinking. The hunters committed crimes of stalking and disorganized abduction. The fishermen were smarter, were more organized."

"Great, so what are you saying, this guy is too smart for us?"

"No, I'm just saying Denninger's smart. He prepared for the time that he would become the focus of law enforcement. He was ready."

"Smart enough not to leave any evidence, to drop the bodies over the side and sink 'em so we'd never find 'em."

"Look at all these photos of the fish he's caught."

She moved the photos around on the table, turning them so they would face Bosch.

"Yeah, we got them from him. He had them on a bulletin board in his kitchen. He was proud of them. He said we could have them."

"Really?"

"He said he had plenty more."

"He's touching them."

"What?"

"In every picture he is holding up the fish or at least touching it in some way."

Bosch leaned forward over the table. She was right. He hadn't noticed this but wasn't sure what it meant.

"Okay," he said.

"Trophies. He likes trophies. He likes to touch his trophies. To be close."

"That's what we were hoping, that he had kept something from the girls and we'd make the link that way. Driver's license, lock of hair . . . anything. But like I told you, we got nothing. His place is clean. His pickup is clean. His boat is clean. The garage where he works is clean. He's Mr. Clean."

"Sometimes the trophy isn't a lock of hair. It's the real thing."

"You're saying he kept the bodies? Impossible. We would have found them. We've put six hundred hours into this case so far. No bodies. He dumped them in the Pacific and we'll never find them again."

Walling nodded, seemingly in agreement.

"I worked more than one case where the bodies were buried and the killer would return to visit. I had another where the bodies were found and buried by their families. Each night of the week the killer would go to a different cemetery to visit his victims. That's where we caught him. It's a strong attraction to be with his conquests, his trophies. Maybe it's the same with water. Maybe he weighted them and they are exactly where he put them in. He visits them on the water."

"Yeah, but how would he mark the locations? He'd have to—"

Bosch stopped as he realized the answer to his own question. Walling handed him the photo of Denninger smiling at the camera and holding up the fish with two hands.

"The console," she said.

Bosch studied the photograph. The photo had been taken from the stern by an unknown photographer. The boat was a twenty-eight-foot open fisher, with a center console and a T-top that offered partial shade from the sun. Denninger was standing by the starboard gunwale, holding up his shining trophy fish. Next to him was the console. Scattered across the top in the shelter behind the windshield was a variety of fishing equipment. Bosch saw pliers, thick rubber gloves, a knife, and a plastic tray filled with lures and leaders and hooks. There was also a small electronic device with an LED screen that Bosch had previously dismissed as Denninger's cell phone.

But now, as he looked at the photograph, Bosch saw that Denninger had his phone clipped to his belt. The device on the console was something else.

"GPS?" he said.

"Looks like it," Walling said. "Small, handheld, perfect for marking fishing spots."

"And the locations of bodies if you planned to come back to visit."

Walling nodded. Adrenaline started to pour into Bosch's bloodstream. Walling had led him right to a solid break.

"There was no GPS in the possessions we searched," he said.

"He hid it somewhere," she said. "He doesn't need trophies. He just needs his spots. So he can visit the girls."

Bosch stood up and started pacing in the small room.

"Where could it be?" he said, more to himself than Walling.

"Who took these photos?"

"We don't know."

"Well, he's got at least one fishing partner. I'd start there."

Bosch nodded.

"Rachel, this is a big help. Thank you."

"The FBI is always glad to help."

Bosch pulled his phone and made a call. Jackson picked up immediately.

"Where is he?"

"He's home. He's gotta know that we're watching him. Did your agent pal come up with anything?"

"Yeah, we're looking for a handheld GPS device. It's in one of the pictures. He marked his fishing spots and he might have marked the spots where he put the girls. I didn't see it on any of the search inventories and I know it wasn't on the boat. You or Tim have any ideas?"

There was a long silence. Bosch thought he heard muffled voices.

"Rick, you there?"

"Yeah, yeah, I'm here. I was just telling Tim. I think we know where it is."

Bosch's eyes darted to Rachel and he held back his first response, which was to ask why the hell the GPS device hadn't come up before if they had known about it.

"Tell me," he said instead.

"I don't know specifically about a GPS because I don't know anything about fishing. I play golf, man. I—"

"Okay, it doesn't matter. Just tell me what you know."

"When we interviewed the guys Denninger plays poker with, a couple of them said they hadn't seen him since he lost a big pot a couple weeks ago and stormed off."

"Okay."

"Well, you know, we asked how much he lost and they told us he lost like six hundred dollars and all his numbers. I said what do you mean, numbers? And they said his fishing spots. They didn't say anything about a GPS device and it didn't occur to me that—"

"Who won the pot?"

"I don't know but we can find out. I'll start calling those guys back."

"Do it. We need those numbers. Call me as soon as you have a name."

Bosch closed the phone and looked at Walling. "Time to go fishing."

Bosch felt queasy. The police dive boat was rocking on three-foot rollers. They had been out almost two hours on Santa Monica Bay and were on the seventh location. Denninger's GPS had twenty-two waypoints stored on it. And it was shaping up as a long day on rough seas.

Harry studied the blue-black water and waited. The captain had said they were in thirty-two feet of water. After a while he looked back toward the coast and saw the bloom of smog that hovered above the city. He thought about having spent his whole life underneath it, and it only made him feel more ill.

He quickly crossed to the other side of the boat and leaned over the side. The captain had given him specific instructions. If he were to get sick, he had to lean over the port side. That way the current would take his vomit away from the dive zone. He heaved twice, two deep exorcisms from the gut. He watched the current take away what was left of his breakfast.

He felt his phone buzz in his pocket. He wiped his mouth with one hand and pulled the phone with the other.

"Bosch."

"Harry, are you all right?"

It was Walling.

"Yeah. Just a little seasick."

"Yes. I wanted to check in. You're still out there?"

"Unfortunately. We're on the seventh location. Nothing so far."

"You sound terrible. Maybe you should go in."

"No, I'm here till we find them. Or till we don't."

"They can look without you. You're not diving."

"If they find the girls, I need to be here." He said it in a tone that ended the debate.

"Okay, Harry. Let me know, all right?"

"I'll call you."

By the time they got to the eleventh location, the sun was high, the wind had died away, and both the seas and Bosch's stomach had calmed. The water had changed color too. It was a lighter blue in the sunlight. More inviting, less severe. Bosch sat on the stern and watched the air bubbles boil to the surface. There were four divers thirty-nine feet down in low-visibility water. The boat captain, the forensics guy, and two deck hands were inside the cabin. Ever since Bosch had gotten sick, they had left him by himself.

Bosch heard splashing and turned to look behind him, off the stern. Two of the divers had surfaced. Between them they were holding up a body wrapped in a plastic tarp and weighted with chains.

Bosch quickly turned back toward the cabin and waved to get the attention of the others. "Hey!"

He then moved to the gunwale door. Before he could open it, one of the deck hands did. Bosch stepped back and watched as the two divers made their grim delivery. The man from forensics followed their progress with a video camera.

The deck hands grabbed the package by the chains and pulled it aboard, sliding it across the deck. It was grim duty, and water slopped over their shoes.

Olivia or Allison? Bosch thought.

Just as the question ran through his mind, the other

two divers surfaced off the stern. They too carried a package of plastic and chains and moved with it toward the gunwale door.

The first two divers backed away from the boat rather than attempt to climb aboard. That was when Bosch knew that Denninger had put more than two bodies into the water here. He went to the corner of the stern and called out to them.

"How many?"

One diver removed his respirator and called back, holding up an open hand.

"Five more coming up."

Bosch just nodded and pulled his phone to start making calls.

Jackson answered right away.

"Where's Denninger?"

"In the house. You find the girls?"

"Looks like it. We've got seven bodies. We're going to be here awhile."

"Holy Christ!"

"We'll probably have to check all the other spots too."

"Should we take him down?"

Bosch thought for a moment. The location had come from the GPS device that Denninger had lost in a poker game. There were gaps in the evidence line, but it still strongly pointed the finger of guilt at Denninger. Even if the recovered bodies did not include those of Olivia Martz and Allison Beaumont, they would make a case against Denninger.

Another detective or a prosecutor might move more cautiously. Keep the surveillance on the suspect, recover all the bodies, and work the evidence until it tightly wrapped around their man. But Bosch couldn't see giving Denninger another minute of freedom.

"Yeah," he said. "Take the bastard down."

"You got it."

"Call me when you're five by five."

Bosch closed the phone and then reopened it. He needed to alert the medical examiner's office that he had a multiple-homicide case and that investigators would need to meet the police boat at the dock. But first he called Rachel Walling back. He needed to tell her that her read on the file and photos had led to the break that blew the case wide open. He needed to thank her again.

As he waited for her to answer, the sun went behind a cloud and the water turned dark again. It was a cold blue on black, and it would always remind Bosch of death.

UNSNAGGABLE

JOHN LESCROART

Meg and Tom Lewis were on the Snake a few miles out of Yellowstone during the second week of August. They'd accessed the river at nine-thirty that morning near a spot where they'd parked by a bridge. Using nymphs since there was no sign of a hatch this early in the day, both of them had hooked into cutthroats in the first pool they'd tried.

Since then, they'd been moving upstream for a little over two hours, covering perhaps a mile total, but spreading out some distance from each other. Both of them were having a good day, averaging about a fish every twenty minutes or less; both wore a whistle on a lanyard around the neck to scare off bear or moose. Both also sported waders, although only Meg wore a belt against drowning—she'd had to borrow it from her husband because she'd forgotten hers back at the hotel room. On a holster on that belt, she carried a large canister of pepper spray specifically for bear. Bear were not an idle concern here, even only a mile off the main road. Grizzlies had attacked three fishermen in the past month, killing one of them.

Meg had tested the anti-bear canister in the parking lot of the sporting goods store where they'd picked up some local flies yesterday afternoon. Careful to point it downwind, she'd pulled the trigger and with an air-horn blast had released a red-misted cayenne spray, which expanded almost instantaneously into a three-by-six-foot cloud out in front of her. "You better not point that at yourself," Tom had said, and she'd replied, "Don't worry. But if you're a bear, watch out."

The river's flow, at about 350 cfs, was moderately fast, making wading, especially in deeper riffles at the heads of the pools, potentially treacherous, so Meg and Tom mostly kept close to the bank. Tom (still not completely recovered from Young Male Immortality Syndrome) was of course without his belt, but he would occasionally venture in a step or more for a promising casting angle. In spite of the current, the water was consistently clear to the bottom, which in most pools was four to six feet down, but in some of the larger ones could get to a depth closer to ten or twelve. There was a lot of downed wood in and around the water, and this sometimes made creek-side walking difficult, but the fallen timber provided good habitat for the fish. It also posed some snag problems for unskilled fishermen, but Meg and Tom did not fit into this category, and neither had hung up more than a few times.

The temperature would soon hit eighty degrees, and there was no sign of cloud in the endless sky above them.

Meg and Tom, both thirty-four, had been married for nine years and had no children. Tom taught seventh-grade math at Ralston Intermediate School in Belmont, and Meg worked as a senior analyst for Oracle. They made their home, a four-thousand-square-foot mock-Spanish mansion worth $2.9 million, on a half acre in the north end of San Mateo, California, a few blocks from where the real estate values became truly stratospheric in Hillsborough.

The difference in their salaries was ludicrous, with Meg earning $372,500 annually, not including bonus, and Tom hauling in about 15 percent of that. Because she was the actual provider, they'd decided not to bother with life insurance for Tom but that Meg should be insured for $5 million. The policy also included mortgage insurance, which would pay off the house in the event of the death of either of them.

After all the wading and walking on shifting gravel, Meg was starting to feel a bit lightheaded—she suffered from mild hypoglycemia and had to keep at least a token amount of food onboard. Looking upstream between casts, she realized that Tom had disappeared around a bend, and she blew on her whistle. After only a second or two, she heard his answering blow, which meant he'd be coming back to meet her.

She stepped away from the riverbank and saw a likely shaded clearing in the woods a hundred yards or so behind her, so she hooked her fly into its little hook keeper in the rod by the reel and, whistling tunelessly, picked her ungainly way across the open rock and gravel streambed from which the raging snowmelt had receded earlier in the summer.

In the clearing, a downed tree provided seating and, taking a shady spot on it, she removed her backpack and laid out a mostly odorless lunch of gorp (the acronym for "good old raisins and peanuts," but augmented, in Meg's case, with dried cherries and M&Ms), a bottle of still-cool Hanzell Chardonnay, and teriyaki beef jerky.

This time, Tom's whistle blew first and she called him to her spot with her answer. Even ignoring his ridiculously young face, which was not always easy for her to do as she watched his strong and trim body effortlessly traverse the difficult terrain, she found herself thinking that he was still a gorgeous man. He'd grown his shock of red hair long over the summer as he usually did, and now as he walked it picked up highlights from the sun.

Tom's prime mantra exhorted him to live in the now.

Although, if he were honest, he'd have to admit that that might not always have been great advice.

Twelve years before, his worship of the now had made him decide that he should get his one-year teaching credential instead of spending three long years in law school. Now, in retrospect, that had clearly been a mistake. If he were a lawyer now, like his thirty-five-year-old next-door neighbor, Dwight Finlay, he'd be making at least what Meg was, maybe more. But he hadn't wanted to put in the time, to defer the gratification. He'd wanted to live in the now, take the pablum teaching courses at community college, get a job that didn't demand too much and that gave him time to do what he wanted when he wanted to do it.

It was doubly unfortunate that in the present here and now, he couldn't even remember what he'd done with all that time—mostly frittered it away, he supposed. He had vague memories of surfing, doing other sports with an ever-dwindling number of nonworking guys, drinking a lot, chasing women, but not even that for too long, since he'd met Meg in his first year of teaching.

Back then, Tom had considered serious, hardworking, ambitious, intelligent Meg to have the bonus of good looks. Or maybe it had just been that her passionate and sensual nature had blinded him a little to any real objective analysis.

Not that she was ugly now, or even close to it. She had definite attributes—shapely legs, no extra weight, good skin, even a killer toothy smile on those rare occasions that it showed itself—but she eschewed even the least invasive intrusions of fashion on her natural looks. And over his time with her, Tom had come to equate this aversion to all things glamorous as simple plainness, even homeliness. She just wouldn't ever even try to make herself prettier.

Long-limbed and as uncoordinated and awkward as a newborn pony, she had feet that were nearly as large as his. Her fingernails, which she never painted, had a spatulate quality, a literal squareness that spoke to him of joylessness, hard work, and somehow, a certain mannishness. Every time he happened to glance at her hands, and those fingernails, the future seemed to stretch before him farther and farther.

It pissed him off that she was just too smart to be bothered to care about her looks at all. They were what they were, and to give too much thought or importance to them was the height of superficiality. She'd told him this in no uncertain terms several times back in the early days, when he'd made a constructive suggestion or two—maybe she should use a touch of makeup or polish on her nails, et cetera. She'd reminded him that she hadn't bothered with that stuff when they'd first been together, hot and heavy, had she? And it hadn't been a problem then. So what was the difference now? They were both going to get old and change, and to fight that fundamental truth was silly and really beneath them.

Now as Tom came into the clearing, he caught a glint of the mottled sunlight reflecting off a portion of his wife's head where the scalp showed through thin hair that she wore short, cropped around her ears for—what else?—comfort's sake.

She might actually be bald before she was fifty.

It was a tipping-point moment for him. He'd been thinking about it for a while now, the titillating idea flitting in and out of his consciousness, more or less a fantasy that he'd never actually realize. But suddenly this remote setting in the now struck him as the right time, the right place.

He could do this. His life could change right here.

Now.

It was perfect.

"Hey," she said.

"Hey, yourself. Killer day, isn't it?"

"Maybe the best ever. How many have you caught?"

"Into the net? Eleven. Four got off."

"I'm nine and two. But one was fourteen inches. Can you believe that? Measured fourteen. Fought me ten minutes at least. Awesome fish."

"Oh, that old guy. I already caught him once before you did. He was tired by the time you got him. I had him when he was good."

She tried a halting smile. "That's what *she* said." But then the smile faded. "Really, though?"

"No," he said, "not really, Meg." He walked up and kissed her. "I'm teasing you. My biggest was ten inches tops. You got me beat."

"It's not a competition, Tom."

"Of course not. I didn't say it was. I caught more. You caught the biggest. That's roughly a tie anyway."

"Even if we tie, it's still not a competition."

"If you say so."

"I do say so." She paused. "What does that mean?"

"What?"

"If I say so."

"Nothing."

"You think I'm seeing our fishing today as some kind of a competition?"

He shrugged. "You're the one who brought up the number of fish caught and the size of fish caught. I was just enjoying the day out on the river."

"So was I."

"And then it just so happened that you caught a bigger fish. And fewer of them got away. And you wanted me to know that. Just in case I forgot you were better at everything than I am."

"I never said that, Tom. I never even thought that. And you caught more fish. Doesn't that count if we're keeping score of these things?"

"Two categories against one. Meg takes it. And wins again."

She drew a deep breath and let it out heavily. "Do we have to fight about this now? I really just wanted to sit down and take a break and have a nice lunch."

"Okay. I want that too."

His neighbor Dwight Finlay's wife, Laura, on the other hand, was pretty much the alpha female among the extremely well turned out women of what Meg called the "country club set." Laura was thirty-one years old.

Much to her embarrassment, Dwight loved to brag about whenever she was mistaken for Kelly Ripa, which apparently happened all the time.

They had been at a block party barbecue about a year before—just after Dwight and Laura had moved in—the first time Tom had heard Dwight going on about this woman at Nordstrom who *just wouldn't believe* that Laura wasn't Kelly Ripa. Tom thought Dwight was a complete tool as he went on and on about this latest misidentification and how often something just like it kept happening. "That's why I married Laura, after all," he'd said. "I figured Kelly was already taken. But then"—the inept recovery/apology, pulling his wife in under his arm—"I found out I got the best one after all."

Tom noticed Laura's pained, pasted-on smile and empathized with her. He also thought that the comparison was odious—next to Laura Finlay, he thought, Kelly Ripa was a skag.

Because both Tom and Laura were married to workaholics who put in regular twelve-hour days, often worked weekends, and frequently traveled, the two mostly-stay-at-home spouses became acquainted over their adjoining back fence at the cocktail hour. It turned out that they had more in common than successful mates. Both believed in living in the now, and the now brought them to bed together for the first time about four months ago.

Once he got over the initial stab of guilt, short-lived and easily rationalized—after all, Meg was gone all the time and they made love only a couple of times a month anyway, she wouldn't even care—Tom let himself savor the sweetness of the feeling he thought he'd never again experience, falling in love. And ironically, this had a positive impact even on his relations with his wife. Suddenly he felt worthwhile, more attractive, confident; no longer a loser, confined to a lifetime of second place. He was easily able to satisfy two partners. It wasn't all about being able to provide and make money; it was about him, the person, the man.

But about a month ago, things changed:

"God, you're a beautiful woman," he said.

It was just after lunchtime, a warm afternoon. Neither Dwight nor Meg would be home for hours, and Laura and Tom had taken full advantage of the long morning. Now Laura had just gotten out of bed and, gloriously naked, was combing her blond hair in front of her dressing table. Smiling, she caught his eye in the mirror, then half turned to him. "You're not half bad yourself." Then, more seriously, "I love you, Tom."

"I love you too."

"No. I mean really."

"I mean really too." He patted the bed next to him. "Come over here."

She shook her head no. "I shouldn't."

"Why not?"

"Because we'll start again."

"Would that be so bad?"

"I don't know. It might be." Finally, she let out a shuddering sigh. "I don't know how long we can keep doing this."

"How about forever?"

Her look immediately grew dark. "Don't say that. Not if you don't mean it. That's not going to happen. It can't happen."

"Sure it can. If we love each other. And I do mean it."

"You mean you divorce Meg and I leave Dwight?"

"If that's where we've come to, you and me, I would do that in a heartbeat."

"And what do we live on?"

"I've got a job, Laura. You're a Stanford graduate. I'm pretty sure you could find work someplace."

"This might sound awful, Tom, but I really don't want to find work someplace. I like my life now and the things in it. And don't kid yourself, I've worked for them, believe me."

"I do believe you." He leaned back against the bed-post. "So what do we do, you and me?"

"I don't know," she said, fighting back tears now. "I can't stop with you. I don't want to stop."

"So . . . what?"

"So we go on the way we are. And then eventually it will end. Dwight or Meg will find out, or you'll find somebody else . . ."

"Never."

"You say that now. But then this will get old . . ."

Sitting back up, he put all he had into convincing her. "That just won't happen, Laura. We've just said we loved each other. What more do we need?"

"We need a way to live, Tom. Isn't that obvious? And you can call me shallow, it wouldn't be the first time I've heard it. But I know what I've done to get to here, and I'm not going backwards. Even if it means staying with Dwight forever."

"What if I could offer you something better?"

"How could you do that?"

"If Meg and I got divorced . . ."

But she was shaking her head. "No offense, Tom. I

love you, but be realistic. You're a seventh-grade teacher. If you divorce Meg and after lawyer's bills get even half of the stuff you own together, then you're a seventh-grade teacher with a few hundred grand in the bank. Dwight makes a few hundred grand every few months." She sighed again, swung back to the mirror, picked up her brush. "Look," she said. "We don't have to talk about this anymore. We can keep on loving each other and hold on to this as long as it lasts. But we can't make it permanent, unless . . . well, we just can't."

"Unless what, Laura? What were you going to say?"

"Unless something changes. But I don't see how that is ever going to happen."

"Gorp, jerky, and Chardonnay," Tom said. "A great combo. Who woulda thunk?"

"It is amazing, isn't it?" Meg said. "I could finish the whole bottle."

"Why don't you? Nobody's watching but me, and I won't tell. How many days off do you get that you can overindulge in anything?"

"You're right," she said. "Maybe I will." Forgoing the plastic glass she'd been drinking from, she tipped up the bottle and poured the rest of the wine into her mouth in a long couple of swallows. "There! God, that's good. But you might have to hold me up when it kicks in. Especially if we get close to the water. Or even in it."

"Whatever. Holding you could never be a burden, fair one."

"Aww." She reached out and put a hand behind his neck, drawing him closer to her, putting her lips briefly against his. "You're so sweet."

"I try," he said, then clapped his hands. "Well, you ready to go back and whack the water?"

"As I'll ever be." She giggled. "But I don't know if that's saying much."

Details were not Tom's thing. He liked to think of himself as more of a big-picture kind of guy, and he wasn't wrong.

As the couple picked their way back over the stones and gravel in the dry portion of the creek bed, he thought he'd just pay attention to changes in Meg's behavior and try to gauge when it would be easiest to make something happen—exactly what it would be still hadn't made itself clear to him. But out here with all the running water and heavy stones and downed timber, it didn't seem that the creation of a plausible accident could possibly be that difficult. Especially since he'd had only a few sips of the wine at lunch and she'd had nearly the whole bottle. Any forensic testing after the fact would show that she was well on her way to drunk when she fell/slipped/knocked her head/whatever. It would be totally believable. Meg had always been a cheap drunk and her alcohol intake seemed to have already kicked in before they'd gotten halfway back across to the channel.

"Are you okay?"

"Fine," she said. "Happy."

"Good to see."

He took her hand and patiently plodded along beside her as she stumbled and picked her way across the rubble. "Step at a time," he told her. "We're doing fine."

At last they got to the water, a wide shallow riffle with very little promise of fish. Meg found a boulder on the bank and sat on it, changing to one of the local hackled dry flies, a grasshopper, they'd bought yesterday, while Tom waded out a few feet and threw his morning nymph a few times, then turned and came back to her.

"No fish here." He went behind her. "You good to keep walking?"

"Definitely." She turned with him and pointed upstream. "I think I saw what looked like a rise in that next pool up. I've switched to dry. I'm going to nail 'em."

"Let's go."

She walked the bank nearer to the water than he did, a couple of steps behind him. Once a good-size stone came loose and turned under her foot, and she went down to a knee, but they were still nearest to a shallow riffle, not a likely place to drown. Tom gave her a hand and pulled her back up.

Sure enough, the next pool, nearly twenty feet across, maybe eighty long, and about plenty deep, was in the beginning moments of a hatch. Suddenly the air above the water was thick with bugs and concentric ripples were popping all over the smooth surface. Walking upstream as they were—and had to be if they expected to surprise any fish, which all hung in the water facing the oncoming current—Tom and Meg came to a stop together at the tail of the pool just before it shallowed out in another riffle.

"They're making it too easy," Meg whispered.

"Don't be too sure," Tom replied. "Gotta get 'em into the net before it counts."

"I hate that rule." Meg blinked a few times, did a few exaggerated exercises with her mouth and the muscles of her face. "I'm a little tipsy," she said. But stepping out onto a flat rock at the water's edge, she unfastened her hook from its place next to her reel. After pulling on the fly to let out more line and a few false casts to gain length, she sent her hackled grasshopper on a perfect trajectory out over the water, where it settled gently into an eddy just off the opposite bank about halfway up the pool.

When the fish hit, at first there was no indication of anything special, just the little flip of water where the fly had landed and then suddenly disappeared. But when she set the hook, she was rewarded by swift and stiff resistance and then a really wonderful explosion of water, followed immediately by an acrobatic series of leaps one after another—three, then four, then five of them! An enormous, impossibly large cutthroat, its red gill gash unmistakable. "Hee yah!" she cried out. "Look at this thing!"

"I'm watching, I'm watching." And in spite of himself, he was.

She let the line run out without an ounce of drag as the fish dove and cut to her left out into the middle of the pool, where it found the central current and pulled into it, then dove again and held. Meg's rod bent nearly double as she tucked the butt of it into her hip to gain leverage. "Don't break off," she pleaded. "Please don't break off."

"You'll get him," Tom said. "Stay cool."

"I'm cool. I'm cool." Sounding anything but.

The fish continued to hold, dead weight, and she had no choice but to do the same for ten seconds, fifteen. Then the line, taut through the deep water, started to rise toward the surface. "It's going to jump again!" And it did, a tail-walking leap of pure electricity and color, at the height of which, all at once, the line went slack and Meg knew that it was over. The fish had thrown the hook.

"Damn, damn, damn!" As she reeled in the line, Meg hung her head and shook it in dejection.

Tom felt the tension go out of his own shoulders as he realized that he'd lost what might have been his best opportunity of the day. While she was standing on her flat rock where the water fell off steeply at the bank under her, absorbed in trying to land the lunker cutthroat, he could have simply sidled up behind her with any one of the large stones everywhere at hand. It would have been the work of a few seconds, then holding her underwater until the thing was done. He could say that he was a hundred or more yards upstream and she, being tipsy from wine at lunch, must have slipped, banged her head, and knocked herself out before falling into the water.

No one would be able to prove otherwise.

Instead he'd gotten caught up in the moment himself.

But at least now—this was the way his ideas developed, in the now—the general outline of what seemed to be an eminently workable plan was coming into clearer focus. There was no question but that another similar, if not identical, situation would present itself over the next couple of hours. Or, it occurred to him, if he played it right, even in the next few minutes. The hatch in the pool continued; Meg still had the right fly tied on, commanded an ideal casting point.

"Hit that same eddy," Tom said. "That's a primo spot."

But Meg shook her head. She still had her fly in her hand, and now hooked it again into its hook keeper up by the rod. She turned to her husband. "It might be a great spot, but not for me. This just proved itself a bad luck pool. If you want to try it, be my guest. I'll even lend you my rod since I'm set up for dry. But I'm done with it."

"That all right," he said. "If Meg calls it a bad luck pool, Tom believes her."

"You saw it yourself," she said. "That was just wrong, that guy throwing my hook."

"It was," he agreed. "So?"

"So." She pointed. "Upstream."

"Lead on."

"But stay with me, would you? I don't like us getting so separated out here."

He gave her a reassuring smile. "I'll be right on your tail."

"Perfect," she said. "Thank you."

At the head of their bad luck pool, the bank rose steeply in a tangle of brush on their side, but a pair of large fallen trees provided a ford to the other side, which looked much more walkable. Upstream of this natural bridge, the water ran wide and shallow, then narrowed and sped up considerably as it sluiced through underneath the logs, probably one of the main reasons the pool had formed where it was, and how it had gotten so large and deep.

Meg paused before she stepped out onto the logs. "Solid and dry," she said back over her shoulder. To her right, downstream, the water boiled in directly under her, continually carving out the deepest cut at the head of the pool. She took a few steps, made sure again that her footing was good, then turned back. "You with me?"

"You with me?" she asked.

"Right here." Tom stepped out onto the nearest log.

Meg, now about halfway across, took a few more steps, then stopped. "What's that?" she said.

"What?"

"Bear, maybe."

She turned to look back at Tom, who was now exactly halfway over the bridge, three or four feet behind her. She pointed to the thick stand of trees that began a few yards back from the stream on the opposite side. Holding up her hand, motioning to Tom that he shouldn't move, she unholstered the bear-spray canister from her wading belt.

Stepping onto the second log, parallel to the first but slightly upstream of Tom, she turned back to him and in one fluid motion, without another word, raised the canister and pulled the trigger, releasing its red cloud of pepper spray into the air in front of Tom's face.

With a scream of terror and pain, Tom raised his hands and fell backward off the log and into the swirling water.

Meg stepped over to where he'd been standing and watched as he floundered under the water. In less than two seconds, he'd already surfaced and let loose with another horrific scream. For a moment after that, her heart was in her mouth as she watched him shake his head in agony, wipe his eyes, and strike out in a strong swimming stroke for the near bank.

But then she noticed that he couldn't seem to get horizontal so that he could actually swim.

Instead, it was as though he was standing in the water on the pool's bottom, except that here the pool seemed to be at least ten, possibly fifteen, feet deep. And all of the motions of Tom's arms were doing nothing to propel him in any direction. Possibly he didn't realize it yet, but effectively he was only treading water. Meg was pleased to note that the reason he couldn't get his feet up to kick and propel him in any direction was that his waders had begun to fill, and were still filling, with water. Because she had borrowed his belt, his waders bloused out under the water's surface, and the water poured in all around him.

He went under again.

But it wasn't over yet. Tom was strong and in a true panic. The water in the bottom of his waders created ballast and the current carried him, still mostly vertical in the water, out some yards away from the bridge into the pool, but he might still succeed in getting to where he could touch bottom and then conceivably make it back to shore.

So Meg, in a hurry now, got herself off the bridge, grabbed a large fallen branch from the bank, and walked along beside where he floated, surfacing again, screaming again, still flailing, still hoping to make any kind of headway toward survival.

A little less than halfway down the pool, the deepest part of the channel cut toward her bank at one point. She had seen this as they'd passed it going upstream and was ready to knock him back in if he extended a hand and managed to gain some purchase on a root or a rock. But as she watched, the weight of the water now filling his waders pulled him under once again, extinguishing his now-exhausted mewlings in a gurgling spray of bubbles.

His progress slowed with the current, and in spite of all the struggle with his arms, he finally couldn't lift his head to clear the water. She watched his arms, moving, moving, trying to force his body up just enough so that he could surface and get one more breath.

One more breath.

But then another burst of bubbles exploded from his mouth and his arm motion slowed, and slowed, and finally changed its character altogether and became truly frantic before at last another strand of bubbles issued from his mouth and nose. After another five or ten seconds, the arms stopped moving entirely. The current had pushed him about two thirds of the way down the pool, and now he hung still in the water where the depth was probably still a good eight feet or more.

Meg, her own breath coming in gasps now, let out a long exhale. With a last look at her husband's body, she walked up the bank to where she could see in both directions. There was no one in sight. They had seen no one else all day. Dropping her branch, she went back down to the water's edge. Tom had been pushed another few feet downstream, but now seemed to have stopped drifting with the current, out in the middle of the pool. His lovely long red hair spread out across the surface of the water.

"You fucking idiot," Meg said aloud. "Did you really think I didn't know?"

After another long moment, Meg got out her bear-spray canister again and, pointing it out in front of her, she pulled the trigger. After letting most, but not all, of the spray dissipate, she stepped into the remains of the cloud, felt the awful sting in her eyes, and then stepped forward into the water.

Three and a half hours later, USFS officers Ted Riley and Lorene Canning moved out of earshot from the distraught widow and their crime scene team. They walked out onto the rock-and-timber-strewn dry riverbed by the pool where an originally hysterical and then progressively more composed Meg had eventually led them to her husband's body. It had taken four men from their team to finally get him out of the water, and now before the long haul carrying the body back to the road, the two forest service officers watched Meg as she sobbed, kneeling over him, her hands gripping his clothes, her head down against his chest.

"That poor woman," Lorene said.

"You think?" Ted replied.

"Of course I think. What else could I think? Just look at her."

"I am."

"And you don't see a grieving wife?"

"I do. But I'm just wondering if she could have gotten him out if she'd have tried."

"Ted. She did try. She couldn't do it. It just took four of our big guys to get him out. She went in and tried, half-blinded even. She was still soaked when she found us, if you recall."

"I remember. And the bear?"

"The bear came at them and she let him have it, but the wind blew the spray back to get them too. And the husband fell in backing away, blind."

"Okay."

"You don't believe it?"

"No. I believe it. That's what the evidence says. I just like to imagine other scenarios. But before we're done, we're going to want to talk to her a little more, find out about their living situation, how they're fixed for insurance, little details like that."

"Of course we'll do that. But I'll tell you right now, we're not going to find anything."

Ted nodded, his jaw set, half a craggy grin pulling at the corners of his mouth. "I'm with you on that, Lor. I completely agree." He took one last glance over to where Meg had by now calmed down, where she simply knelt on the rocks by the prostrate body of her husband. "I don't think we're going to find anything."

DARMSTADT

ANDREW WINER

"All over."

That was the foreigner's reply, in English, to my wanting to know where he was from. I looked at him, starting with his shoes and then moving up his cuffed pant leg and coat until I reached his face, because the way you look at someone new—well, I mean the order in which you look at them—is fucking fundamental, especially if what they're doing is illegal. (To fish the Waldsee, a mud hole masquerading as an angling pond in the middle of nowhere Germany, you have to belong to our piece-of-shit club: the Angelsportverein Wall-dorf.)

"You are not a member of the club," I said.

I considered delivering this in a death metal growl, but checked myself at the last moment in case I needed to play that card later.

The foreigner turned his gaze to the outhouse we call the club office, then to the Darmstadt-Frankfurt freeway, which white-noises the far end of our pond. His dark eyes seemed to cloud with sadness. "I think I'm entitled to a guest pass," he said.

He was roughly my age, taller, yes, but thinner, and I believe we both knew that I could've handled him easily, bounced him from our club property in a way that would've made him think twice about ever re-turning to the midlands of Hessen and maybe Ger-many itself. Yet he took his time reeling in his fly

(*fly*-fishing the Waldsee!) and blinked sleepily at the brown water, almost as if trying to amplify an appearance of fearlessness.

"What is your name?" I asked.

"Aschenbach."

I looked at him. He looked at me.

"*Scheisse*," I said, rolling my eyes. Which means "shit," but also a thousand things beyond that, at least for me. It expresses the power of despair, but at the same time the power of hope. You can cry when you say the word "*Scheisse*." It's a way of staring at the world and saying: *Really?* That's why I say it like a landlubberly Hessian, positing it as a question, slowing it down with a clayey *z* rather than *s* sound (to the foreigner, to any person who spoke English, it would have sounded like "sh—*EYES*—uh?"), because, after all, if you live in the state of Hessen for any amount of time you will inevitably look around at some point and ask, *Really?*

"Really?" I asked.

The foreigner was focused on disassembling his rod.

"Because—Aschenbach: I am not an idiot. I know the reference. You are testing me, I know that too. But even here, in Walldorf, where the year's big event is ChickenFest (we slaughter all of the chickens, then we get shit-faced: it's brilliant, Aschenbach), we read our Thomas Mann in school. So why don't you tell me your real name?"

"Cohen."

"Cohen?" I said dumbly. And even more dumbly: "It is really Cohen?" And then dumbest of all due to the fact that I was trying to drown out my dumbness:

"I am supposed to believe that name?"

"It's representative."

"You are scaring the shit out of me."

I didn't really say that. I said, "You have to leave now," and escorted him past the club office out to the dirt parking lot where Welcome to Hell, my old Renault hatchback, was parked. He had no obvious means of transportation, and turned down the road without saying goodbye, his tin fly-rod case tucked under his arm and pointing at me as he walked away.

To make sure everything was okay, I went back to the pond and inspected the narrow gravel shore where he'd been standing, but I felt stupid: what could the foreigner do to the Waldsee? It wasn't some precious wild trout stream. We weren't catch-and-release. We were catch-and-kill: the Waldsee was manmade, dug from a leased tract of mud beside a farmer's field in the 1950s by two local men, Guril and Mönch, former soldiers who'd lived through Hitler's Russian campaign and then the Allied bombings and who apparently had a leftover need to landlock something in order to catch it and kill it. I didn't become Kommisar of the club until fifty years later (after dropping out of music school in Cologne and coming home to find no other job open), but when I look into the faces of Guril and Mönch—I keep their photographs above my desk in the club office—I believe I understand them. Like me, they weren't pretty men; they resembled the fish that they declared (in the club charter) should be put in the pond: pike, eel, catfish, and sturgeon. No trout, only the basement tenants who prefer darkness and murk, where they can survive forever, maybe see things hidden from human sight. Sometimes I think of Guril and

Mönch when I'm releasing fresh spawn into the water, or when I'm playing guitar with my band and we're inflicting danger on the thrashing crowd. The eel hatchlings already look pummeled, like they've absorbed blows out of nowhere, or are swimming from questions put to their blunted foreheads by an unidentified judge. Moments such as that, when the eyes of a hundred swarming dwellers of the unlight meet mine with expressions of ceaseless doubt, are a lot like being on stage and making eye contact with strangers in the mosh pit. There's love in those exchanges, mixed with cruelty. Really they are the only times when hope ever comes to me and confirms my belief that life lands on the side of the ugly. You try to reach out and touch a few slithering things, to shake off what doesn't feel true and believe that you and they fit together into some kind of pattern. Can you tell I'm the lyricist for our band?

I climbed into Welcome to Hell after grabbing the guitar I'd left over the weekend in the club office (which was the only reason I'd come out to the pond on a Monday, when we're closed), and was halfway down the long frontage road leading to the highway when I passed the foreigner. He didn't even look up, and that infuriated me. I slowed to a stop, eyeing him in the rearview mirror until he drew abreast of my car and I rolled down my window.

"All right, in fact I have not read *Death in Venice*," I found myself saying, to my surprise. "The only reason I know your idiot reference is because Aschenbach happens to be one of the four greatest bands in death metal history. Do you want to hear them?"

"Not particularly."

"Are you hungry?"

"Hungrier than you could ever imagine."

"Is that why you were fishing our pond illegally?"

"You could say that."

And then I invited him to join me for a Big Mac and *pommes frites* with mayonnaise at my favorite McDonald's, twenty minutes away in Darmstadt, several doors down from the pool hall where my band always meets and not far from Morbid, where we regularly gig. I took the back roads through the fields, driving extra fast around the turns and blasting Aschenbach's *Greatest Hits* for the foreigner's benefit. He clearly didn't understand how to smile. During very humorous parts of the songs, he just sat there in the seat being glacial, metaphysical, as if measuring the fluctuations in his soul's temperature. At last, the song "Tadzio" came on, in which Thomas Mann's protagonist follows a little boy all around Venice for several stanzas before trapping him in a dungeon and fucking the shit out of him and finally eating him for dinner.

"Do you like this music?" I asked the foreigner.

That brought on an instant of complete absence, when the foreigner's glance suddenly hung in the void.

"I like it very much."

"Scheisse."

The foreigner refused to eat his Big Mac. Instead, he experimented with an order of *pommes frites,* using his toothpick like a delicate surgical instrument to extract certain fries from the carton and place them in his mouth without ever touching his lips, his eyes passing over the mayonnaise every now and then with a look of such disgust you'd have thought it was a plate of vomit I'd put between us. This didn't bode well for introducing him to the seven madman carnivores who along with me make up the band Todeslied (in English: Deathsong). Sure enough, when we entered the smoky pool hall, they all stopped playing and stood around the table staring at the foreigner, even after I said, "Cunts, this is Mr. Cohen."

Helmut, who, like drummers the world over, specializes in group diplomacy, was the first to break the silence, employing his best high school English. "Shall I take your coat, Mr. Cohen?"

"I'd prefer to keep it."

Directly across the table stood our five other guitarists: Udo, Dirk, Jens, Manfred, and Reinhard. You could see the tattooed flames on their shoulders going rigid.

"Where do you hail from, Mr. Cohen?" asked Udo, making a point of speaking not only in German but also in the most throaty and yokelish Hessian dialect.

"All over," I interjected.

Udo threw me a stern look.

"He is from all over," I clarified.

"All over?" our bass player Dudek said to the foreigner. Dudek flicked a long coil of hair away from his eyes. "So how are you finding it *here?*"

"I only came down this morning."

The foreigner met Dudek's gaze straight on, and Dudek was clearly trying to decide if he should be insulted, but before he came to an answer I said, "Mr. Cohen was fly-fishing the Waldsee."

That brought laughs all around, and somehow, really it was a miracle, the tension vaporized, as if there was no more audience for it, and soon the foreigner was part of the group, in fact beating us all very badly over many rounds of pool. Later, the guys convinced him to come with us down the block to Morbid. No bands were playing, but it was death metal night, and the DJ blasted all the good stuff, allowing us to give the foreigner a history lesson, starting with Sodom and Slayer of course, well, and Kreator and Celtic Frost, then moving on to Autopsy, Necrophagia, Atheist, and Obituary, before taking him through Nihilist, Entombed, Dismember, Pestilence, Hate Eternal, Disembowelment, and Zyklon.

I've never seen someone pay such close attention: the foreigner asked us to repeat certain facts, clearly taking notes in his head, particularly about the bands Zyklon, Hate Eternal, and Atheist. He even challenged us on our theories—you'd have thought he already had a degree in death metal. Before we knew it, he was out on the dance floor, arms extended, throwing his head up and down, eyes closed like he was comforted by the music, relieved. The eight of us closed ranks around our circular table and just watched.

"I love this guy," Dirk said.

"Then you're a queer," said Udo.

"You think he's gay?" I asked.

"Has to be," Jens said. "Look how pretty he is."

Jens was right. For some reason, I hadn't seen it before: the foreigner was beautiful. He had a strong nose and jaw, yet his skin glowed like a woman's, and you could make out his eyelashes from our table, even. If there was anyone who loved this guy it was I. Not because I'm a queer: I'm not. But I was drawn to him, I had to admit—in the way you are drawn to tell a particular person the most shameful thing about yourself, and drawn afterward to hate him for it.

"I believe it's more than that," I announced.

All the guys turned to me at the same time.

"More than he's a *queer?*" Udo asked. "What kind of nonsense are you talking?"

"Maybe he's a pedophile," I said.

"Fuck you!"

"Fuck *you.*"

Udo lit up one of the crappy cigarettes he liked to roll himself from cheap Ukrainian tobacco. He was trying to pretend like it all meant nothing to him. So was I.

"Tell us what you know," he said, exhaling.

I didn't know anything, least of all why I was saying what I was saying. Yet I pressed my forefinger hard into the middle of the table and continued: "Earlier today on the drive over here?"

"Yeah?"

"I played him Aschenbach's 'Tadzio.'"

The guys raised their brows at me.

"*And?*" Udo said.

I tilted my head, rolled my tongue against my cheek, then just put it out there: "He said he liked it very much."

For ten seconds, we all looked at each other. Then, in the synchronized way that only a band that's been together forever can pull off, we said:

"*Scheisse!*"

"*Scheisse!*"   "*Scheisse!*"

"*Scheisse!*"   "*Scheisse!*"

"*Scheisse!*"   "*Scheisse!*"

"*Scheisse!*"

Unfortunately, the foreigner walked up at that very moment. He squeezed into our circle and the silence was terrible. "What were you talking about?" he asked, looking around the table.

No one was going to speak, so I did. "We were having another laugh about you trying to fly-fish the Waldsee."

"Yeah," said Dudek. "No catfish fuck is going to rise for a fly."

Here, Udo chimed in with an exaggerated glee. "Christ, Cohen! What were you *thinking*, man?"

The foreigner smiled at us. "I was thinking that even what's lowest must look upward sometime."

I was so ashamed about calling the foreigner a pedophile to the other guys that, at the end of the night, when he revealed he had no place to stay, I offered him the fold-out couch in my apartment, ignoring the knowing glances and comedic smirks of my shit-faced band mates. And that was how the foreigner came to live with me for the rest of that spring and early summer. He was an easy roommate, hardly there but to sleep, cleaning up after himself, regularly bringing home supplies without my asking him to. If he ever ate in the apartment, I wouldn't have known it, and at the end of each week I'd come home to find an envelope waiting for me on the table with a hundred fresh-smelling Euros in it. Passing all that time near someone I still knew nothing about made our rare encounters awkward. But, well, fuck, they were really no different than accidentally catching a glimpse of an old friend's penis at the urinals and then catching him catching you. No different than when a voodoo impulse compels you to say hello to the villager you've seen for years in the bakery. At most, you might feel a little electricity in your chest—the way you do when spotting a fish rise for a bug that's fallen in the water. When, like I'm saying, tiny events erupt on the surface of regular life.

But in June came an event, an eruption, an encounter (okay, it wasn't really an encounter: I saw the foreigner, he may not have seen me) that was so big, it left life anything but regular—and it sent ripples that not only lasted for weeks but also fanned out across the whole state. It certainly sent *me* all over Hessen—in a Welcome to Hell that was, due to a failing fuel pump, at last living up to its name.

It happened on a Tuesday, my other day off from the pond. In a small warehouse we sometimes rent in Mörfelden, the band had spent the afternoon laying down a new track I'd written—"Meet You in Perdition"—and afterward, as I was walking on Langgasse toward the train station (Welcome to Hell had refused even to start that morning), I spied the foreigner fifty meters ahead of me, staring into the window of a ground-floor apartment. I had no idea if he saw me, but *something* made him leave the window abruptly and rush away up the street until at Darmstädter Strasse he turned out of sight. I approached the apartment, looking around to see if anyone was watching, taking on the guilty pose of a man behaving suspiciously himself. But when I reached the window, guilt turned to anger, because inside was a half-dressed boy, no more than six years old, watching cartoons while lying on his bed, happily oblivious to my gaze.

I didn't go home, *couldn't* go home—not right

away. Instead I walked the suburban streets of Mör-felden, little curving lanes I'd always hated for being cute and boring but now found to be filled with the burning chance of real evil. The light was disappearing, yet everything flashed in my eyes each time I turned a new corner and checked to see if the foreigner might be peering into the window of another unsuspecting house. Of course my behavior made no sense: instinct told me he'd left long ago and was probably back at the apartment. It was like I'd tripped and fallen, only to rise and find that Satan was wearing a new face—a face I was drawn to even now as I was wasting time in shitty Mörfelden just to avoid seeing it.

I won't lie to you: I was glad the foreigner wasn't around when I came home that night. He wasn't there in the morning either, but I remembered hearing him enter and then leave the apartment at some point while I'd been asleep. All day, and all that week (I hadn't seen him again), I sat in the club office wondering where he was and if he was doing harm to the boys (I guess because of the song "Tadzio" I didn't even con-sider the girls) of our local villages.

Then, on Sunday evening, I walked into the apart-ment and found him at the table, hunched over a map of all the fishing holes in the state of Hessen. Spread across the kitchen counter were hooks, thread, wire, feathers, and animal hair of every color, several pairs of pliers, and a vise. The foreigner followed my eyes to these things he was obviously using to tie artificial flies.

"I'm running low," he offered with a weak smile.

And that was half of his explanation for where he'd been. The other half came when he jabbed a finger at the ponds he'd circled on the map and mumbled something about having unusual luck, trying to convince me, I guess, that it wasn't the local boys but our fish that he'd been doing harm to all week.

I remained standing near the door and said, "It's against the law, what you're doing."

At this the smile returned to his face. I couldn't read it; he looked insane to me.

"Whose law?" he asked.

I was sure he was trying to find out what I knew, and I should've said something about the rules of each angling club's charter, or the laws of private property, but in my anger I blurted out: *"Germany's!"*

Now he was all victory, beaming at me—I'd just confirmed that I was onto him, maybe even that I'd spotted him on Langgasse leering at the little boy through the window.

"Germany's?" he echoed with defiance. "Its laws mean nothing to me."

Would you believe I found him back at the same window on Langgasse in Mörfelden the following day? This time I was on my way *to* the warehouse, and I stopped before he could see me, retreated, and walked a big loop to get there—all so I wouldn't have to face him again.

With the guys in the band I didn't share any of it. I was to blame for telling them the foreigner was a pedophile in the first place. Yes, that is what I felt . . . that I'd brought this on our suburbs, brought the problem into the world by giving it a name. And all on a lark, because I'd suddenly seen the foreigner's beauty!

Whose responsibility was it but mine to follow the foreigner now? Well, of course I should've gone to the police, but I didn't like the idea of passing on a problem I'd started, didn't like the idea of the police, period. These were the excuses I kept telling myself over the next three weeks when I'd call up Ulla, our club secretary and my incredibly-ex-girlfriend, and ask her to cover for me at the pond again. "I've caught something really bad," I told her when she pressed me, "and just need to figure out what it is and get it to go away." But during the long drives when I'd be following a taxi the foreigner had hired to take him to some distant village, there was enough time for me to face the real reason I didn't call the police: a vision of the foreigner sitting there in jail while I went to work every day and shot pool with the guys and played gigs at Morbid. I couldn't turn him in.

So I trailed him—to Altengronau east of Frankfurt, where he stood all afternoon in front of a gray house on the main road; to Eckardroth, where he sat in an ugly park for an entire day; to Wohra and Dillich, Tann and Vöhl and Schmitten; to Asslar and Fulda, Villmar, Lohra, Angenrod, Pohl-Göns, Rhoden-Wrexen . . . He'd leave early each morning, fly-rod case under his arm, but in none of these villages or suburbs did I spot him fishing, despite the frequent nearness of a pond, lake, or brook. Of course I wasn't able to track him on every one of his outings, either because I had to work or because I'd lose his trail en route (more than once, he'd take a train to some rural hamlet and then hire the only local taxi, leaving me at the station with nothing to do but wait for a train back to Walldorf).

At home we weren't speaking to each other anymore—at least we didn't until I asked him one night, very casually, how much longer he was going to stay. My apartment building is one of the latest additions to Walldorf, so it stands at the edge of the woods that separate us from the runways of the Frankfurt airport. He was sitting by the living room window, watching distant planes emerge from the treetops and rise up into the clouds. Whatever he'd been thinking, my question pulled him out of it and seemed to leave him confused. He turned to me like a distracted father finally acknowledging a child who's been pestering him.

"I'm not done yet," he said.

And then circumstances forced me to stop following him. At the end of June, right in the heart of the summer fishing season, an epidemic broke out, fouling our local ponds and lakes: reports of fish die-offs were coming in almost daily. The Waldsee was still uninfected, and I felt a duty to somehow stave off the threat, though the biologists hadn't yet figured out the cause. I closed down the club, and even put parking cones across the frontage road to block anyone but me from driving in. And I *did* drive in, every day, sometimes even in the middle of the night, to look for that first dead fish. When I wasn't standing vigil at the edge of the pond, I was at my desk in the club office, checking the Web for updates, talking to colleagues I knew from the network of angling clubs around Hessen, or sometimes just staring at the photo of the founders, Guril and Mönch. The fish they'd selected to stock our pond with weren't made for this world (I was convinced that's why Guril and Mönch had loved them; it's why I loved them) and now it was my strange job to keep them *in* the world—strange, because like the founders, I'd always been fishing, one way or another, for Death.

I was so preoccupied with the pond that a month went by quickly. Given how little time I spent in the apartment, I couldn't have told you anything about the pattern of the foreigner's comings and goings during that period, and I confess that the fish became an excuse for me not to think as much about him. When I did, I drowned in guilt—especially when I'd walk past a child in the street.

It was nearly mid-August when the foreigner stopped me one morning in the kitchen; by then, several weeks had passed without a significant incident of fish fatality anywhere in Hessen—the Waldsee was apparently going to come through okay—and I already felt that a load was being lifted from me. So when he told me that he was "almost done" and would be leaving soon, which meant he'd be relieving me of this other huge problem in my life, I found myself saying we'd have to celebrate. In my eyes it was no accident that Welcome to Hell was scheduled to receive a new fuel pump that day. When I picked up the foreigner in the evening for the drive to Darmstadt (our plan was to celebrate at—where else?—Morbid), I had some old Sodom screaming from the speakers, the countryside was warm, and, as I accelerated out into the fields thinking of the fish and of the foreigner's upcoming departure, I believed I could literally smell Hessen's newfound well-being.

Why, then, did I roll up the windows all of a sudden and tell the foreigner that I had a secret to share with him: a very different kind of music, something my own band mates didn't even know I listened to? The foreigner eyed my iPod with apprehension. He seemed to be groping toward a choice, and I made it for him by choosing a play list I'd cryptically titled "D" long ago. One grating gong filled the car, followed by a frozen silence. Then all at once we were swimming in a flood of instrumental disorder: howls, pings, electronic whirrs and buzzings.

"Stockhausen!" I yelled above the sonic dissonance.

The foreigner was still staring at my iPod—only now as if it were a bomb. And it *was* a bomb, the way I used it, skipping through tracks, setting off a whole series of explosions from the Darmstadt School—composers who'd created new organizing principles in the wake of World War II, going against the old ordered system of chords, erasing any leftover traces of melody from modern music. I hit the foreigner with some atonal atom-splitting by György Ligeti, then a serial music monster by Milton Babbitt. I brought on Boulez and Feldman and Maderna, and an army of more contemporary composers who'd taught at the International Summer Courses for New Music.

"I studied with some of these men!" I shouted over Górecki's *Epitafium*. "Well, only for a few summers— at a very famous place not far from Morbid. I took this same road, playing these songs just like we are now! If you ask what the world is *for me,* it is driving to Darmstadt, through these fields, listening to this music, which is on the other side of comprehension, yes, which seems maybe incompatible with how humans extract information from the air."

The foreigner was looking ill, as if the music was disturbing much more than the ambience of the car, its notes striking deeper than the ears, a traumatism of the soul.

I don't know exactly why I went on. I thought maybe I was trying to soothe him, ease him past his resistance to experimental music, but that wasn't the whole truth. Because it was wonderful to speak to the foreigner like that. To turn the volume even higher, and shout as loudly as I could: "THERE IS NO HIERARCHY! I DO NOT FIND MYSELF IN THIS MUSIC! THESE ARE THE SONGS FOR SOMETHING ELSE, SATISFYING NO ONE, HARDLY BELIEVABLE!"

As soon as we entered Morbid, the foreigner started drinking, his face concentrated in pain, like he was thirsting for eternal relief after having to listen to my secret music. He was shit-faced and stumbling around the dance floor by the time the other guys joined me at my table and asked what was wrong with him. At that point, I too was drunk and told them the truth: "What's wrong with him is that he's spent the last three months traveling all over Hessen in search of little boys."

Udo, Jens, Helmut, and the others all looked at me, looked at each other, then lifted their beers in the air and toasted the foreigner's health, yelling for the waitress to take a beer out to the man right away. They didn't believe a word I'd said.

And it filled me with rage—so much so that, after watching the foreigner enjoy the beer they'd sent over (he downed it without pausing, then raised it toward our table in acknowledgment), I got up from my chair and walked straight at him. He saw me coming, but it only made him put more zest into his dancing, and in fact he seemed to lose himself in the song that was playing—a growling blackened death number, by an obscure Norwegian band, about sexually penetrating God in every orifice, including the eye sockets.

"Find *this* music more to your liking?" I said, getting right up in his face, and at the same time surprised to be taking a moral tone against music I'd been defending forever.

The foreigner kept dancing. "You were right about the songs you played for me," he shouted. "They're not for humans—they're for someone else!"

"Fuck you," I said. And then I shoved him in the chest.

He reeled back in wide-eyed surprise, all the while spewing more words than I'd ever heard come out of him. "You people can't just make up new rules! That's not your right. The rules came before you, and they're forever." He jabbed a finger toward the dance floor. "*This* music acknowledges the rules. It expresses the good, if only by identifying what's evil."

I lunged forward, getting my hands around his neck. "Is that what you told your little Tadzio? That by doing what is evil to him you were *expressing the good!*"

The foreigner threw his brows up in confusion.

"Langgasse, asshole," I said. "I saw you at his window!"

He tried to answer me, but my thumbs were firmly implanted in his larynx, and he only managed to emit a wet throaty sound.

"Oh, you're speaking Hessian now?"

And that was the last thing I said to the foreigner—ever.

His last words to me came after a bouncer threw a massive arm around my own neck, pulling it—and, by painful extension, me—away from him. The foreigner spoke at once, as though he weren't even winded.

"Not Tadzio. *Erez*. The boy's name is Erez. And I'm not done yet."

Who else but our diplomatic drummer Helmut could have talked a very angry club owner out of calling the police and banning our band from ever playing Morbid again? I was too far gone to gather all that he said, but I recall that his argument hinged on the foreigner being a certified pedophile, and I remember laughing when the other guys chimed in, the sight of seven hairy barbarians standing there with their tattoos and crossbones and insisting that I'd only been doing Morbid a service by trying to rid it of the nasty element. I don't know whether they actually came to believe that the foreigner was a pedophile, and it's irrelevant now anyway because I don't believe it.

The guys took me home, and I didn't wake until noon. The foreigner had disappeared—not just from the club, but also from the apartment, from Hessen, maybe even from the planet. I'm not kidding.

His few belongings were gone from my place, except for his state fishing map, which I found folded up under the couch, and took to the kitchen table to flatten out. A shaft of sunlight from the window seemed to set the whole map on fire—I was in pain looking at it—and, when my eyes finally adjusted, I noticed that since the last time I'd seen it he'd done a lot more than simply circle fishing holes. With a fine-point pen, he'd made notations—in tiny block letters—beside hundreds of towns, villages, and cities all over Hessen. Of course my eye went first to the places where I'd spied on him. The gray house in Altengronau where I'd watched him stand out on the sidewalk for an afternoon: FRANKFURTER STRASSE 3, INTERIOR RAVAGED, RITUAL OBJECTS DESTROYED, NOVEMBER 9/10, 1938, CURRENT USE: RESIDENTIAL. The ugly park in Eckardroth in which he'd sat all day: QUERGASSE (EARLIER JUDENGASSE), BUILDING DESECRATED, NOV. 9, 1938, SYNAGOGUE BURNED TO GROUND BY CHILDREN, SEPT. 1944, CURRENT USE: PUBLIC SQUARE. And the apartment building in Mörfelden where little Erez lived: LANGGASSE 2, BUILDING SET ON FIRE—BURNED OUT AND DESTROYED—RUIN, TORN DOWN AFTER MAY 8, 1945, CURRENT USE: MULTI-TENANT RESIDENTIAL, JEWS, FAMILIES ABRAMSON, SKLAR, LAFER, ZIPSTEIN.

I read the rest of the notes late into the afternoon, but it wasn't until I came to the city of Angenrod—whose synagogue was a warehouse now—that my eye landed on nearby Sandsee, one of the fishing spots he'd circled. In the middle of the pond, he'd written "1953" with a pencil. He'd done the same for all the other ponds he'd circled too: Badesee Zeppelinheim, "1950"; the Wasserhof of Crumstadt, "1956"; Sandbach Griesheim, "1962"; the Steinrodsee, "1958"; Gross-Zimmern, "1952"; and our own Waldsee, "1950"—that was the year Guril and Mönch had broken ground. Only then did I realize that every one of these ponds was within striking distance of a synagogue no longer in existence. And every one of them had been hit during the summer with a fish die-off—except the Waldsee.

For once, Welcome to Hell responded brilliantly to

my demands for speed as I raced the back roads from my apartment to the Waldsee, but it was all for nothing. Even before I mounted the rise at the edge of our club's parking lot, I could smell the fish. It was still fresh, but the oldest smell in the world.

The fish were arranged along the gravel shore in rows, according to their kind. The sturgeon lay in the first row, some of their prehistoric tails needling the water. Eel were next; many of them had begun to coil from contraction brought on by the sun's heat. The pike made up the third row, followed by the catfish, a number of which were still twitching. All of them were belly-up, and at least five hundred in number. The pond had been emptied. I was sure of it.

In all the years I'd been Kommisar, I'd never batted an eye when members of the club had come and killed their catch. This was something different, and I was frightened, standing there at the top of the beach. Many of the fish at my feet had been planted in the pond by me, when I was younger and still had dreams of getting out of Hessen. Others, the oldest and biggest ones, had been planted by Walldorf men before my time—Guril and Mönch and their successors—who'd had their own youthful dreams. We'd all been part of something, perhaps even moving toward the *same* thing, as long as the sturgeon and the pike and the other fish were in the pond.

How'd they gotten out?

When I walked down among the fish to look more closely, I found all the proof I needed: caught in the throats of several of them were artificial flies.

It's funny how, with the biggest questions, you end up staking everything on the smallest of evidence. Did

I really believe that the foreigner had caught all those bottom dwellers by fly-fishing? I did. The fish must've wanted the dark brightness above. They must've finally longed to be freed from their fate. *Even what's lowest must look upward sometime.*

I finally did. I stood there by the water's edge and looked upward, thinking back to that first day when I'd found the foreigner standing on the same spot. And it occurred to me that I'd caught him, broken the rules, and hauled him up out of somewhere unseeable, the dark depths of the cosmos, or even my country, I hope not my own character.

CHERCHEZ LA FEMME

DANA STABENOW

There is one in every village.

They don't have to be young, they don't even have to be pretty, but there is one woman in every Alaskan village whose very presence short-circuits something in the nervous system of the male of the species, resulting all too often in events that spiral into intervention on the part of a professional peace officer.

In the case of Dulcey Kineen, the femme fatale came in a pleasant enough package, medium height, nice curves, regular features, but with Dulcey it was more attitude than pulchritude. Her hair was thick and black and she wore it long, in a shining cape she could toss around her shoulders, made a man think about wrapping it around his fist and hanging on for wherever the ride took him. Her eyes were a warm, wicked brown, and they had a way of peering from beneath already-thick lashes so heavy with mascara, it seemed her lids couldn't be strong enough to hold them up. She had a habit of using her tongue to toy with her teeth and the corners of her mouth, which she left open much of the time, as if she were about to take a bite out of whatever was nearest, fry bread, smoke fish, that sensitive spot beneath a man's left ear.

Most women hated her as much as their men loved her, of course. Margaret Meganack had erupted into Bobby Clark's house when Marvin, that morning's guest on Park Air, had strayed from the advertised topic, which was the current red salmon run or lack thereof, to wax eloquent on what Dulcey hadn't been wearing at the Roadhouse the night before. Dinah had banished both Meganacks from the property and interdicted Marvin from being an on-air guest ever again, and given the subsequent repair and replacement bills, you could see her point.

And then there was the time Dulcey ran for Miss Niniltna and won, allegedly on the strength of the blueberry pie she baked for the talent competition. That was fine until Auntie Vi accused Dulcey's cousin Norma Ollestad of baking the pie for her, which no way Norma would have done because of that little episode a while back involving Dulcey, Norma, and Norma's boyfriend, Chuck. Turned out Dulcey really had baked the pie, but she was stripped of her crown anyway. Never a good idea to show up on the auntie radar, and Dulcey had made what Auntie Vi, with uncharacteristic restraint, had described as a nuisance of herself with more than one of the boarders at Auntie Vi's B&B. Auntie Vi could give a hoot what Dulcey did with whom, but she resented the need to wear earplugs to bed every night in her own home.

Sergeant Jim Chopin said that fully a third of the local callouts to the Niniltna trooper post involved Dulcey Kineen in some way. Either she was enticing men at the Roadhouse to drink so she could drink with them, or she was seducing men away from their wives and sweethearts, or she was vamping men for cash, moose backstrap, or a free ride to Ahtna with Costco privileges thrown in, or spurned suitors were getting drunk and wreaking mayhem and madness on a town too small to ignore either. The incident the previous winter involving Dulcey, Wasillie Peterkin, and the road grader was still a painful subject for everyone concerned.

Dulcey and the Balluta brothers. Anybody should have been able to see it coming. But nobody did, until it was far too late.

There were three Ballutas, Albert, Nathan, and Boris. Their father had been a fisherman, their mother had worked as his deck hand until Albert was seven and big enough to take her place. She returned to their house at the edge of the rickety dock across the river from Niniltna and seldom left it again, the last time when they buried her next to their father out back. She'd been a quiet woman and her eldest, Albert, took after her. He was twenty-eight now, a steady, serious, capable, reliable man. He'd inherited the *Mary B.* outright, along with his father's Alaganik Bay permit, and fished it every summer, coming in high boat two out of three years and piling up a healthy balance in the bank in Cordova. Winters he worked on the *Mary B.* in dry dock and on his gear in the net loft over the dock.

Albert's inheriting the *Mary B.* was a source of friction with the youngest brother. Boris was twenty-two and self-involved, opportunistic, loud, and lazy. He fished subsistence when he worked at all, but his smoke fish was the best on the river and, packed in fancy balsa-wood cases, twelve eight-ounce jars to a case, sold at a hefty premium to the clientele of Demetri Moonin's high-end lodge up in the Quilak foothills. He made a mouth-watering saviar from the eggs too, for a list of subscribers from as far away as New York City, every batch sold out months before it was in the one-ounce jars. It was enough to keep him in beer and Edwin jeans. Boris was also a bit of a dandy who had been known to fly all the way to Anchorage for the right haircut.

Nathan, twenty-five, was a typical middle child. He worked summers for Demetri, guiding his clients to the best fishing streams in the Quilaks so they could beat the water for record kings. Winters he worked on the *Mary B*.'s moving parts, paid minimum wage by the hour, and kept all their vehicles running for fun. He was cajoling and conciliatory and could charm the most obstreperous client out of a sulk, which made him invaluable to Demetri, who paid him accordingly.

They all lived together in their parents' house, managing to coexist for the most part in peace, until Dulcey Kineen came along.

Well, Dulcey didn't come along, exactly, she'd always been there, born a Park rat to a typical Park rat family, part Russian, part Aleut, part Norwegian. Her father fished and drank. Her mother had babies and drank. The eldest, Dulcey, fell heir to the babysitting and housekeeping chores early on. When her mother died, her father began to use her as a stand-in for other things as well. She stood it until she was sixteen, when Nick Totemoff told her he loved her. It was the first time anyone had ever said that to her, and she eloped with him to Cordova that night.

Nick had been motivated by what young men are usually motivated by and he'd disappeared within a month, leaving her on her own. She got a job bartending at the Alaska Club and the tips allowed her to rent a tiny mother-in-law apartment. It was her own home, her first and, as it turned out, her only, because her father came into the Alaska Club in the middle of the following fishing season and tried to haul her out across the bar. The damages included her job. The next day, Jim Chopin brought her the news that on the way back to his boat her father had fallen into the small boat harbor and drowned.

Her next-oldest sibling was fourteen. There was no one else to take care of her three brothers and two sisters. She went back to Niniltna, sold her father's boat and permit to Anatoly Martushev, and that and their quarterly NNA shareholder payments, their annual PFD from the state, and their parent's Social Security death benefits managed to keep the family together in the little log cabin with the loft, no running water, and an outhouse out back. Cramped, crowded, everyone took turns splitting firewood for the oil drum stove and no one went hungry.

Which didn't necessarily turn Dulcey into a pattern card of respectability. There were men. There were a lot of men. She had been forced to a realization of her power early on, she knew how to use it, and it didn't help that she was a walking, talking example of chaos theory.

And so, inevitably, Ulanie Anahonak, that self-appointed moral arbiter of village and environs, took exception to Dulcey's behavior, and further, took it upon herself to call DFYS. They didn't show for almost a year. When they did, they spent five minutes investigating the situation before scooping up the five minors and shipping them off to four different foster homes in Ahtna, Anchorage, and Valdez.

Dulcey didn't fight them. Some said she just didn't care. Others said she was relieved to be rid of the burden. Some thought she figured she couldn't win against the state so why try. Instead, she got a job waiting tables at the Roadhouse, in spite of stiff opposition from Jim Chopin, who was already spending too many duty hours breaking up brawls between Suulutaq miners and Park rats fighting over the same girl. Putting Dulcey in the Roadhouse seemed to him like rolling a nuke into a firefight. The resulting explosion was predestined and the fallout would be toxic to everyone in range for a long time.

To his surprise, indeed, to the Park's collective surprise, Dulcey managed to suppress whatever incitements to riot were hard-wired into her DNA for the hours she was on duty. Off duty was another matter, and most of her off-duty hours were spent at the Roadhouse. Hard to tell when she first started hooking up with the Balluta brothers, and no one ever did figure out if it was serially or concurrently.

Everyone remembered the fight Nathan and Boris got into that April, though. It had already been a notable evening, what with Pastor Nolan having confessed his affair with Patsy Aguilar, and his wife sitting right there at the congregational table. Then there was the group of climbers who, having summited Big Bump, had come in for their requisite shots of Middle Finger. It was always fun to see their expressions when Bernie took down the unmarked bottle of Everclear with the finger floating in it.

And then the fight had erupted and spread to engulf Pastor Nolan's parishioners, the Big Bumpers, and the quilting bee in the corner, where it upset three of four Irish coffees. The aunties were pretty pissed about that. So was Dulcey when she had to clean up the mess, and it then became blindingly obvious what the fight had been about, as Nathan and Boris vied with each other to rush bar rags to the scene and then got into another fight over who was allowed to carry the dirtied rags back.

Dulcey twitched her fine behind around the bar and fixed Bernie with a fiery glance. "I didn't start that."

"I saw," Bernie said, and got out the baseball bat. Fortunately Albert walked in and broke it up before Bernie had to break any heads.

Now, you'd think that would have been it, spleen vented and honor satisfied, but instead things seemed to escalate. That spring Nathan guided a couple of salmon hunters to one of the secret streams where Kanuyaq River kings of trophy size came home to spawn, and found Boris there already, tromping back and forth in hip waders, muddying the waters and scaring everything with a fin two creeks away. He was carrying a dip net. Said he was fishing for female kings so he could make his saviar. Nathan's customers, who had had the look of very good tippers, didn't so much as get their lines wet.

A couple of weeks later Boris was fixing to set up his fish wheel. It was a lot of work and Boris didn't put in that kind of effort unless he was certain of a return, so he'd spent the previous week watching the river, counting red runs, and coming up with a pretty fair estimate of when they'd hit his beach. Once the fish wheel went into action it stayed in action until he'd caught his limit, then he packed up the whole shebang and brought it back to the house for smoking and canning.

Only this time, once he'd put all the parts in his pickup, driven the forty miles to the trailhead, humped all those same parts down a mile of rough and more or less vertical trail to the creek, and started to assemble the wheel, he found all the bolts missing.

There were other incidents, and the queer thing was that in between them Boris and Nathan would show up at the Roadhouse and take turns courting Dulcey. Under Bernie's watchful eye they were as polite as ever they could be, to each other and to everyone else.

"It's real amusing to watch," Bernie told Jim, "but it feels like sitting on top of an unexploded bomb."

Jim talked to Albert, who shrugged. "What am I supposed to do? Give 'em a time-out? They're adults, they screw up, you can lock 'em up."

"Maybe it's Dulcey oughta be locked up."

That earned him a sharp look. "Not her fault my brothers are making fools of themselves over her."

Jim, ashamed, said, "I know. I'm just worried somebody's going to get hurt."

The *Mary B.* strained at her moorings. "Boys aren't dumb. They'll figure things out eventually. Meantime, I got a tide to catch tomorrow and too much to do between now and then." Albert laid a hand on the gunwale and vaulted on board.

The Park waited, holding its breath.

The very next day Jim was in his office at the post when he heard a commotion in the outer office. He got to his door in time to see Boris Balluta, covered in blood, yelling, "She's dead! She's dead, I'm telling you, she's dead and he killed her!"

"She," it transpired, was Dulcey Kineen, and it wasn't Boris's blood, he'd just acquired it when he went to Dulcey's place, went in and found it on the couch, on the coffee table, and on dishtowels and hand towels wrung out into the sink. He'd torn the place apart looking for a body and hadn't found one, which he guessed was how he'd gotten blood all over himself.

Jim went to the tiny little cabin. Dulcey wasn't there. Neither was Nathan. The scene was about as bad as Boris had described it, and since Auntie Edna lived next door and kept a weather eye out for the goings and comings of her neighbors, she had seen Boris go in that morning and come out again not five minutes later not quite as spick-and-span as he had gone in. He had placed no bundles in his pickup and buried nothing mysterious in the yard, although he had shouted greetings at Albert, chugging downriver on the *Mary B.*

Jim, his heart sinking, drove around looking for Nathan's pickup and found it parked in front of the post office and Nathan himself coming out the post office door. He gaped at Jim's questions. No, he hadn't been to Dulcey's place in the past twenty-four hours. He hadn't seen Dulcey in five days, come to that, he'd been up at the lodge guiding Demetri's fishermen to trophy mounts for their corner office walls. At the post Nathan saw Boris's red-stained hands and launched himself at his brother. Jim pulled out the Cap-Stun, told the dispatcher to vacate the premises, and emptied the canister on the brothers. He followed Maggie outside and held the door closed until they stopped screaming and started sobbing. Afterward, he put Boris in one cell and Nathan in another, over the vociferous objections of both.

No Dulcey, a lot of blood, and two brothers in a fierce competition for the affections of the same woman. Demetri Moonin confirmed Nathan's alibi. Auntie Edna confirmed Boris's.

Jim went back to Dulcey's cabin with his murder bag.

One room with a loft for sleeping, the cabin's floor plan was a familiar one. On the ground floor there was a woodstove for heat, an oil stove for cooking, a sink in a counter with shelves above and below, a small dining table with mismatched chairs, a battered couch, a coffee table, some brick-and-board shelves. Electricity had been added post-construction and there were wires tacked to log walls everywhere.

The dark blue corduroy couch was stained with blood, only at one end. He took photographs.

The coffee table, a relic of George Jetson's living room circa 1962, was staggering on the corner nearest the stained end of the couch. Upon closer examination, that corner had a preponderance of blood on it, along with a quantity of short dark hairs.

On the table were two place settings—plates, knives, forks—and the remains of a pork chop, green bean, and applesauce dinner, for the most part unconsumed. Meal, interrupted.

Upstairs, the bed looked like it had been hit by a tornado, covers slid to the floor, bottom sheet holding on by one corner, mattress crooked on the box springs. Dulcey's clothes were stacked neatly on more brick-and-board shelves under the eaves, though. He couldn't tell if any were missing. He took more photographs, bagged some samples from couch and coffee table and sink, and returned to the post, where he spent some time writing a timeline of events, and some more time in thought.

Then he sent for Kate.

Kate Shugak was a lifetime Park rat and a private investigator who took on the occasional job for the state at his behest. Five feet, 120 pounds, hazel eyes tilted at the corners, short cap of black hair, she had a presence that reminded him of that line somebody, maybe Shakespeare, had written: "Though she be but little, she is fierce." Her size was indeed deceptive, for she was strong as an ox, quick as a snake, and smarter than the average bear. She was also related to most of the Park either by blood or by marriage, which made her a walking, talking repository of Park history going back generations. Whoever was voted most likely to, odds were Kate knew them, knew where they lived, and could bring them in without mess or bother. She was sort of like shorthand for the Alaska state trooper presence in the Park.

She listened without comment as he ran down the story of Dulcey's disappearance, said, "I'll be back," and left without speaking to Boris and Nathan.

"You unbelievable morons," Kate said two days later—pretty dispassionately, Jim thought, under the circumstances. Kate's tolerance for idiots was very low. "She's not dead."

Both brothers sat up at this. "What do you mean?" Nathan said.

"I saw the blood!" Boris said.

"It was all over you!" Nathan said.

"Shut up," Kate said.

They shut up.

"She and Albert eloped," Kate said.

"What?"

"What!"

"They took the *Mary B.* to Cordova. Dulcey was hiding below when Boris and Auntie Edna saw Albert heading downriver." She looked at Jim. "Whatever you said to him that day convinced him to talk to Dulcey."

He waited. Nathan waited. Boris waited. Finally Jim said, "And?"

"Jim," she said. "It's Dulcey."

"Oh," he said, and then repeated, "Oh."

"It turned into a very long talk. It lasted all night." Her expression dared him to laugh. "The next morning Albert, uh, tripped and hit his head on the corner of the coffee table in front of the couch."

Jim remembered the goo solidified on the corner of the coffee table.

"Dulcey mopped him up as best she could and they got on the *Mary B.* and went to Cordova, where they were married that afternoon." She sat back and watched their various reactions, not without a certain mean satisfaction. "Boris, when you found all that blood, you said it was Nathan just for meanness. You knew he was working up at the lodge, didn't you?"

Boris wouldn't look at her. He wouldn't look at anyone.

"Nathan, Jim tells me you jumped Boris here at the post and he had to pepper-spray you to pull you off him."

Nathan wasn't making eye contact, either.

"One way or another, you boys have made a spectacle of yourselves and caused a great deal of annoyance for the whole Park for the last six months. There will be consequences."

Everybody wondered what that meant. They were not held in suspense for long.

"I talked to a few people on my way back here, and we've come up with something that looks a little like justice." Kate looked at Nathan. "Nathan, you're going to care-take Demetri's lodge for him this winter. You get minimum wage, board and room, and a box of books. I'd recommend at least one of them be written by Deepak Chopra."

"Who else is going to be there?"

"No one."

Nathan swallowed hard. "I'm going to be up there all alone?"

"Yes."

"I won't go." He looked at Boris, at Jim. "I won't go, Kate."

"Yeah, you will," she said. "You earned this, Nathan. You've pretty much proved yourself unfit for human companionship, at least in the short term. Take this winter and think about it."

She looked at his younger brother. "Boris, the mayor of Cordova has finally convinced Shitting Seagull to use all his accrued vacation time. You'll be the acting harbormaster from October one to April one, and yes, that does include keeping space open in transient parking for alien spaceships on their way through to Delta Epsilon. You'll be living in Gull's quarters in the harbor and you'll be on call twenty-four seven for the whole six months."

"What! Why, you—"

"I can think of no punishment better suited to fit your crime than to spend six months serving the public. You'd better be polite to them. If I get to hear otherwise . . ." She let the words trail off into an artistic silence.

"So Dulcey Kineen's alive and well and in Cordova with Albert Balluta?" Jim said in his office. Mutt, the half gray wolf, half husky who let Kate live with her, was waiting for her favorite man, with the usual adoring look in her great yellow eyes.

"No, actually, she's in Anchorage. They both are."

"What for?"

"They're at the Division of Family and Youth Services, applying for custody of Dulcey's younger siblings."

"Really." Jim let the word stretch out. "So that was her price."

Kate shrugged.

"And Albert's?"

"Ratio of men to women in the Park used to be seven to one. Since the mine opened it's probably more like twenty to one. And you know how long most women stay here who weren't born to it."

"Um. Well, Albert's got one of his very own now. Let's hope he doesn't know he has a tiger by the tail."

"Albert's the head of his family," Kate said. "Dulcey's the head of hers. They do sort of fit, if you think about it. I don't know that it's a happy ending, but it may actually be the right one."

"Well, you have to hand it to her. She went through every guy in the Park until she found the right one. And speaking of tigers, just what happened that morning?"

"Well." Kate looked as if she were trying to decide how much it was good for him to know. "Things got a little . . . athletic out."

He let his eyes drop down over her body, lingering here and there. "I can see how that might happen."

Her answering smile was long and slow and full of promise.

Jim left the boys locked in the cells, dimmed the lights, and went home, promising to let them out the next morning.

An hour passed. Another. The July sun tracked around the walls, lessening in intensity but still omnipresent.

Of course Nathan spoke first, and of course it was conciliatory. "She sure was cute." He spoke of Dulcey in the past tense, as if she was dead.

A long silence. "Yeeaaaah," Boris said, drawing it out. "Did you see that little tattoo on the inside of her—"

"Yes, Boris," Nathan said. "I saw it." He sighed and rolled over to look at his brother through the bars.

"I guess now all three of us have seen it."

Silence. A reluctant rumble sounded from the other cell.

A moment later, they were both laughing.

SANDY BROOK

DON WINSLOW

Jerry Donovan has never been a very good fisherman, but he has a naive faith that he can turn his luck around on Sandy Brook.

His devotion to the narrow little stream is absolute. Every time that Jerry sets out to dip a line into one of the Berkshires' many, and better, trout streams, he always ends up changing his mind and going to Sandy instead.

Perhaps it's his belief—all external evidence notwithstanding—that detailed stream knowledge is the key to successful fishing, and *that* Jerry certainly has of Sandy Brook. He knows every pool, fall, drop, and eddy. He knows each rock and sunken log—especially the latter, as they're festooned with his hooks. Jerry is familiar with every overhanging branch, similarly generously decorated with his hooks and line, and where each shadow falls at what time of the day or evening.

Jerry Donovan knows Sandy Brook.

He's out there all the time during the Connecticut fishing season. The locals who drive on Sandy Brook Road, the windy two-lane blacktop that flanks the stream, would be surprised to make the trip and not see Jerry's beat-up old Chevy Nova—color of dull silver, bright rust, and Bondo—on one of the dozens of dirt pull-offs.

Truly, if you want to find Jerry (although not many people do, except for his ex-wife, Brenda, when the alimony is overdue or he blows a car payment), the way to do it is to drive the five-mile road until you spot his car on one of the pull-offs, and then walk the stream from fishing spot to fishing spot until you see Jerry not catching fish. What you mostly see Jerry doing is untangling his line, trying to pull out a snag, clipping his hopelessly fouled line, standing on his tiptoes reaching toward a branch that is arched as tight as a drawn bow, trying to grab his tackle box before it floats farther downstream, or slipping off a rock into the water.

Jerry's ineptitude is the stuff of legend among the denizens of the Riverton General Store, the locus of all fishing knowledge hard by the point where Sandy flows into the larger Farmington River. The serious fishermen chuckle about the time that Jerry cast his entire rod and reel into Sandy and then chased it all the way downstream. Or the time that Jerry spent twenty minutes hauling in a submerged log in the belief that it was a record-breaking brownie, or when he became entangled in his stringer, tripped, and fell into the deep pool beneath Big Rock, or, truly epic, when he hooked his own crotch and jerked his rod tip up . . .

The stories are funny, but not really mean-spirited. The guys like Jerry, everybody likes Jerry, maybe because he's such a good-natured loser. He's just a nice guy, and they can't help but admire his single-minded, quixotic quest to bring in a "keeper" from Sandy Brook.

That's all the guy wants—a "keeper"—one twelve-inch trout.

He pursues it with an almost religious devotion interrupted by only by his stretches in the state penitentiary.

Jerry boosts trucks.

Cigarettes, alcohol, home goods, you name it—Jerry is the number-two man on a crew out of Waterbury that works Connecticut and Rhode Island. He makes a living—*just*—ask Brenda—and didn't need much money in prison, where he kept himself sane during seven- and five-year terms by mentally fishing Sandy Brook. In his imagination, Jerry hauled in long fat brownies and rainbows that fought long and heroically, finally surrendering to Jerry's superior skills. He released all but the record trout, carefully unhooking them under the water and letting them go, watching them wiggle away in a beautiful silver flash toward the freedom he gave them.

Fifty-three years old now, Jerry has nothing.

No wife, no girlfriend, no house, no money, no future.

No keeper.

And he has to report tomorrow for his third stretch, a ten-to-fifteen grudge sentence for a repeat offender.

So he's out there on Sandy Brook.

Last chance at a keeper for a while.

This particular June evening, Paul Harris walks into the General Store and orders a roast beef sandwich with red onions and mayo on a French roll, because it's impolite to ask for information and not buy something, and because the General Store is famous for its sandwiches, piled thick with meat and good value for your money.

While Ed's slicing the roast beef, Paul asks if he's seen Jerry around lately. Jerry's name brings a smile to the couple of fishermen hanging around the counter.

"He was in this morning," Ed says, "getting his mealies."

"Sandy Brook?" Paul asks, smiling.

"Where else?"

Paul pays for his sandwich, buys a Snapple iced tea to wash it down, and walks across the road to the little park by the river. He sits down at a picnic table and watches the fishermen standing out in the water.

These are serious guys in serious equipment—waders, vests, floppy canvas hats, and long, expensive fly-rods and reels. To Paul, they're yuppies or preppies. Paul doesn't come from that kind of place—he's from Waterbury, where they used to make tools and mortgage payments and now they don't make either. Still, the fly-fishermen are nice to watch, graceful in their movements, and the sunlight is soft on the water.

Paul finishes his sandwich, crumples the wrapping paper, and throws it into a green trash can. Then he gets into his car and goes to look for Jerry.

Jerry ties another hook onto his line.

His last hook is embedded in an underwater log.

Tying the hook isn't easy with his pudgy fingers and it takes several efforts to wrap the line six times and then push it through the loop. He had to take off his sunglasses and put on his reading glasses to even see the line, and now he holds it up close to his eyes. His pole, leaning against his shoulder, slides off and clatters on the rock.

Jerry's not a fly-fisherman.

He's a ham-and-egger, rod-and-reel guy who has nothing but contempt for the fly-fishing snobs who mostly come from nose-in-the-air towns like Litchfield and Sharon. Or they're doctors and lawyers from Hartford, and Jerry hates lawyers. He figures he's paid for their expensive fly-rods and what did he get in return? Two stretches in the joint and another one on the way. Even now there's a bill from a fly-fishing lawyer sitting unopened on the table in his motel room. Guy gets you a Hamilton but he still wants to get paid.

Jerry has the rod and reel he bought at K-Mart.

And Jerry doesn't use flies, he uses worms.

Earth, or mealie.

Jerry basically has two fishing techniques: Either he casts the worm to the far side of a pool or the downstream end of a ripple and reels it back across, or he hooks a worm under a bobber and lets it sit for a minute or so before casting to a different spot. He flirted with lures for a while but couldn't afford to replace them, given the considerable attrition rate, so he went back to the worms.

Now he opens his tan plastic tackle box—also from K-Mart—and fumbles for a split shot. Finally getting one between his thumb and forefinger, he opens it, puts it on the line about eight inches above the hook, and squeezes it shut. Then he reaches into the little plastic tub, finds a mealie, drops it, and watches it fall into the water, then grabs another one and succeeds in getting it onto the hook.

Jerry stands on a gently sloping rock above and to the left of a long riffle. He picks up his rod, casts into the riffle, and lets the bait float downstream until it reaches a shallow pool where he expects the waiting keeper to hit.

Nothing.

He clicks his bailer, reels it back up, and repeats the

process five times until he decides to move along. His strategy this evening is to work upstream, finishing up in the late dusk at his favorite spot, a long shelf of rock at the base of a cliff that Jerry has named Cliff Rock.

Jerry picks up his tackle box, realizing too late that he hasn't fastened the lid, and watches the contents spill out on the rock. Putting his reading glasses back on, he spends the next few minutes bent over, struggling to pick up the split shots, hooks, bobbers, and nail clipper, and his belt buckle digs into his belly. Brenda was always after him to lose the spare tire, and he did do sit-ups for a few weeks during his last stretch, but Brenda should talk, right? The woman had her lips around Sam Adams more than Mrs. Adams ever did.

He takes off his reading glasses, sets them down, puts his sunglasses back on, picks up his tackle box, and remembers that he left his reading glasses on the rock. He turns around to get them and hears them crunch under his foot.

The right arm is twisted, and the left lens is shattered, which is about what you can expect of a pair of glasses when you set two-and-a-half bills down on them. It's going to be a problem, because he can't see to tie a hook without them, but he experiments with closing his left eye and just looking through the right lens, and that seems as if it will work all right.

And they'll fit him with new glasses in the joint.

He puts the mangled glasses in his shirt pocket and walks up to his next spot. You'd think Jerry would be discouraged, but he isn't. He believes, really believes, that this is his night, that he's going to get a fat keeper on his last try.

Jerry can't believe that God would let him go another ten-to-fifteen without granting him this one small request.

Paul spots Jerry's heap on the pull-off.

He parks his Focus behind it, gets out, and walks through the trees down to Sandy Brook. It's easy, he just follows the foot trail in the red dirt where probably hundreds of fishermen over scores of years have walked.

Jerry's not there.

Paul looks upstream and downstream but doesn't see him. Doesn't spot his short, pudgy body with that old, sweat-stained blue porkpie hat pulled over his thinning ginger hair.

This annoys Paul, because it means he's going to have to haul his ass up and down the rocky, muddy shore of this creek. He just bought new Adidas sneakers and doesn't want to mess them up. But Jerry is scheduled to report the next day, and Paul has promised to take him, so it has to be done.

He looks downstream again. The stream is fairly straight here, he can see a long way and Jerry's fat ass is nowhere in view.

Paul walks upstream.

Jerry hides behind a boulder.

On the other side is a deep pool, and Jerry *knows* that a keeper is waiting on the far end of the pool just below what Jerry calls Big Rock.

He has a plan.

Leaning against the boulder, he's going to lob his bait like a hand grenade and let it bounce off Big Rock into the pool, where it will be irresistible to the big trout doubtless lurking along the edge of the rock.

Jerry takes a deep breath and makes his cast, which lands in the branch above Big Rock. This isn't part of the plan, and Jerry's concerned that the noise he'll make freeing the hook will alert the trout to the danger, so he pushes his eyeglasses up on his nose, takes the clippers out of the tackle box, and cuts the line.

He spends the next five minutes tying on a new hook and getting the mealie on, and tries again.

The next cast is good.

It strikes the rock at precisely the spot that Jerry intended, but it hits a little hard and the mealie worm pops off the hook and falls into the water. Peering over the top of his boulder, Jerry sees a swirl of water as the trout hits the worm, and he knows that his plan was a good one. Excited, he hopes that the big trout is still hungry as he reels in and hurries to hook a fresh mealie. He lobs the hook again, and while the placement isn't perfect and the bait strikes the rock a little higher than he wanted, the mealie slides down the rock and into the water still fastened to the hook.

Jerry feels the fish strike the bait. He forces himself to wait for an interminable moment and then jerks back the rod tip.

The trout is hooked. Jerry scrambles up the boulder, gets his balance, and sits down, keeping his rod tip high and the line tight. It's a big fish, bending the rod, and he feels it fight and struggle, trying to take his line deep. Jerry reminds himself to be patient, take it slow, and not try to horse it in, but his heart is racing and for a second he's afraid he's going to have a heart attack as he reels in and has the fish halfway across the big pool.

The fish jumps.

It's a big brownie, a definite keeper.

It plunges back into the water and Jerry reels in a little tighter, and now he has it right beneath the boulder and it's only a question of landing it. He can't just haul it straight up the boulder because it might wriggle off in the air, so Jerry slides down the boulder onto the rocky shore, desperately trying to keep the line taut as he does.

His feet land on the round, wet stones and he slips, falling hard on his butt and, as he does, the line slackens and the fish slips off.

Jerry can feel the sad, empty absence of weight at the end of his line.

It feels like heartbreak.

He picks himself up and moves to the next spot.

Paul finds broken glass on a flat rock.

At first he thinks that someone dropped a bottle, but on closer inspection he sees that it's the remnants of a thick eyeglass lens.

Could Jerry, that doof, have broken his friggin' glasses?

Of course he could, Paul thinks. He's Jerry.

He remembers the time Jerry dropped them coming off the back of a truck and was on his hands and knees looking for them when the truck backed up and almost ran over him. Fifty-eight times he tried to get Jerry to go in and get contacts, but Jerry never had the money and didn't have health insurance. Anyway, Jerry would probably poke his eye out trying to get the lenses in, so maybe it was a good thing.

This last job, Jerry was a horror show. Couldn't get

the ski mask over his glasses, couldn't see without them, so blew off the mask, which was really bad because the driver had a wingman who picked Jerry out of the known felon book and then a line-up. Which put the whole crew under the gun, although the witness couldn't make a positive ID of any of them.

But still . . .

It looks like Jerry has been going upstream.

It's pretty here, Paul thinks, in the dusk. The trees that line the far side of the stream are deep green and leafy, the light is pretty on the limestone cliffs, the stream is broken by rocks, boulders, and fallen logs. It's a nice peaceful spot, and Paul can see why Jerry likes it so much.

Paul feels a sadness coming over him.

But he often does at sunset.

He walks upstream.

Jerry stands on the flat shelf of stone beneath Cliff Rock.

A strong chute of whitewater runs past Cliff Rock, breaking into a shallow ripple just below. Downstream to Jerry's left, the stream breaks over a small waterfall into a short but deep pool, and it is on this place that Jerry places his last hope.

It's tricky.

He knows that a submerged log, a veritable hook trap, lies at the base of the waterfall, so he has to fasten his slip shot close to the hook, keeping the bait shallow, and float the line at exactly the right spot in the stream to miss the log but still hit the pool. And it will require a strong cast to get it out into the stream, but you can't get much backswing because of the cliff directly behind and an overhanging tree limb. So it has to be done side-arm.

Jerry's never made this cast before—he's always screwed it up and put the hook in the branch, or in the wrong spot in the stream, and ended up snarled in the underwater log. But his record of past failure doesn't affect his present confidence.

He knows he can do it.

He has to.

The sun is already down below the trees, the light is leaving, and Paul will be coming soon.

Do the math, he tells himself—you're fifty-three now, add ten or fifteen to that and when you get out, if you get out, you're going to be too old to get down the steep path to this spot. And even if you can, you probably couldn't make the climb back up. Not with your bad knees and weak ticker.

He puts his broken glasses on his nose, adjusts the split shot, and hooks on a mealie. Then he plants his feet, takes a deep breath, and makes his cast.

Paul runs out of shoreline.

It stops abruptly at the base of a big cliff and he has to climb up a steep trail, holding on to tree branches to pull himself up. When he gets to the top, he looks down and sees Jerry standing on a rock at the base of the cliff.

Paul's new sneakers are a muddy mess and his nice 501 jeans are smudged with red dirt. He takes the .22 out of his waistband, plants his ass on the steep path, and slides down.

The cast is perfect.

Jerry's thrilled as he watches the line float dead-center in the stream, and then he holds his breath as it drifts over the waterfall and—

glides safely over the log and—

drops into the pool.

Bang!

The trout hits it like a truck. Jerry waits, then sets the hook and feels it set, nice and strong, as the trout races out of the pool and pulls into the stream of whitewater. Jerry's heart pounds and a grin comes over his face as the fish jumps. It's a rainbow, flashing silver in the soft light. It dives under again. Jerry keeps his rod tip high but lets the fish take more line, which zings out of his reel almost like it's singing with excitement.

Then he starts to reel in, now fighting both the fish and the current. The trout fights back, zigging and zagging, but Jerry stays with it, reels it across the ripple into the slower water downstream of the pool. He can see the trout now, flicking its tail violently back and forth, but he can also see that the fish is tiring.

So is Jerry. He's sweating and breathing hard with exertion and excitement as he reels the trout in.

Then he feels something behind him.

"Just a second, Paul," Jerry huffs. "I almost got him in."

"Take your time." Paul sits and leans his back against the cliff.

The fish is played out, and Jerry pulls it in toward the rock at his feet. Keeping the line tight, he squats down and looks at the beautiful rainbow—fifteen inches at least.

A real keeper.

"Nice fish, Jerry."

"Yeah, it is, isn't it?" Jerry says, admiring it again. He looks up and around at Sandy Brook, so beautiful and warm in the dying light of a summer evening. "I can't do another bit, Paul."

"The guys were worried about that."

"I thought maybe they would be," Jerry says, looking down at the trout, now resting from its struggle. "Let's just do it here, Paulie, okay?"

"Yeah? That's what you want?"

"Yeah, it is."

Paul gets up. Jerry hears the metal of his pistol scrape on the rock. He sets his rod gently down and bends over toward the fish. "One second, huh?"

Jerry puts on his broken glasses, reaches into the water, and with a newfound grace takes the trout with one hand while with the other he finds the hook and gently pulls it out of the trout's lip. He holds the beautiful keeper for a moment longer, then opens his hand and lets it go.

The trout flicks its tail twice, then scoots off downstream.

Jerry watches it go.

Then he says, "Yeah, okay."

Paul pulls the trigger twice and Jerry's already in heaven when he topples into Sandy Brook.

THE NYMPH

MELODIE JOHNSON HOWE

The stench of the outhouse seeped deep into Colette's skin. Dim early morning light slid in through the spaces between the wooden slats. The door rattled from Ford's pounding. She tensed.

"What are you doing in there, for Christ's sakes?" he demanded.

"There's no toilet paper."

"Where do think you are, the Plaza? This is Montana. Use what's there. The sun will be up and the goddamned trout will stop biting."

Colette peered at the two torn-out pages from *Life* magazine. On one page was a picture of Marilyn Monroe looking so vulnerable, so beautiful, so available. On the other was the baseball hero and now soon to be Marilyn's ex-husband, Joe DiMaggio. The year was 1954, and Colette knew she could never wipe her ass with a picture of her favorite movie star. She grinned, delighted that it was left to Joe.

Gingerly pulling her jeans up, she winced as she zipped them against the bruise that spread across her belly. Ford hit her or kicked her only where it wouldn't show. She folded Marilyn's picture and slipped it into her pocket.

Outside she found Ford Adams, rods in hand, pacing. His khaki-colored canvas hat was pulled low over his blond hair. His eyes were a mean blue in a large red face. The tall, lean man named Zimmer waited patiently.

"I never should have let you come," Ford snapped, then turned and strode angrily down the hill toward the river, leaving her with Zimmer. Leaving her feeling like a child.

"Sorry," she murmured.

"It's all right." He tipped his battered cloth hat to her like a gentleman. She blushed.

The night before, the three of them had met in a Billings bar run by the Judge. (Though she wasn't sure if the Judge was really a judge.) Ford made her wear the silver mink stole he'd bought her. She felt embarrassed and out of place in it, but Zimmer had put her at ease. He took the fur from her shoulders, folded it, and placed it on an empty chair at their table.

Drinking too much, Colette had listened as the two men discussed the differences between lures and flies. Zimmer made his own flies, and she'd learned he was famous among dedicated anglers. Ford was at his best when he was with someone he wanted to impress. The bully that waited inside of him would disappear, and his charm would take over. Zimmer and he talked about fishing as if it were an art, as if the process was more important than the actual catching of a fish. She had been impressed with Ford's knowledge and sensitivity for fly-fishing. She had never seen this side of him.

Colette had come on the trip because she thought she might catch Ford in a lie. She didn't believe he was fishing when he said he was. She was sure he was off with another woman or worse, his wife. It was all those frozen trout that ended up in her freezer when he returned from his trips. Every time she opened the door there they were, beady eyes staring at her and mouths slightly open as if they had just made a smoke ring. She had begun to wonder if he had bought the trout at a seafood store. She was here to see the "big fisherman" fail, to see him reduced to what he was: a brutal blowhard.

But last night she even forgot her bruises when he began talking with Zimmer. He became the man she wanted him to be, thoughtful, knowledgeable, the man she thought he was when they first met.

When Zimmer and Colette arrived at the river's edge, Ford was already in the water. The river lapped against his waders. Sitting on a fallen tree trunk covered with moss that felt like velvet, she pulled her windbreaker tightly around her and watched in awe as Ford expertly cast his line.

"He's very good." Zimmer stood beside her.

"I didn't know."

"I thought he might talk a good game but when it came down to it he wasn't the kind of man who had the patience for it." He looked at her. "You know what they say?"

"What?"

"The biggest fan of fly-fishing is the worm."

Colette laughed. Ford glanced over his shoulder at them and smiled winningly. Colette waved. For the first time in the two years she'd been with him she felt proud. Was it possible to fall in love again? To feel the way she had when they first met? He was so graceful standing in the river, it was like he could never hit anyone, she thought.

Colette turned and looked at the golden-green meadow that spread out behind her. A single cow stood in the far distance. Zimmer followed her gaze.

"Cows get lonely," he said.

"You mean they feel loneliness like we do?"

"In their own way." He moved toward the river and told Ford he was going farther down to try his luck. Ford nodded. Colette watched Zimmer, gear in hand, disappear around a bend.

The early sun was hardening, warming her face. She was surprised by the quiet of the countryside. The stillness soothed her as she observed Ford skim the fly over the water, tantalizing the trout. He was in his element as much as she was out of hers. And yet she felt calm and unafraid.

She thought of some of the beautiful flies Zimmer had made. All that craftsmanship just to fool a fish. She hadn't understood it last night. But this morning she was beginning to have a sense of its power. Besides, fishing with fake flies didn't seem that different from a woman bleaching her hair, changing the shape of her nose, wearing a padded bra and false eyelashes, just to fool a man.

Colette peered back at the cow. It was slowly moving in her direction. Its big long face hung toward the ground. Its large stomach billowed from its narrow bony back. She closed her eyes and enjoyed the safe comfort of her reverie. Smiling, she remembered Zimmer, flirting, had told her there was a fly named the nymph. She felt a shadow fall over her. Opening her eyes, she looked up into Ford's face. Her body stiffened.

"Are you finished?" she asked.

"Do you see me with any fish?"

"No." She blinked.

"Then I'm not finished."

He threw his rod on the ground and took another from a canvas carrying case.

"I like watching you fish."

He smiled. "That's not fishing. That's technique. That's some goddamned philosophy."

"You talked about it so . . . beautifully . . . last night. I never heard you sound that way. It was as if you cared about something other than yourself. I remember you once talked about me the same way." She tried to sound flirty but her voice was bitter.

"I was just throwing the BS with Zimmer last night. He's the big poobah of fly-fishing. Keep a lookout."

"For what?"

"Zimmer."

"Why?'

"Because I'm gonna catch me some trout. More than he will. I don't want him to know I'm using bait."

"Why?'

"Jesus Christ, you're like talking to a child. I want him to think I caught the damn fish with flies and not bait. Get it?"

From his vest pocket he took a small soiled paper bag. His hand came out with a worm squiggling in his fingers. He plunged the worm onto a hook. She gasped. He grinned.

"Why can't you fish the other way?"

"Because this is easier."

"You're always looking for the easy way."

"That's why I went for you, baby. You rolled as easy as a lump of dough."

His words dug deep. She stared back at the cow, which was now trotting toward them, its belly swaying side to side with the effort.

Ford crept like a burglar toward a group of rocks where the river had formed a small pool. She got up and stood next to him, looking down into the water. She could see her image reflected over the shimmering sleek trout that gathered there. She was still young enough. Still pretty enough.

He shoved her away. "You're casting a shadow on the water. You want to scare them?"

"No." *Yes,* she thought, *I want to scare the fish away from you.*

He carefully dropped his line into the water. She held her breath, hoping he wouldn't catch anything. Then she saw the line jerk, and Ford flipped his wrist, pulling up, feeling the hook catch. After a few give-and-takes he reeled the trout in.

"See?" He held up the fish. "Like shooting monkeys in a barrel."

"I never understood what that meant until now."

Ford furtively peered toward the river's bend while reaching into his pocket for another worm. The silver-speckled trout flapped desperately on the dirt, its gills pumping.

Colette grabbed the fish and threw it back into the water. The trout listed. She should have anticipated the blow, but she was too intent on watching the fish right itself and swim off. The power of Ford's fist knocked her off her feet. She landed in the shallows. The water was shockingly cold yet felt pure. *Can you feel purity,* she wondered, waiting for the kick she knew was coming. He jumped down the bank. His foot dug hard into her side, pushing all the breath out of her.

He returned to the pool and peered in. "You bitch, the trout are all gone."

Gasping and shivering, she sat up. Her hand found a flat rock about the size of an evening bag, only heavier. Getting to her feet, she staggered up the bank. Her clothes clung to her, weighing her down.

Ford, big barrel chest pushing toward her, snarled, "You trying to cut my balls off in front of Zimmer? Is that what you want?"

"I want you to fly-fish!" she screamed.

Behind Ford, the cow sauntered up close. She was surprised at how quietly it moved. She thought nature would be noisier.

As Ford's hand went back to strike her again, she slammed the rock into the side of his head, knocking off his hat. Blood streamed from his temple. As he lunged for her, the cow let out a deep mooing bellow so deafening it stunned him. He whirled around to face it. His body turned rigid as if he'd been shot. He grabbed his left arm. His skin turned an awful gray. He gaped at the cow, then at Colette, as if both of them had betrayed him. Gasping for air, he fell backward into the water.

The river washed over Ford. His empty blue eyes stared up at her. The cow mooed again and she saw big tears roll from its eyes.

Cold, her body shook as Zimmer approached. She didn't know how long he had been standing by the mossy log.

"I . . ." she faltered. "I didn't . . ." She wanted to explain that she just needed to hit Ford back. Just once. Not kill him. But the words wouldn't come.

Taking the rock from her hand, Zimmer threw it far away into the deepest part of the river. Then he got her to kneel so he could wash the blood from her hand.

"A cow will scare the livin' daylights out of a man, sneaking up on him that way," he said softly.

His eyes were as dark and as intense as Joe DiMaggio's. She hadn't noticed that earlier. She remembered the picture of Monroe folded in the pocket of her jeans. It would be all crumpled and wet now. Zimmer held on to her hands even when she tried to pull free. She felt powerless, as if she were being transferred from Ford to him.

"I . . . I didn't know cows could cry," she finally said.

TIGHT LINES

JAMES W. HALL

"A handgun on a fishing trip?"

"For protection," I said.

"Oh, come on, Logan. Don't do this."

"I'm not doing anything. I'm taking a gun, that's all. And Dad's ashes."

She glanced at the door to my study as if she were considering barricading it. Anything to prevent me from going off with a pistol.

"Remember *Deliverance*," I said. "All they had was bows and arrows. Twenty miles downriver, stalked by maniacs, they wished like hell they'd brought firearms."

"Don't joke about this, Logan."

"I'm trying to be lighthearted. I'm trying to be upbeat."

"Look, you can't fake your way through this. You're depressed, walking around in a black funk, now you're heading off into the middle of nowhere, and you're taking a goddamned gun? That's crazy, Logan. Crazy."

"I'm fine. Really, I'm a lot better."

"No, you're not. You're not sleeping, you're skipping work. You're a zombie."

"So I'm still grieving. I'm allowed to grieve, right?"

"He's been gone for two months. It's time to move on."

"That's exactly what I'm doing, Nadine. I'm going

fishing. I'm going to the Lost Lagoon. That's getting on with my life. Right? I'm trying."

"Going back to where you found his body. You ready to face that?"

"That's why I'm doing it," I said. "To answer that question."

My dad's suicide had shocked everyone. Most of all me. And I should have been the one to see it coming. I was, after all, closer to the old man than anybody in his family or his wide circle of friends. I was a partner in his cardiology practice, his only child, his duplicate in matters of temperament and personality. But Dad had hidden his state of mind from even me. He'd fooled me completely. A week after my mother, his wife of fifty-three years, died of a heart attack, Dad was back at work, acting perfectly normal, making his rounds, seeing patients, playing golf with his same buddies, mowing his grass, preparing his own meals.

Then in January, only a month after Mother died, the old man vanished. No note of explanation, no warning. No one had an idea where he'd gone or why. The police merely went through the motions. After four days with no word, I decided to check our secret fishing hole.

Dad had discovered the Lost Lagoon as a boy. It was out in the far reaches of the southern Everglades. He and I had camped and fished there since I was a boy. It was our golden secret. Only Dad and I knew its location. If there was one place Dad might go to revive his spirits, it would be the Lost Lagoon.

Across the room Nadine paced back and forth, giving the Smith and Wesson in my hand dark looks while she combed a hand through her long red hair.

"Think of the gun this way," I said. "It's for whatever invasive species have arrived lately. Pythons, monitor lizards. The Everglades, you never know what's out there. It just makes me feel safer. That's all it is, Nadine. I swear to you."

She walked over to me, got her face inches from mine, spoke in a whisper.

"You've chosen him over me," she said. "One more time, even when he's gone. He's more important to you."

"That's not true, Nadine."

But it *was* true, and we both knew it. My lie hung sour in the air.

She couldn't bear to look at me.

"Just promise me one thing," she said.

"All right."

"You won't do what your dad did."

Nadine was never one for small talk.

I tucked the .357 into the waterproof pouch. Nadine looked away and squinted out the bedroom window at the palms tossing in a dawn breeze.

"I'm fine, Nadine, really. I'm going to sprinkle his ashes, sob for an hour or two, catch some fish, commune with the stars, and come home. That's all."

Nadine shook her head slowly. Resigned to losing this argument, perhaps even resigned to losing me.

For the two decades we'd been married, she'd heard hundreds of stories about my fishing trips with Dad. Most of them hammed up by the old man—the drinking games, the close calls with gators and sharks, the swamped canoes, violent thunderstorms, and stories about all the glorious fish we'd caught and cooked out there in the wilderness.

He and I were pals, best friends, far closer than any father and son I'd ever met. We had a bond that made some people nervous, as if it were somehow unnatural that two men, even father and son, could be such kindred spirits.

We had our fishing expeditions down to a ritual. A pair of canoes launched from Flamingo National Park, just me and Dad paddling for hours across bays, up and down twisting rivers into the remote northern fringes of the Everglades, then paddling another hour through the claw and snag of mangrove branches, cramming through narrow breaks in the foliage, places so tight even the canoes got hung up sometimes, and finally, five, six hours from the docks, an hour or two beyond all the known fishing grounds, we glided into a lagoon Dad had discovered more than a half century earlier. The lagoon bent like a beckoning finger, north then west, and was no more than thirty yards wide at any point.

Because the spot was isolated and virginal, it was primo fishing grounds—tarpon over fifty pounds, badass snook, reds, even some freshwater bass cruising the brackish water. The lagoon was all but invisible from the air, did not appear on any chart or GPS, and was surrounded by flats too shallow for anything but canoes or kayaks. A place so hidden, even the bugs and birds had a hard time zeroing in.

While Nadine watched in grim silence, I finished packing. I wedged a coil of heavy braided rope into my duffel. Repairs to the platform usually were necessary. A loose board, a broken branch.

Tucked into one corner of the lagoon was a flat shelf of cypress planks. When I was a kid, too young to be taken along on the fishing trip, I remember Dad sliding cypress planks into his car and driving away. One by one he had lugged the boards out across those miles of water, and gradually constructed a platform high above the waterline, lashing it to the sturdy mangrove trunks.

Even after brushes with hurricanes and the wear and tear of half a century, the platform was still sturdy. It was a ten-by-ten-foot deck where Dad and I rolled out our sleeping bags, set up the cookstove, lay back, and watched the stars. That's where I got to know my father, listening to him ramble through stories of his youth. After a six-pack of beer, he even spoke of the war, his time in the jungles of Southeast Asia, stories of the women he'd loved before Mom. I knew things about him that not even she had known, things about his wild, adventuring mind, his restless imagination, and a sadness in him that came from putting his dreams on permanent hold as he settled into a lifelong marriage, parental duties, and a job that brought him into daily contact with the sick and dying.

I could feel Nadine watching me as I took the cardboard carton off my desk. My dad's ashes filled a white box that was as anonymous as a takeout carton from a Chinese restaurant. Pork-fried Dad.

I thought of saying it out loud. Something to break the gloomy mood, get Nadine to smile. But I checked myself. It was a bad joke. Like so many things I'd been saying lately. Off-key, out of sync. As though some crude teenage kid had taken up residence in my body.

I looked Nadine in the eyes.

She wore only a lacy pink bra and a matching thong. She moved to the doorway of the study with her arms crossed beneath her lush breasts, giving them a subtle lift. The body language of a woman meaning to ambush me before I could get out the door, lure me into the four-poster so we might spend the afternoon twisting the sheets.

With my spinning rod in hand, I came over. She relaxed and cocked her head back an inviting inch and I bowed my face into her cleavage and inhaled her scent. Coconut and warm honey, like a tray of a macaroons fresh from the oven—an aroma that had triggered countless sexual episodes between us.

Until Dad died, our sex had been frequent and spirited, but in these past two months I'd lost my appetite for her, along with all the other reliable pleasures.

I let her scent fill my lungs and held it in like dope smoke, trying to feel the familiar erotic high. But nothing stirred in the hollow reaches of my chest.

She pressed her hands against the back of my head and forced me deeper into that tempting flesh. In another moment, I saw my father's stern face, heard his commanding voice. Nadine's spell over me was broken, and I drew away.

"No," I said. "I have to go."

"Four days at home in bed. It could be nice. Like old times."

"You're evil."

"I'm a woman," Nadine said. "We're all evil."

I drew my face from the melt of her breasts and saw in her smile that she wasn't kidding.

"When I get home," I said, "I'll make it up to you."

Nadine stepped back and folded her arms across her breasts.

"Don't take the gun, please."

"I won't use it, Nadine. Unless it's absolutely necessary."

"At least tell me where to find your body if you don't return. Draw me a map. Do me that kindness."

I shook my head.

"You know I can't do that."

I parked in the western edge of the huge parking lot at Everglades National Park and hoisted the canoe off the rooftop and carried it overhead to the dock. I eased it into the canal, lashed it to a cleat, then trip by trip, I transported my gear and rods and tackle. One spinning rod, one fly, a small plastic box of hand-tied lures, and a few jigs. I wasn't fussy about casting only flies. Whatever the fish were biting was good enough, that was Dad's philosophy, and it became mine. Better to catch a few with plastic bait than lay down flies all day with no results.

As I went through the drill, I felt a presence shadowing me. More than once I stopped and swung around as if I might find Dad standing close, a huge grin on his face as he sprung yet another of his elaborate practical jokes. But nothing was there. Nothing but the muggy morning air, the cries of gulls, the sulfurous vapors that rose from the stagnant waters near the dock.

By noon I'd paddled several miles across the length of Whitewater Bay. I saw my last motorized skiff by three o'clock. The wind was light from the west, the sky cluttered with wispy, unthreatening clouds. The forecast called for a week of sun, only the remotest chance of rain. I didn't care one way or the other. Let it rain. Dad and I had been out there once for six solid days of rain. But it hadn't mattered. The rain just made the trip more memorable. The fishing out there was always good, no matter what.

I glided past the last chickee hut where campers were allowed to pitch tents and build cooking fires. A narrow dock of weathered pine jutted from a nameless mangrove island. Back in April it was to that very dock that I had transported my father's corpse and laid it out as if this had been his final resting place.

It was a ghastly journey, hauling his rotting body in the small canoe. My father lay at my feet as I paddled, his face destroyed from the pistol blast and the days of rot. There were missing chunks of flesh and long lacerations where scavenging animals had feasted on him.

Ever since that afternoon those images haunted my dreams and waking hours and the vile gas of his decay still gagged me at unexpected moments. The horror of that hour alone with his body had driven me to a despair beyond simple grieving. I couldn't fathom what he'd done. I couldn't connect the images of the ravaged and shriveled corpse with the vital, dynamic man I'd revered from my earliest days.

When I found his body in the Lost Lagoon, I had not debated it for a moment. I knew the authorities would be required to thoroughly investigate his death, and their presence in the Lost Lagoon would forever desecrate the place. By relocating his body and washing down the original death scene, I'm sure I committed numerous crimes, but neither the metro detectives nor park rangers had seemed suspicious of the body's location. The investigation was hurried and minimal.

It was ruled a suicide. The gunshot to the head and

the weapon still in my father's grip made it obvious. Even if the police had tried to dig deeper, it would have been difficult to prove anything. After days of decay and the ravages of vultures and raccoons, and several hard thunderstorms, forensics was all but impossible.

I paddled on beyond the nameless island, retracing the route I'd made two months ago. By the time I crossed the final bay and slid the tip of the canoe into the mouth of Homestretch Creek, my shoulders were aching and blisters were forming on both hands. Homestretch Creek was our private name for the narrow twist of water that led into the Lost Lagoon. Neither the lagoon nor that narrow creek had official names, for neither showed up on any navigational chart. The creek was a half-mile long but usually took an hour to negotiate, threading beneath the slick and knotty mangrove limbs, bumping past their exposed roots. It was barely wide enough for a canoe to pass, and on every trip Dad and I had to clip back a few encroaching branches just to wedge through. From anywhere out on the bay, a passing boater would see only an impenetrable wall of green.

As I paddled deep into the snarl of branches, ducking and twisting out of their way, small green herons eyed me from the shadows and spider webs shone in the golden afternoon light. Overhead, against the empty sky, a flock of snowy egrets drifted by like the spirits of departed souls, in no hurry to get where they were going.

Fifteen minutes into the thicket I came upon a fresh-cut branch.

I held my paddle still. I peered around me in every direction into the tangle of green and brown leaves but saw no movement. Off in the distance an osprey shrieked in alarm. I smelled the fetid stew of mud and exposed barnacles and a fishy incense that breathed through the mesh of vegetation. I dragged the canoe close to the snipped branch and bent its pointed edge down. The meat of the wood was still green. It looked clean and new, but I was no expert on such matters.

I sat for a while till my heart calmed.

There was no way anyone could have discovered this sanctuary. The place was too remote, too hidden, too veiled by growth. Several million people lived only fifty miles away to the north and east in Miami and Fort Lauderdale, though this part of the Everglades was as primeval and desolate as the far side of the moon. It was legally off limits to gasoline-powered engines, and the few kayakers or canoeists who journeyed this far into the wilderness invariably camped at the National Park's primitive sites, which were at least an hour's paddle west of Lost Lagoon. In all our years here, Dad and I had never seen another soul within two miles of the lagoon.

The cut branch, I decided, must have been from my last trip out. A snip I had made in my haste on that frantic afternoon when I'd come searching for my father, hoping beyond hope that I would discover him alive. Sorting out my mother's death, trying to revive his spirits.

I forged on, paddling a few strokes, then I had to drag the canoe by hand past overhanging branches and intruding roots. It was just after five o'clock when I squeezed through the final narrow passage and coasted out into the calm waters of the lagoon.

The smooth surface of the water was pocked here

and there by fish rising to feed. I caught the silver flash of a single tarpon cruising deeper into the lagoon.

After tying off the canoe and lifting my gear onto the platform, I fortified myself with a long breath and climbed up onto the shelf of cypress.

There was no sign of his blood. No evidence of violence. The bullet that exploded his skull had left no trace in the surrounding shrubs. I had a momentary dizzy sense that none of what I remembered had truly happened. As though some terrible nightmare had taken root in my memory and borne its poisonous fruit.

I sat on the edge of the platform and looked out at the gathering darkness, at the metallic water, and watched the green mangrove leaves shiver as a sunset breeze passed through. With Dad gone, the isolation I felt in that place was total. No one knew where I was. No one knew such a place existed. If I chose to use the pistol and end my life, there would be no son to find my body. I was lost to the world.

It was when I was laying out my supplies, placing them into the customary corners of the platform, that I noticed the photograph thumb-tacked to a branch at eye level in the northwestern corner of the deck.

I inched over to it, peered at the image. It was a faded black-and-white snapshot, a vintage photo so washed out that the two figures in it had almost disappeared. A man and a woman were leaning against the fender of a '57 Ford. The man was most certainly my father. He was maybe nineteen or twenty at the time, a few years before he married my mother. There was a jaunty expression on his face. Tight jeans and a snug T-shirt showed off his athletic build.

The woman snuggled in beside him was black-haired and smiling. She had large dark eyes and heavy eyebrows and wore a light-colored summer dress, and the garland of flowers in her abundant black hair had come undone, a strand of it falling down along her smooth cheek. It was not my mother. It was no one I recognized.

On the previous trip, in my frenzied state, I must have missed the photo. For some reason my father had fixed it there as he struggled with his fateful decision. Was this the love of his life? A woman he returned to in his imagination after my mother's death? A haunting reminder of the romance he'd lost as his existence was gradually defined by routine family responsibilities and the grind of work?

He had told me about some of his early loves and I had imagined them vividly, but this young woman's face did not match any of the images in my mind. She was too stunning. Somehow both a classic beauty yet strangely exotic—as though her heritage was a wild mix of Slavic and Caribbean.

I studied the photograph until the light was nearly gone, then I rolled out my sleeping bag, ate the turkey sandwich Nadine had made for me, downed a beer in three swallows. I watched the stars appear, listened to the changing of the guard in the mangroves, night creatures stirring, the creaks and sighs of the branches. A splash, then another, as the warfare between the predators and prey resumed.

I took out the pistol and held it in my hand. Its heft was oddly reassuring. The despair, the bleak hopelessness I'd been feeling was still there, but it had subsided by a degree or two, like the momentary dulling of a migraine.

The photograph seemed to glow through the darkness. Two lovers leaning against that old car. A beautiful woman whose memory had some deep and special significance to my father, but not enough to save him from his suicide.

I raised the pistol and touched the barrel to my temple. Held it there for several seconds as I listened to the wilderness around me. I felt a communion with my father in his final moments, a gun at my head, death so close by. A slight tightening of my finger could end it all. Such power, such finality, such terror.

I exhaled and lowered the pistol and set it on the platform beside me. I could feel my bones trembling.

For decades I had marched side by side with my father, matching his stride, harmonizing my values to his. No other friends I had, not even Nadine, could compare. He was my model, my ideal. Calm, commanding, full of joy and fun, engaged in the rough-and-tumble world, smart and inquiring, endlessly curious. That he had gone off to this spot to end his life still seemed an unfathomable mystery. My mother's death had shaken him, of course, but my father was too strong-willed and independent to succumb to suicidal despair. Unless there was a side of him that he'd managed to hide from me.

I squinted at the pale unnatural moonlight shining from the photograph. Dad would have known that only I could have found it. Which meant he must have left the photo for that reason, like a confession, or the key to a puzzle he meant for me to solve.

I climbed into the bedroll and stared at the endless sky. The pistol lay at my side within easy reach. The scrape of branches and plinks and splashes and rattle of leaves kept me company for an hour or two as my eyes roamed the heavens.

When sleep came, it was agitated and cluttered with scraps of dream. My father was alive again, wearing the same ghoulish mask of death he'd worn on the last day I'd seen him. His jaw was missing, one eyeless socket wept blood, deep gouges grooved his cheeks and throat. He was speaking in a hysterical gibberish that sounded like two raccoons locked in a mortal battle. As I tried to speak his name, my father's hand reached up and took hold of the flesh of his cheek and peeled away the macabre mask as if it were rubber. His normal face was revealed. He smiled in his sheepish, good-natured way, yet I could see the smile was not for me, but for someone beyond the frame of the dream.

I groaned and broke away from sleep, my heart flailing, sweat soaking my clothes. For the rest of the night I lay with my eyes shut, asleep and not asleep, my body clenched and feverish until finally a gray light began to fill the Lost Lagoon.

Still groggy, I felt the platform trembling beneath me.

I lifted my head and squinted. Five feet away, sitting on the edge of a platform, a naked woman held my spinning rod. Her line was tight. A big fish was bending the rod almost double, but her arms and back seemed unstrained by the tension.

This had to be a continuation of the nightmares I'd been having all night. She had the dense black hair of the woman in the snapshot. The knobs of her spine gleamed unnaturally as if her skin were translucent and the shadow of her skeleton was visible through the sheer flesh. I could see the muscles flex and relax as she worked the fish closer to the platform.

I tried to sit up, but discovered I couldn't lift my head more than a few inches from the planks. I fingered my throat, and felt the braided cord I'd brought along. I tried to tear the noose away, but it was knotted too well. I traced the single strand, finding that it was wrapped around one of the cedar planks, leaving just enough slack so I could lift my head a few inches.

"Tarpon," the woman said. "A hundred and five pounds, maybe one ten."

She horsed the fish to the right and made it jump, a wild silver flailing before it crashed against the surface of the lagoon. Bigger than any catch my dad and I had ever made in these waters. It jumped a second time and a third, my rod bending so deeply I thought it might snap.

I fumbled with the cord around my neck, but the fibers were so tough, even if I'd had a knife at hand, it would've taken half an hour to saw through it. I clenched my eyes shut and opened them again. This was no dream. The pain was real, and the woman too. I lifted my head, straining against the ropes to see the tarpon jumping again high into the dawn light.

When she'd reeled the tarpon close to the deck, she stooped forward and with one hand she held the tarpon's mouth and with the other she pried the hook free. I could hear the swoosh of its departure.

"Who are you?"

She stood up and turned around, smiling with the glow of her catch. She set my rod on the deck in the same place my dad and I stored them.

Her body was long and lean and tanned all over. She was a few years younger than I, with large brown eyes and a plump lower lip. Her breasts were small and her hips boyish. A swimmer's body, or a long distance runner's.

She came over to me and squatted down and picked up the white carton that contained Dad's ashes.

"The woman in the photograph. You're her daughter."

"That's right."

I gripped the noose and tugged.

"Let me go. I won't hurt you."

"You couldn't hurt me if you tried."

"So let me go."

She eyed me for several moments.

"That tarpon," she said. "That's the smallest one I've caught in a month. You ever caught any that size?"

"No."

"I didn't think so. I guess I got the fishing genes."

"What do you want?"

"I wanted to meet you. Face to face. See what you're made of. It took you a damn long time to return here. I've been out here for a month. I've been eating so many fish, I'd kill for a hamburger."

"You're his daughter? He brought you here, to this place?"

"Oh, yes. You and I have been sharing him," she said. "We've been dividing the old man all our lives. But you didn't know that, did you? You thought he was all yours. All those conferences he went to, the golfing trips, that was my time with him."

"Let me go."

"That makes me your sister," she said. "Half sister."

"No, you're not. I don't believe it."

"So don't believe it. Keep your fantasy. You and the

old man were best buddies. You and the old man had a unique bond. You had this secret place. Well, you didn't. None of that was true. He was unfaithful to you, unfaithful to your mother. He was living a parallel life."

"You're lying."

"You can't wish me away. I'm here. I've always been here."

I lay still. I looked up at the sky, where a single pelican was coasting past.

She knelt beside me and worked at the knots with one hand while she held the white carton in the other. I could smell her aroma, like a bale of hay baking in the sun, or wildflowers withered on the stem. She was smiling at something, her eyes off in the distance as if she were listening to a voice.

When I was free, she rose and stepped away.

I struggled to sit up, feeling faint and weak.

"Sorry about the noose," she said. "I had to be sure I could handle you."

"Give me the ashes," I said. "Give them to me."

"Pork-fried Dad," she said.

I couldn't speak. I felt the blood drain from my skull.

"It looks like Chinese takeout," she said. "Moo shu Dad."

I saw my father's irreverent smile on her lips.

"You're an illusion," I said. "A figment of my imagination."

"Yeah, right. Dream on."

"What do you want with me?"

"My mother's gone now, in case you were wondering. She died a month before your mom went. That's what did Dad in. The double whammy of losing both his lovers. I'm not married. Never have been. So I don't have a family. No one knows about this place but the two of us. Unless you told Nadine today."

"Dad told you about Nadine and me?"

"No," she said. "He pretended you didn't exist. But I figured it out. Tracked you down. It wasn't hard."

"You figured it out."

"I'm a woman. We're good at things like that. Seeing through our men."

I looked at the paper carton in her hand.

"So," she said. "Let's do his ashes. Then we'll decide who stays, who goes."

"What does that mean?"

"You know what it means, Logan. Only one of us is going to leave here."

I looked around for the pistol, but it was no longer lying by my bedroll where I'd set it last night.

"Why?"

"Think about it. Are you willing to throw away your past? Revise your memories, spend the rest of your life adjusting to this new state of affairs? I know I'm not. I want Dad to myself. I want this place to myself. I want you gone."

I looked past her at the lagoon. At the morning light filtering through the dense green growth, the dazzle of sunlight on the water. For a moment I pictured Nadine back in Miami, waiting for me, wondering if I would return at all.

I thought of my own betrayal of her. The long years when she was second in line for my affection. How she must have longed for the larger part of me, the part I reserved for Dad. And I saw again the resigned look in her eyes as I left yesterday. Or was that a look of finality? A farewell to the man she had squandered her life on?

"You ready, Logan?" She was holding the carton above the water. "I was thinking I should sprinkle half of it and you sprinkle the rest."

I stepped closer to her and saw the pistol's rubber grip exposed at the edge of my sleeping bag.

"All right," I said. "You first then."

She gave me a look that was both wary and amused, one eyebrow cocked just as Dad used to do.

She held the box over the water and tipped it, then swept it from one side of the platform to the other. A breeze sent the gray cloud swirling across the waters.

"Now you," she said, turning to me.

The smile on her lips grew solemn as she saw the gun in my hand.

"Ah, yes. The inevitable pistol."

"I don't want to do this," I said. "But you give me no choice."

"Of course," she said. "I'd do the same. I don't blame you. Not in the least."

"Where's your canoe? Where's your gear?"

She motioned to the waters beyond the bend in the lagoon.

"I have to do this. I have to."

"Of course you do."

I aimed at her left breast. She would fall backward into the lagoon and be carried by the tide deeper into the mangroves. I would sink her canoe, then pack mine and paddle back to the main dock and drive home. Her body would decay and would never be found. I would do what I could to repair my marriage. I would make love to Nadine with a fervor I hadn't shown in years. I would start my life anew. I had seen death a thousand times. I had looked into the dazed eyes of the dying as they breathed their last. I could do this.

But her hand swung up and my father's dust blinded me. In a second she was on me, as strong as any woman I'd ever known. She chopped at my hand and the pistol clattered onto the deck. I stumbled backward over my sleeping bag, clawing at the air in a sightless frenzy. She had her hands around my throat, and I got my hands around hers.

In a moment I felt the fibers giving way beneath my fingers and I heard the crackle of my own ligaments beneath her powerful grip. The dim light grew dimmer as I staggered to the side, pulling her with me in this awkward dance. The deck swayed and rocked and I heard the creaks of the old ropes that held it in place.

I gasped and heard her gasp. My knees sagged. Tiny sparklers fizzled. I smelled the sweet burn of apples and saw my father in his prime, hiking beside my mother and me across a mountain orchard on one of our family vacations. The reel of my childhood began to flash, scenes of my father and me on boats and with bats and balls in fields of play, swimming in a motel pool, riding a Ferris wheel, shooting beer cans off fence posts with a .22, falling asleep side by side beneath the Everglades stars. I felt the ache in my throat and watched blackness swell from the frame of my vision.

On Whitewater Bay, I paddled with even strokes, making it to the docks by noon. I loaded my car with the fishing gear, strapped the canoe on the roof rack, got behind the steering wheel, and waited.

I watched the families come and go. Winnebagos and station wagons and SUVs. Men with their sons. Men with their daughters. Men with only their wives or girlfriends. Backing their fishing boats down the ramps, heading off for a day in the wilderness. I watched tourists park their rental cars and walk aimlessly around the parking lot. I watched birders with their binoculars combing the trees.

At two o'clock she arrived. She wore shorts and a red T-shirt and tennis shoes. She hauled her canoe from the water, carried it to a VW van, and fixed it in place. She sat inside her van for a while, then started it and drove away.

I followed her out the entrance drive, then spent the next half hour shadowing her back to Florida City, staying a good half mile back. When she turned south on the interstate, I turned north. I didn't need to know anything more. She wouldn't return to the Lost Lagoon and neither would I. We had spoiled it for each other, contaminated the place with our savagery.

It was an hour back to the house. I left the canoe on top of the car and sprinted to the front door. I swung it open, ran inside. I called out Nadine's name. Called it out again and again as I searched.

I found her sleeping in the guest room. The TV was on the Weather Channel and a man in a suit was promising more days of sun.

"You're back," Nadine said, as I staggered into the room. "What happened? You look terrible. What happened, Logan?"

I dropped to my knees beside the bed and held her. At first her embrace was stiff and uncertain, but in a moment it softened as though there were no sins she couldn't forgive, no limits to her mercy.

"Your eyes, Logan. What happened to your eyes?"

"It's nothing," I said. "I was crying. That's all. Just crying."

I rubbed at my swollen eyes until my vision finally cleared.

EVERY DAY IS A GOOD DAY ON THE RIVER

C. J. BOX

The guide, Randall "Call-Me-Duke" Conner, pushed them off from the sandy launch below the bridge into the river, and within seconds the muscular dark flow of the current gripped the flat-bottomed McKenzie boat and spun it like a cigarette butt in a flushed toilet. The morning was cool but sunny and there was enough of a breeze to rattle the dry fall leaves in the cottonwoods that reached out over the water like skeletal hands. There were three men in the boat. Jack, who'd never been in such a boat before, cried out:

Is this safe, Duke?

Ha! Of course. Just let me get at the oars and get us turned around. Everything'll be fine. It's a good day on the river. Every day is a good day on the river.

Duke stepped around Jack, who had the front fishing seat in the bow. The boat bucked with his weight. Jack reached out and grasped the casting leg brace in front of his seat and held on and slightly closed his eyes until Duke got settled in the middle of the boat and it stopped rocking. The guide grasped the oars and with two quick and powerful strokes—forward on the left oar, backward on the right—stopped the boat from spinning and righted it within the flow.

See, we're perfectly fine now. You can relax.

It's Jack, isn't it?

Yes, Jack.

Duke laughed, then spoke in a pleasant soft voice. What he said was well rehearsed.

This is a McKenzie drift boat, Jack, the finest of its kind. It was designed for western rivers like this. Flat-bottomed, flared sides, a narrow pointed stern, and extreme rocker in the bow and stern to allow the boat to spin around on its center like a pivot. It's not sluggish like a raft or a damned tank like a jon boat. We point the bow toward one of the banks downriver and keep the stern upriver and we use the power of the river to move us along. That's why it's called a drift boat! I use the oars to keep us in the right place for fishing. Hell, I can shoot this boat from side to side across the river like a skeeter bug to get you fishermen in the best possible position for catching fish, Jack. That's why we float at a forty-five-degree angle to the current, so both of you will have clear fishing lanes and you won't have to cast over each other. It's stable as hell, so don't be afraid to stand up in that brace and cast. Just make sure you keep balanced, Jack. And try not to hook me in the ear on your back cast!

Duke had a deep laugh that Jack would describe as infectious if he were in the right mood.

Jack found out his fishing seat would turn on its pedestal. He released the leg brace and cautiously spun the seat around so he could watch Duke work the oars. The guide was a magician, an expert, and he could move the boat with a flick of either oar. Duke was tall, with powerful shoulders from rowing, no doubt. He had a big sweeping mustache and a dark tan. He wore a fishing shirt, shorts, and river sandals. His eyes were hidden by dark sunglasses fitted with a strap so he could hang them from his neck. Forceps were clipped to a breast pocket as were clippers strung from a re-tractable zinger. He had a big wolfish smile full of perfect white teeth. Jack thought, *He's a man's man.*

Jack watched as Duke turned around and looked over his shoulder at the other fisherman, Jack's host, in the seat in the bow of the boat.

And you're Tim, right?

Yes. I'm Tim.

Tim looked small and slight and scrunched up in comparison with Jack. Jack thought Tim looked like a wet mouse, even though he was dry. Maybe it was the way Tim sat, all pulled into himself, hunched over in his seat, his chin down against his chest. He wore an oversized rain jacket, waders, and a ridiculous hat with hidden earflaps tucked up under the band. Jack shot a look toward the northern horizon to see if there were thunderheads rolling. Nope.

Jack and Tim. You guys seem like a couple of hail fellows well met. Did you say you've fished this river before?

Jack said he was new to drift boat fishing, but he was willing to learn the ropes. Jack confessed:

I've never fished with a guide before. This is all a new experience. But when Tim asked me to come along, I jumped all over the opportunity. So just tell me what to do, I don't mind.

That's a good way to be, Jack. We'll have a good time. What about you, Tim?

Tim didn't answer. He stared at the water on the side of the boat as if the foam and bubbles were the most fascinating thing he'd ever seen. The only sounds were the metal-on-metal squeak of the oars in the oarlocks and the rapid *lap-lap-lap* of the water on the side of the fiberglass hull.

Tim, what about you?

Finally, Tim looked up. There was something mean in his eyes, and his lips were pulled against his teeth so hard they looked translucent.

Duke, why do you say our names every time you ask a question, Duke? Is that so you'll remember our names, Duke? Is that one of your guide tricks, Duke?

Then he added, in an icy tone Jack had never heard Tim use before:

Your name is Randall but you go by Duke. I think I'll call you Randall, Randall.

Duke flashed an uncomfortable smile and looked up at Jack instead of over his shoulder at Tim. As if trying to get Jack to acknowledge Tim was out of line. The silence between them grew uncomfortable until Duke finally shrugged it off and filled it.

Someone wake up on the wrong side of the bunk this morning? Well, never mind that, Tim. Everything will change, Tim. Every day is a good day on the river. We just haven't caught any fish yet because we haven't been fishing. So let's just get you fellows rigged up. I'll pull over here into this little back eddy and drop the anchor and get you rigged up. Everything will be fine once you hook up with one of these monsters.

What crap. Jesus Christ.

Jack had never heard Tim talk with such sarcasm before, and he was a little shocked. He tried to cover for his host.

Tim's been all over the west on all the famous rivers. The Bighorn, the Big Hole, the Wind, the Madison, the North Fork, and of course here on the North Platte. He always tells me about his trips. So when he invited me on this one, man, I jumped at the chance.

You've gotten around, eh, Tim?
I'm not the only one, Randall.

Jack thought: *Bitter.* Then: *Maybe rich men treat guides this way.*

Jack heard a heavy splash and he turned around in his seat again. He'd seen the anchor hanging from an arm off the back of the boat and now it was gone. The anchor was ten scarred pounds of pyramid-shaped lead. It was triggered to drop by a foot release under Duke's rowing bench. Jack could feel the boat slow and then stop when the anchor bit into the riverbed and the boat swung around into the current.

Duke spoke to Jack as if he hadn't heard Tim's statement.

We'll get you started with nymphs and an indicator. When we get rigged up, throw it out there and keep an eye on the indicator, Jack. If you see it tick or bounce, you raise the rod tip fast. Sometimes these fish barely lip the nymph. So if you see that indicator do anything at all, set the hook.

Okay.

It's easy to get mesmerized by the indicator in the water, so don't worry about that. We only have one place on the river where it gets a little hairy, and that's the place downriver called the Chutes. You've probably heard of it.

I have. Didn't somebody die there last year?

About one a year, actually. There's rocks on both sides and some rapids. But as long as you hit the middle squared up, there's no problem. I've done it a hundred times and never flipped a boat. That's the only place you'll need to reel in for a few minutes and you may get a little splash of water on you since you're in front. Otherwise, don't worry about a thing. Tim, do you want me to tie on a couple of nymphs?

I'll do it myself.

Suit yourself, Tim.

I will, Randall.

Jack really didn't know Tim all that well and he couldn't really claim they were friends. So he was surprised when Tim called him at his construction company the week before and offered to host him on a guided fishing trip on the North Platte River. Jack had said yes before checking his calendar or with his wife, Janey, even with the odd provision Tim had requested.

Later, Jack had told Janey about the invitation and the terms of the provision. She was making dinner at the stove—spaghetti and meat sauce—and she shook her head and made a puzzled face.

He wants you to make the booking? I didn't think you knew him all that well.

I don't. But yes, he asked me to use my credit card for the deposit, but said he'd pay me back for everything afterward, including the flies we use and the tip. He wanted to make sure we were scheduled to go on the river with the owner of the guide service—somebody named Duke—and no one else. He said it was important to go with the owner because we'd catch the most fish that way. Who was I to argue? Tim wants the best, I guess.

But why you?

I guess he remembers I was the only one who never gave him any shit in high school when we were growing up. Everybody else did because he was such a weird dude. And he was. You've seen that picture of him in the yearbook. But hell, I guess I always sort of felt sorry for him. For some reason, I liked him and I kind of felt sorry for the little creep. His parents were real no-hopers, and for a while the whole family lived in their car. That car was just filled with junk—sleeping bags and crap. They'd drop him off for school on the street we lived on, so nobody would know, but I saw him get out once. He was real embarrassed, but I didn't tell anyone. I guess he appreciated that. He told me once he never wanted to live in a car again. A high school kid telling me that, I don't know. I was sort of touched. Man, I sound lame.

She laughed.

You do, honey, but that will be our little secret. Then he invented that thing—what was it?

You're asking me? Hell, I'm not sure. Somebody explained it to me once but it didn't take. Something about a circuit for a wireless router or something.

Whatever it was, it made him millions.

And he moved back home to Wyoming. I always thought that was strange.

Yeah, me too.

If you made tens of millions would you move?

Jack snorted and rolled his eyes. *We won't have to worry about finding out. I'll never have to make that decision, so you better keep your job.*

And he got married to that bombshell. What is her name?

I can't remember.

I saw them together once. Beauty and the geek, that's for sure.

Maybe he wanted to prove something to all the

jocks and high school big shots who used to pants him and hang him upside down from a tree, like, Look at me, losers!

But he asked you to go fishing with him.

Yeah, and I want to go.

Maybe he thinks you're his best friend. That's kind of sweet and pathetic at the same time.

Oh, bullshit. I just want to catch big trout with a five-hundred-dollar-a-day guide. That's the big time, baby.

Every man wants to fish with flies and catch a big trout. Here's my chance.

Jack caught two large trout before noon with the nymphs and missed at least five more. A rainbow and a brown. The trout were big, thick, and sleek and reminded him of wet quadriceps muscles that happened to have a head, fins, and a tail. When the fish took the nymphs, it was as if an electric current shot up through the line to his rod, as if they'd like to pull him out of the boat and into the water. He'd whoop and Duke would drop the anchor with a splash and reach for his big net. Jack couldn't remember when he had so much fun.

Tim caught ten but netted them himself without a word and Duke simply shrugged and said: *Let me know if you need any help.*

I don't. I do things for myself.

The rhythm of the current lulled Jack. He stared at the indicator until the image of it burned into his mind and its bobbing mesmerized him. At one point he looked up and thought the boat and indicator were stationary in the river but the banks were rolling by, and not the other way around. There were bald eagles in some of the trees—Duke pointed them out in a way that suggested he did the same thing every day—and they floated by mule deer drinking in the water and a family of river otters slip-sliding over one another on some rocks.

Duke kept up a steady patter.

River right there's a nice hole.

Nice cast there, Jack.

Don't forget to mend your line. There, that's the ticket.

If you hook up again, use your reel. That's what it's there for. Don't grab the line. Don't horse it in.

What a beautiful day. Every day is a good day on the river, ain't it?

All of the land they were floating through was private, with just a few public spots marked by blue diamond-shaped signs mounted on T-posts. There were few houses or buildings along the shores and it seemed to Jack they were the only people on the river or, perhaps, on the planet. There were no takeout spots anywhere, and the truck and trailer would be miles ahead by now, he guessed.

He thought: *Once you're on the river, you're on the river for the rest of the day. You can't stop and go home. You can't get out. There's nowhere to go.*

Although he was concentrating on the gentle bobbing of the strike indicator, Jack saw—or thought he saw—an odd movement in his peripheral vision from the back of the boat. When he turned his head and looked directly, he saw Tim pulling his arm back and jamming his hand into the pocket of his coat. There had been something black in his hand and his arm had been out-stretched, but whatever it was was now hidden, and Tim wouldn't look up and meet his eyes. Instead, Tim made a beautiful cast toward the opposite bank.

Jack shook his head, and rotated back around in his chair. What had been in Tim's hand? And why did he think it might have been a gun pointed at the back of Duke's head?

Then Jack thought: *Stop being ridiculous.*

Duke backed the boat to the bank and dropped the an-chor on the dirt with a heavy thud and said, *How about some lunch, guys?*

Jack had already reeled in because he could hear the increasing roar downriver. The sound was heavy and angry.

Is that the Chutes up ahead, Duke?

That's it, all right. But we'll grab some lunch here first.

Jack was hungry and it felt good to step on hard ground and stretch his legs and back. Duke had said the camp was leased from a rancher exclusively for Duke and his fishing guides and it had a picnic table, a fire pit, and an outhouse. Tim headed for the out-house first, and Jack followed. Duke stayed back at the camp and started a fire in the pit and dug items out of his cooler.

When Tim finally stepped from the outhouse, Jack smiled at him.

I really want to thank you again for inviting me along. This is really special.

Sure, Jack.

Jack hesitated, wondering how to put it. Then he said: *Is everything okay, Tim? Are you feeling okay?*

Why do you ask?

Is there something between you and Duke, or am I just imagining things?

Tim looked hard at Jack, as if searching his face for something or wondering what he should reply.

A while back, I looked in the back of the boat and I thought I saw something.

Really?

Yes. But I might have been imagining things.

Tim reached up and patted Jack's shoulder as he walked past him.

I shouldn't have gotten you involved. I'm sorry.

Involved in what?

But Tim was gone, walking toward the river far to the right of the camp to be alone.

Jack and Duke sat at the picnic table and ate hamburgers. Jack ate two, and half a tube of Pringles. He washed it all down with two cans of Coors Light.

I can't believe I'm so hungry.

Being outside does that to you.

The burgers were great, thank you.

You're paying for them.

Duke laughed, then shouted to Tim, who was still standing alone on the bank, watching the river flow by.

Tim, are you sure you don't want lunch? You've got to be starving, man.

Tim didn't reply. Jack leaned across the table and lowered his voice.

To each his own, I guess. Is he always this surly?

No.

I never got his last name. What is it?

Hey, I really don't like gossiping about my friend, if you don't mind.

Sorry, I shouldn't have asked. You're right. Oh well, I've had worse in the boat. Luckily, I'm a people person. You have to be a people person to be a guide.

I guess you get some characters, eh?

You have no idea, Jack. You have no idea.

Duke packed up the lunch items and secured the cooler to the floor of the boat with bungee cords. Jack waited on the bank, looking downriver toward the roar.

You say there's nothing to worry about, right?

Right. I've done it a million times and haven't lost a fisherman yet. And right past the rapids is one of the deepest holes in the whole river. You'll need to be ready to cast out as soon as we clear the rapids. We'll for sure pick up some fish in there.

Jack, I'll take the front.

Jack turned. He hadn't noticed that Tim had joined them. Tim's face was ashen, and he looked gaunt.

Are you sure?

Yes.

Duke says it gets a little splashy in front.

Please, Jack, step aside.

Tim shouldered past Jack and stepped into the front of the boat and took the seat. He swiveled it around so it was backward and he faced Duke, who was already on the oars. Duke ignored Tim and spoke to Jack.

I'll swing the boat around so you can get in the back easy.

Tim had his hand in his parka pocket and when he drew it out there was a snub-nosed revolver in it. He pointed it at Duke's face, not more than two feet away from him.

Start rowing.

Hey! What the fuck are you doing?

I said start rowing. Pull up the anchor. We're leaving Jack here. He doesn't need to see this.

Jesus, this is a joke, right? It's a joke?

Jack stood on the bank with his mouth open. Tim spoke to him out of the side of his mouth without taking his eyes, or the muzzle of his gun, off Duke.

I'm sorry, Jack. I'm sorry I used you and brought you along. But I was afraid Randall would recognize my name if I made the booking. I'm sure Amanda told him my name.

Jack noticed that the blood had drained from Duke's face. Amanda, that was Tim's wife's name. Amanda.

Right, Randall? Right? She told you my name.

She called you and told you when I was going on a business trip? Or a fishing trip? So you two could get together and humiliate me in my own hometown? Right in front of dozens of people who know me? I know all about it, Randall. Did you laugh at me when you were in my bed? Did you laugh because I was so stupid?

Look, it was Mandy's idea. Really. We never laughed at you.

Mandy, is it? She never asked me to call her Mandy. It's a stupid name. Like Randall. Or Duke.

You don't have to do this. This is crazy. Look, I'll never see her again. I fucking swear it, man.

No, you'll never see her again. You're right about

that. No one will ever see her again.

Oh, God. No.

Yes. This morning. In that bed you know so well.

She thought I was bending over to kiss her good-bye. And in a way, I was.

Jack didn't realize he was unconsciously stepping away from the boat until the picnic table hit him in the back of the thighs. The roaring in his ears drowned out the sound of the Chutes. Tim shouted to be heard over it.

I'm sorry, Jack. I'm sorry to leave you here. But there's a ranch house a couple of miles away. You'll be fine.

Tim, don't do this. Please, Tim.

Too late, I'm afraid. They laughed at me, Jack. That's the worst thing anyone can do to me. Remember how they used to laugh at me in school?

That was along time ago, Tim. You're a big man now. You're a good man.

No one laughs at me.

Jack watched Tim say something to Duke and the boat slipped out into the current and was gone. Because of the heavy brush downriver, he lost sight of it quickly but began to run parallel to the river, hoping he could catch them ahead on a bend. Hoping he could persuade Tim to pull the boat over before it picked up too much speed entering the Chutes and he'd lose them. And before Tim did something he'd regret.

Jack stopped when he heard the sharp crack of a shot. Then he lowered his shoulder and forced himself through the brush. Thorns tore his flesh and his clothing, and his face was bleeding when he broke through and stood knee-deep in the cold water.

The boat was a long way downriver. Beyond it Jack

could see the huge boulders in the river and the foam of whitewater. Duke was slumped over on the oars, his head forward, his arms hanging uselessly at his sides. Tim had swiveled his chair back around, facing downriver. Tim stood up in the fishing platform and braced himself. He tossed the gun aside into the water and reached up and clamped his hat on tight and then raised his chin to the oncoming rapids.

Jack shouted but couldn't even hear himself.

The boat began a lazy turn sideways.

DEATH BY HONEY HOLE

VICTORIA HOUSTON

Early evening late May. Temp midsixties. Light breeze out of the west.

Boyd Martell plunked his butt down on the open tailgate of the Jeep Grand Cherokee and leaned forward to pull his boots on over his waders. He was late getting out this spring, but then so was the hex hatch on the bog.

He tied a double knot on each boot, well aware that even if he tied a *triple* knot the damn things would come untied within the hour. He made a mental note to buy himself a new set of waders—the kind with the built-in boots.

Whew. That done, he straightened up, slipped his arms into his fly-fishing vest, and checked to see he had the right fly boxes. He needed the one holding a half dozen size 12 Royal Wulffs and it would be good to have the box with the wet and dry flies he had tied with the flash of fluorescent orange that these brook trout found irresistible. *Hmph,* Boyd grunted: took him only twenty years to learn orange works!

A whisper of a splash off to his left prompted him to jam on his hat, grab his seven-foot three-weight fly rod and step into the spring-fed bog that was his personal honey hole. Only his wife, Julie, knew where he spent his first evening of fly-fishing every season. And she had sworn on pain of death to keep it secret.

Julie, Julie, Julie—where the hell did you go? he

asked himself for the umpteenth time as he hung on to a handful of tag alder branches so he wouldn't slip as he let himself down into the water. Eight months since she had disappeared. Gone without leaving a note, without calling from somewhere to demand a divorce. Just . . . gone. And man, what a mess she left behind.

It wasn't just the small comforts of good food, bright lights in the windows as he entered their driveway on cold winter nights, and the knowledge someone was around to take care of the dry cleaning, buy groceries, pay bills . . . He actually missed the woman he had taken for granted for so long. *What's the saying?* thought Boyd. *You don't know what you got until it's gone. So true.*

His professional life had suffered as well. Suspicion alone had taken a nasty toll on his medical practice. Even after all this time, he was still under surveillance. That cop must think he's stupid not to see the police cruiser hunkered down behind the arbor vitae shrubs lining his neighbor's drive. He'd spotted her out there at midnight as recently as a month ago.

Too bad, too—Lewellyn Ferris may be a cop, but she is also a very attractive woman. Though she was hardly his type, but he found it difficult to take his eyes off her.

Oh well—let's not think about that now. The brookies are waiting, the air is crisp, the sky is glorious, and I've got the perfect trout flies.

Pushing through the waist-high water toward the sunken log on the far shore, he cleared his mind of all extraneous thought. For the next two hours it would be just himself and the brook trout. No work, no women, no missing wife.

Boyd had considered a spring-fed bog to be such an unlikely source for brook trout in this region of rivers, lakes, and trout streams that when a grateful patient had first offered him access to the bog on his private land Boyd had resisted the offer. But the old man twisted his arm, insisting that he join him for just one evening of fishing, and that was all it took.

Boyd was seduced: the bog held native brook trout averaging six to eight inches and even a few at twelve. Tough little fighters. Fantastic fishing. Now, years later, with the old man gone to fish in heavenly waters, his widow had given Boyd a key to the front gate. The key, which he kept on a rack in the kitchen, was as prized a possession as one of his bamboo fly-rods.

Ten feet from the sunken log, Boyd paused and began to feel his way forward with care. The water, stained dark from the tannins, made it difficult to see the deep hole just in front of the log. The brookies loved to hang near the log or along the bank that cantilevered over the pool. More than once he had filled his waders when he'd gotten too close. And he didn't need to do that tonight, not with the water as cold as it was.

"Jeez Louise." He extended his right foot a few tentative inches. "Can't someone design a sonar unit for fly-fishermen so we don't have to fall in to find our way?"

He had to be close . . . Sliding his left foot through the muck along the boggy bottom and anxious to make that first short roll cast, he raised his fly-rod. The toe of his boot stubbed something and he toppled forward.

Boyd managed to catch his balance before falling. He peered down into the water. Something metallic was catching the fading sunlight. Under his feet he could feel a hard, slippery surface. Checking the bank, he noticed for the first time that the nearby brush was crushed and broken. Had a car or a snowmobile driven off the logging lane that circled the bog? His own vehicle was parked back behind this spot so he hadn't noticed the damage earlier.

Boyd paused, rod in hand, thinking. What to do? Ruin a good night's fishing by alerting the authorities that there might be a problem here? The widow who owned the property was still in Arizona so she wasn't available to get help. Eh, maybe he should just fish and then call someone.

He shuffled around until he could be sure that it was the roof of a car or a small van that he had stumbled on. Had one of the estate's caretakers dumped a vehicle into the bog, thinking no one would ever find it? Claim insurance on a stolen car?

It wasn't until he imagined that someone might be *in* the car that Boyd made up his mind: he could not in good conscience fish over a ghost. He'd better get this situation checked out.

The tow truck arrived within twenty minutes of his call to 911 and, unfortunately, the baggy jeans held up with red suspenders adorned with vertical lettering that spelled DA YOOPERS were a little too familiar. This was not one of his lucky nights.

"Yo, Doc, you needing a haul out *again*?" said the driver in a gruff voice as he launched his bulk from the cab of the truck. "Guess water hard or soft just don't work for you, huh?" he said, chuckling at his own wit.

"Thank you, Emil," said Boyd, striking a tone he

had learned to use when advising patients of the gravity of their pending surgery ("I have a twenty percent chance of losing you on the table."). At the moment it was a tone he hoped made clear he found no humor in Emil's remark.

"I'm afraid someone else may have a problem this evening." He pointed down from where he was standing on the bank on of the bog. "Right under here is a deep hole . . ."

"How deep?" Emil sounded worried. "Do I need to hire a diver?"

"Not too bad. Six . . . eight feet maybe?"

Just his luck it had to be Emil they sent out. It was Emil who had righted his car the night after a combination of ice on the road and too many gin martinis had ended with Boyd upside down in the ditch with that cute young nurse—the one with the frizzy red hair and the stud in her tongue. The one who kept calling even after their little affair had run its course. He didn't like being reminded of that fiasco. Plus, he had tipped Emil fifty bucks that night and still the story had got around town.

"Chief Ferris said to tell you to wait right here, Doc."

"How the hell did she get involved?"

"I dunno." Emil shrugged as he pulled the heavy chain from the back of the tow truck. "They call me, I don't call them."

The police cruiser came bouncing down the logging lane just as the roof of the submerged car surfaced. Boyd watched the vehicle emerge from the bog with enough muck and weeds sliding down its sides that it was difficult in the dark to see what color the car was. It didn't hit him at first. In fact, it wasn't until Chief Ferris was standing alongside him that he realized he was looking at Julie's Lexus.

"Oh . . . oh, my God . . . that's my wife's car." He turned toward the police officer beside him. For a crazy moment, he thought that his identifying the car might convince her finally that he was innocent, that he had had nothing to do with his wife's disappearance.

The car was still half submerged when Lewellyn Ferris leaned forward to shine a flashlight into the interior. Stepping back, Boyd felt his entire body shudder: He wanted to know, he didn't want to know.

"Who is it?" he said in a whisper.

Lewellyn gazed at him for a full thirty seconds, then said, "We have a body inside the car, Dr. Martell. It appears to have been here quite a while but we'll need to be sure . . ."

"That it's Julie?" he offered, his voice weak. "Do you need me to . . . ?"

"No. We'll handle the ID through the dental charts. May take a day or two but I'll call as soon as we have the results. Don't leave town until you hear from me. Understood?"

Boyd got the message.

As always, Chief Ferris was brusque. Was it just him or was she like this with everyone? He sensed she didn't like him. Of course, he hadn't helped his case by inviting her to dinner a few months back, wheedling in his usual style and saying, "Hey, looks I'm single again, Chief."

"Really?" The frosty black eyes had been challenging: "You *know* you are or you *think* you are?"

Big fucking mistake, Boyd, he told himself for weeks after that little contretemps. *Big fucking mistake.*

Boyd Martell had to admit it: the only person in town who hadn't known he had an addiction to women was his wife. Sweet and trusting, she had always believed him when he excused the random calls from angry ex-girlfriends as, "That has got to be a wrong number, hon." Or, "That woman is a disturbed individual who has fantasies about all her docs—just ask Brian, as she called his home too."

What was odd about his attraction to Lewellyn Ferris was that she was the opposite of the women who usually caught his eye—the ones lush and curvy but slim through the hip. Taking care to preserve his own good looks and stay fit, he saw himself as a slightly older version of the tall, lanky, good-looking basketball player he'd been in his youth: the guy who always dated the cutest cheerleader. Cute, perky, adoring girls—that's how he liked 'em.

And that had been Julie—twenty-two years ago. But twenty-two years had changed things. Seventy pounds had changed things. How many times had he urged her to do something about her figure? Do something outside the home more interesting than baking cookies, cleaning closets, dusting roses? But she had resisted, happy to keep house and afternoons filled with her bridge club, her garden club, and the "girlfriends' birthday club."

He should have been happy. Thanks to his money and Julie's willingness to work with interior decorators (at his insistence since Julie's taste was a little unsophisticated), they had a lovely home. She was good at keeping the fridge stocked with his favorite snacks and a home-cooked meal was always waiting on the random nights he forfeited to be home. Bottom line: she knew how he liked things and she didn't argue.

Nor did she complain about the lack of sex. Instead she seemed relieved that she no longer had to undress in front of him but could huddle in her own closet to pull on her pajamas. Her lack of interest assuaged his guilt over his flings as if, had she known, she would have understood. And so it was that they had drifted into an agreeable but flat life together.

Yet every once in a while Boyd would feel a flash of hate: hate for the pounds accumulating year by year, hate for the drooping of the once perky breasts, hate for the nattering on about her friends' health problems, their annoying kids, their new living room sofas. Boring shit.

If only Julie had some vestige of what drew him to Lewellyn Ferris. During the interrogations following Julie's abrupt disappearance, he found himself mesmerized by her direct, succinct manner. Add to that the masculine uniform of the police department, which hardly hid the swell of her breasts and hinted at a fit, interesting body. The very fact she was a woman he couldn't intimidate made her even sexier.

Only once they had veered off the subject of his missing wife. That was to talk fly-fishing—the rods they used, favorite trout flies, the emotional pull of rivers and streams. But that was as far as she had ever let him in. He hoped for more. He had tried once but she proved as hard to hook as a brook trout.

Boyd followed the tow truck out of the property, turned left in the direction of his home, and was soon pulling into his driveway. He entered the kitchen through the back door and hung the gate key on the rack in the mudroom. A Billy Joel refrain announced a call on his cell phone.

"Hey, where are you?" Alicia's voice struck him as a little too cheery.

"Home. Just got here. Why?" He was really, really tired of these calls and she was the last person with whom he cared to share the grim details of the evening.

"Well, honey, I worry about you."

He softened his voice. "I appreciate that, Alicia. Let me call you later—I have a patient on hold."

"Sure."

Boyd hung up and stood rocking back and forth on his heels, hands thrust deep in his pockets. He had learned the hard way that when he was done with a woman it was wise not to be blunt. Don't ever say "It's over." Do that and they go ballistic: key your car, call your wife, harangue your best friend. No, no, no—the right approach is to let things fade. Ease off. Be busy. It may take a while but they do get the message eventually. He would not return Alicia's call.

He knew now that he should never have gotten into it with Alicia. Not only was she the wife of his hunting buddy who was also his stockbroker, but she was a regular in Julie's circle of friends. That should have warned him off, but no. Late at a party on a pontoon just over a year ago he had found her intoxicating: pretty, bubbly, endowed with a great body and a sexy voice, and quick with the quips and funny stories. She was everything Julie was not. Oh, and how she had adored him.

"Four hundred!" He remembered her squealing in amazement when she had quizzed him as to how many women he'd slept with.

"Yeah," he had answered. "But over fifteen years. That's not too bad, is it?" He was rather pleased with himself.

"Ever get caught?"

"Nah, Julie doesn't pay attention. She knows I have lots of meetings." That was true. Seldom had he slipped, and on the few occasions that Julie might have suspected something, he had managed to find an explanation. Never had he hurt his wife's feelings.

Indeed, he had compartmentalized his flings quite nicely. Once a month he made the trip to Madison where he attended medical meetings to keep current with new research. Whether entering a meeting room, a restaurant, or a bar, he knew within minutes which woman he would connect with. Most were like himself: bright, attractive, and looking for fun. Just fun. A couple had been mistakes and hung on too long but he'd found a way to shrug them off over time.

Alicia was his first big mistake. He couldn't have been more stunned when she up and left Jerry. He sure didn't see that coming. He had thought they were one of those couples that had the kids and the vacation homes to keep them together. Who wants to divorce after twenty years? That costs major money. He had just assumed Alicia, like himself, needed a little spice in her life.

Too late he realized that Julie's house, Julie's husband, even Julie's jewelry had long been on her radar. He had underestimated her ambition.

When Jerry moved out and Alicia started dealing with the realities of divorce, she stopped being fun. Boyd didn't like hearing that Jerry was overextended between credit card debt and mortgages. He didn't like the note of desperation that had crept into Alicia's voice. She even made the mistake of mentioning marriage.

Oddly, it was Julie's disappearance that ruined their affair. Once he was free to see Alicia more often, it wasn't the same. It was like . . . it was too much like marriage.

And so he had started to backpedal. But the more he backed off, the more she pressed. Calls to the clinic, to the home phone, to his cell. E-mails on his business account—some of which were a bit too graphic. He worried over the impression her e-mails might make on the hospital techs monitoring the IT system.

Alicia set the phone down. He wouldn't call. She knew that. She also knew about the new girl. And the one before that. She wasn't worried—if she could get rid of Julie, she could handle anyone. But she was a little uneasy. Julie had proven to be less predictable than Alicia had expected.

Today—nearly four months from the one-year anniversary of her disappearance, Julie still had not filed for divorce. Alicia figured she must be waiting the full year and then her lawyer would call: prepared to take Boyd for all he was worth. Or so Julie might think. State law protected half of Boyd's assets. That plus the fact his career was hardly over meant he was still worth plenty.

The odd thing was that though her purse and wallet were missing, Boyd said that he saw no use of their credit cards, nor had she tapped into their bank accounts. "She must have tucked some family money away after her dad died," said Boyd a month after her disappearance.

Alicia thought back over that afternoon when she had dropped by Julie's kitchen to deliver the news, to show her the photos, to suggest a reasonable exit strategy. Julie's face had tightened in a way that surprised her. She had expected her to burst into tears or even take a swing at her. As many times as Alicia had gone over that confrontation, she was still puzzled. Julie had been so calm. So *quiet*.

Eight months and three days earlier

Julie had just pulled the apple charlotte from the oven when Alicia smiled at her through the back-door window. She waved her in.

"Hey!" said Alicia, closing the door carefully behind her. "Got a minute? We need to talk." She laid a manila folder on the kitchen table and pulled out a chair.

"One second," said Julie as she turned the oven off and wiped her hands with the dishtowel. Only later would she recall that Alicia's voice had sounded a little too tense for a friendly chat rehashing their recent bridge game or the atrocious novel they had to read for book club.

"Want some tea?" asked Julie.

"No, this won't take long." Then Alicia had pulled the photos from the manila folder. At first she laid them upside down. She put her elbows on the table, laid one hand over the other, and leaned forward.

She inhaled deeply, then spoke. "I'm leaving Jerry."

"Oh . . . I'm so sorry, Alicia." Julie was shocked. She knew they bickered but this was serious. "How can I help? Do you need a place to stay?"

"I love Boyd—"

"And we love you too."

Alicia hit the table with her right fist. "Will you shut up and listen? I love Boyd and he loves me. He wants a divorce . . . so he can marry me."

Julie heard the words as if through a hollowness in her head. She felt a sudden dullness, the same dullness she'd felt that afternoon she got the call saying her father had died. Listening to Alicia's words from a great distance, her heart left the room.

"We've been seeing each other for a year and he wants out. But he's prepared to make a very fair settlement, Julie. Once the divorce is finalized—" Alicia paused. "I can see from your face you don't believe me."

"I believe you. But, Alicia, you are hardly the first."

"Oh, that I know. Boyd said he's slept with over four hundred women since he married you. Now what does that tell you?"

Julie said nothing.

"You still don't believe me. I knew this would happen so I brought these . . ."

She turned over the photos. There were three, and from the appearance of the bedclothes all were taken the same night.

Julie studied them as if she was looking through a seed catalog. She saw the pleasure, real or faked, on Alicia's face. She saw her husband's long, athletic body entwined with Alicia's. She saw the glee on Boyd's face.

How many years since *she* had seen that expression on his face?

"May I have these?" She yanked the photos off the table. Caught off guard, Alicia tried wrestling them back. The two women half-rose from their chairs, nearly tearing the photos until Alicia let go and threw her hands up.

"Goddammit, keep them. I can print more."

"Leave my house. *Now*," said Julie, getting to her feet, her voice a harsh growl.

Alicia slammed the door behind her. Julie stood where she was for a long, long time. She stood waiting for hate, for despair—for some emotion to hit her, but none did. Instead she felt relief: the enemy was known.

She remembered now a moment, six months ago, during a dinner party when Alicia had walked behind Boyd's chair and brushed his shoulder with her hand. Julie realized that intuitively she had known right then. That explained the ensuing panic attacks, which had become so debilitating she had had to ask Boyd to prescribe antidepressants.

At the thought of Boyd, currently in Madison for his bimonthly medical conference, she decided to act immediately. Given he wouldn't be back until tomorrow morning, she had the entire evening to plan. Her goal was simple: avoid the humiliation of a divorce and make Boyd pay.

Reaching up behind the salad spinner on the third shelf, she felt for the box of Andre's Swiss chocolates that she kept hidden there. Candy in hand, she picked up her household notepad from the kitchen counter and sat back down at the table. She remembered the advice of the therapist she had seen after her father's death: "When facing a tough decision make a list of the positives and the negatives." Julie titled her list "Life after Divorce."

An hour later, she had the answer. The positive list was short and it held a brutal truth: after a divorce from Boyd she would have no life. They had no children. Both her parents were dead. She was an only child and Boyd had a sister and an elderly mother who would, of course, side with him.

She would get house and money but that was all— just two "positives." Her women friends were her life. Their golf games, bridge games, cooking classes, and shopping trips were the pleasures that filled her days. But her women friends, like Alicia, were also the wives of Boyd's friends.

After the divorce, the men would align with Boyd and so would their wives. At first, the girls would pity her, then they would include her only when Alicia wasn't likely to be there. Eventually she would be dropped. She would have a big house, a nice bank account—and nowhere to go, nothing to do.

It wasn't about losing Boyd. It was about losing her life.

Well, she thought, I still have control over how that happens, don't I. She made up her mind right then to exit on her own terms.

She mulled her husband's predictable daily patterns. She considered his prized possessions: his British shotgun, his expensive golf clubs, his bamboo fly-rods . . . That's when it struck her: fly-fishing. The secret honey hole, the spring-fed bog that only he and the owner's family had access to.

More than once he had called for her to deliver a late-night sandwich so she knew the way in and she knew he liked to fish the deep end. She had another thought, one that made her smile: if she could pull this off, he would be asked a lot of questions.

But how did she feel about drowning? Julie didn't like that thought. On the other hand, she had all those antidepressants that Boyd had prescribed for her anxiety. She could refill the prescriptions. Not only would they take the edge off, they would let her drift away. With the car sealed tight, she wouldn't have to drown. She could simply fall asleep.

And so she planned into the night. With each decision, the sense of satisfaction grew stronger. Her last thought before she slept was the number that Alicia had thrown at her: four hundred. Wow, when had he found the time?

Julie woke early the next morning, showered, grabbed a sugar donut from the fridge, and was on her way to Wausau, a good sixty miles from their town, before Boyd would have parked in the hospital lot. She found a small hardware store on the north side and paid the old man who copied the key a buck and a quarter.

Then she drove home. On the way, she had another thought—one that would perfect the plan: provide evidence that she was planning ahead. She recalled reading in a novel that her book club had discussed recently that a woman planning to commit suicide does not plan ahead. They had all agreed how true that was.

Once home, she didn't check for phone messages or even the mail. Instead, she scanned the phone book for the number of the divorce lawyer whose wife was in her bridge club. She immediately called his office and pressed for an immediate consultation because she was leaving town later that day. The ruse worked: she got an appointment for late that afternoon with one of the young associates.

Before slipping the photos into a large envelope, she wrote a note to herself and paper-clipped it to the photos. The note contained the phone number for the law office and the name of the young associate—also bullet points detailing the information she wanted to share. As suggested by the receptionist at the law office, she went into Boyd's study, found a copy of their last tax return, and slipped that in as well. One of Boyd's briefcases caught her eye and she put all the documents into it. That would definitely make it look like she had serious business in mind.

Then she swallowed the pills, got into the car with her purse and the briefcase, and drove to the gate guarding the entrance to the bog. She leaned through the car window to unlock the gate, drove in, then got out of the car and walked back to lock the gate behind her.

After parking where the road ran alongside the deep end of the pond, she waited over an hour until she felt drowsy. Stepping out of the car, she threw the gate key into the pond at a spot far from the honey hole, got back into the car, made sure the windows were tight, and released the emergency brake to let the Lexus roll down the bank and into the water.

As she drifted off, she resisted a wave of sadness. She was doing it her way and she knew it was a good, smart plan. Little did Boyd know she had it in her.

Eight months and three days later

The morning after Julie's car was found, Boyd woke with a start to find Alicia standing over his bed. "Alicia—w-h-a-a-t?"

"Boyd, I just heard the news on the radio. They found Julie's car. I'm so worried for you."

"Alicia, please." He struggled to push himself up on one elbow. "I'm fine and I'd just as soon be alone right now. How did you get in?"

"You always leave the side door open—the one to the garden. Remember?" Alicia sat down on the edge of the bed. "Gosh, that reminds me of the night we spent here when Julie was in Milwaukee with . . ."

That was it for Boyd. "Alicia, stop. We're over. I don't need to remember. And please, do not come into my house like this again."

"But, Boyd, aren't we . . . ? Doesn't this mean . . . ? Boyd." She leaned forward. "We need to present a united front."

"What on earth are you talking about? We had an affair, we had a good time together—but it's over. O-V-E-R."

She handed him a manila envelope. "You might want to check these out before you make up your mind." Her tone was cool as she got up and waited, arms crossed.

Boyd hoisted himself up in the bed and slipped the photos from the envelope. He gave them a quick glance, feeling his stomach turn. "Why? Why did you keep these?"

The photos had been taken early in their affair on a night when too much wine, heady sex, and Alicia's new digital camera had enticed them into setting the timer to capture and relish their fun—photos Boyd had assumed would be deleted the next morning. Evidently not.

"That's why I'm here. I'm worried because . . ." She sighed. "Because I made the mistake of showing these to Julie and she kept the copies I had with me that day."

"Are you crazy? You showed these to Julie?"

"I thought they would convince her that we wanted to be together."

Boyd waved her away. "Please leave. If the photos become an issue, I will be very honest about our relationship and how . . . how they happened. Alicia, I really don't understand why you did such a stupid thing."

With her teeth clenched in an attempt to smile, Alicia said, "I guess I decided a long time ago that if I couldn't have you—no one could. I still feel that way."

"You're insane."

"Crazy with love, sweetie." She backed toward the bedroom door. "Crazy with love."

Later that day it was confirmed: the body in the submerged vehicle was Julie Martell. Chief Lewellyn Ferris drove to the Martell home and met Boyd at the door. "Dr. Martell," she said, "I have a warrant to arrest you on suspicion of first-degree intentional homicide. The medical examiner has determined that your wife did not drown." Boyd was speechless.

Bail was set at one million dollars. By six P.M. that same day, he was able to make bail.

It didn't take long for what remained of his practice to evaporate. Soon he was seeing patients only three days a week, then two, then the bill for his mal-practice insurance arrived and the hospital administration, which had covered it in the past, refused to do so any longer.

Meantime, the three friends with whom he made an annual fly-fishing trip to Jackson Hole decided to make the trip without him. Shortly after, he heard from one of his partners in the deer shack: "Boyd, I really hate to be the one to make this call but we, all the guys that is, would prefer if you didn't hunt this year. Maybe next year when things are straightened out, okay?"

Three months after the car and Julie's body were found, a preliminary hearing was held. Boyd, his lawyer beside him, sat in stunned silence listening to Chief Ferris run down a list of incriminating evidence.

First, the toxicology results showed that Julie's death was due to an overdose of antidepressants—allegedly overprescribed by her husband, Dr. Boyd Martell. The body was too decomposed to determine exactly how the drugs entered her system.

Second, there was scant reason to believe she committed suicide as she had made an appointment to see a divorce lawyer. In fact, along with her body, in a briefcase that had protected its contents from water damage, was a note containing the details she planned to share with the lawyer. In the same briefcase were photos of Dr. Martell naked with a woman not his wife.

The woman in the photos was a local resident who had chosen to cooperate with the authorities. Alicia Cummins had volunteered her cell phone records, which showed hundreds of calls to Dr. Martell at his office and on his cell phone—calls that took place during the year before his wife's disappearance. She was also willing to swear under oath that Dr. Martell had told her at least once, "I hate my wife. Some days I could just kill her." She admitted to sending the photos to Mrs. Martell anonymously in hopes they would spur her to leave her husband.

But the most incriminating evidence disclosed during the hearing was the fact that only three people had keys to the gate leading to the spring-fed bog. The owner's widow, Mrs. Dickson, said she and the caretaker for the property each had a key—as did Dr. Boyd Martell. Not even her two sons who drove up from Chicago to fish the bog had keys.

Since Dr. Martell's key was found hanging on a rack in his home—and since the gate to the bog was locked at all times, it was assumed someone other than the late Mrs. Martell had to have driven the Lexus onto the property.

Through his lawyer, Boyd asked the court why he would have been so quick to report finding a car beneath his feet if he had been the one to put it there.

The question was answered by Police Chief Lewellyn Ferris: "Knowing that Mrs. Dickson's sons would be fishing there shortly and that their father had shown them the honey hole too—both myself and the prosecution suggest that Dr. Martell thought that he could finesse the investigation if he was the one finding the car. We believe he overlooked the fact that he had locked the gate after leaving his wife, drugged, in the deep end of the bog . . ."

The case went to trial. Convinced by circumstantial evidence, the jury found Dr. Boyd Martell guilty of first-degree intentional homicide. He was sentenced to mandatory life imprisonment.

One year later, Alicia Cummins's divorce was final and she joined the dating Web site match.com. Among her hobbies, she listed "photography."

THE BLOOD-DIMMED TIDE

WILL BEALL

Ballard played dead while four stone-eyed gangsters from MS-13 dropped him on the deck of the trawler. They were compact men with sinewy limbs. Every visible inch of skin scrimshawed by gothic MS tattoos, even their faces. Ballard made them for gangbangers called up to the majors, culled from the street ranks of Mara Salvatrucha to play for the cartel.

They were a few miles off the Santa Monica Pier now. Ballard could see the neon spokes of the Ferris wheel and he heard the sea lions bellowing from their buoy as two gangsters lifted chum sacks out of plastic paint buckets. They punctured them with knives, spattering the deck with reeking cow's blood, and dangled the sacks from the stern cleats of the trawler. Then one of them tossed the dead coyote over the side. Ballard doubted sharks got much coyote.

The *soldados* now yanked Ballard up off the deck and he decided he would fight them if they tried to throw him into the drink now, but they dropped him down the stairs instead. He pitched forward, tumbling into the galley, landing hard on his knees and elbows. His wrists, bound with his own handcuffs, were already blue and swollen. Ballard's head throbbed, his eyes adjusting to the dark. The only light in the room came from a desk lamp on the galley table. Next to the lamp, Ballard saw a glass of ice, a pair of bolt cutters, and a fifty-milliliter vial of Lidocaine. So he knew he was in for a long night.

They hauled Ballard to his feet and forced him to sit in a plain aluminum chair. Then they shoved the chair up against the galley table, causing the ice to rattle inside the glass. One of them was holding a towel double-pressed over his ear, the towel soaked with blood. Graze wound. Ballard hoped he had given it to him.

The wounded gangster wore an AK-47 slung over his shoulder. With just seven moving parts, Mikhail Kalashnikov's carbine would fire caked with mud or submerged in water, but it wasn't the right weapon for close-up work. This dipshit probably just carried the thing because he'd seen it in Grand Theft Auto. Christ, Ballard thought, his AK even had a 40 mm grenade launcher mounted under the barrel. If that thing went off in here . . .

Ballard sensed the presence of someone else in the dark, maybe seated at the far end of the table, but Ballard could not see him until the man leaned forward into the light, like something conjured. The man popped a kitchen match with his thumbnail, held it to the tip of his brown cigarillo, and sucked it to life. The flaring glow filled his face with raw red light. He looked like a chainsaw sculpture in a black *guayabera* and Wranglers. He had the sun-punished skin of a life-time soldier, masonry cheekbones showing some mestizo blood. His mustache was a frowning crescent of baleen, yellowed at the tips. He shook the match out and blew smoke from his broad nostrils. "Do you know who I am?"

"Wild guess." Ballard said. "You're an asshole."

The man nodded to his *soldados*. They took hold of Ballard's head and held Ballard still while the man leaned forward and pushed the end of his lit cigarette into Ballard's right eye. Ballard squeezed his eyelid like a fist, heard it sizzling. Ballard screamed, bucked, and twisted in the chair. He could smell his own cooked flesh.

"Okay, okay, Jesus!" Ballard said, gasping. He shuddered and sighed. "Evidently, you're the asshole with the lit cigarette."

"Yes." The man chuckled, donning a pair of latex gloves. "But that is only half of who I am to you now." He snapped the gloves over his wrists and leaned in again to inspect Ballard's eye. They held Ballard's head still while the man forced Ballard's burned eyelid open, but this time his manner was strangely gentle. The man clucked his tongue as though lamenting the injury Ballard had just inflicted upon himself.

"I am an asshole, yes." He said, peering into Ballard's damaged eye. "But I am also an angel."

He reached into the glass, fished out a gleaming ice cube, and weighed it in his gloved palm. "Later, I may remove your fingers, and you will hate me for it," the man said, resting his palm on the bolt cutters. "But you will be so grateful after I inject those bloody stumps with Lidocaine that you will tell me anything." Rivulets of water ran down the wrinkled latex glove as the man held the ice cube over the cigarette burn on Ballard's eyelid.

Ballard's entire body slumped with relief and he almost cried. He told himself he probably deserved this because he'd killed the Red Ranger, practically killed him, as good as killed him. "You see?" The man whispered. "We're friends again. Now." The man pulled the ice cube away from Ballard's eye, popped it in his mouth, and crunched it. "Where the fuck is my money?"

Ballard's foot touched the lamp's cord under the table.

Detective I Shane Ballard rolled over and knocked the phone off the nightstand. He wasn't supposed to be catching tonight. So let someone else handle the spatter, the casings, the homicide scene trampled all to shit by curious uniforms. He would have torn the cord out of the wall, but it was a cordless phone. No one had any other kind anymore.

"Ballard?" The voice on the line was familiar, but floating so far out of context here on Ballard's home phone at one in the goddamned morning that he didn't recognize it.

"Who the fuck is this?"

"Who you *think* it is?" It was Everton, his playful petulance giving him away. Everton James, a.k.a. Twin from Boot Hill Mafia, calling an LAPD detective at his home.

"How'd you get this number?" Ballard asked, sitting up now. He could almost hear Everton holding the phone out away from his ear, scowling at the stupidity of the question. That was like asking Santa how he managed it all in one night.

They said when Everton was a kid, he'd developed a cyst the size of a watermelon in his gut and it wasn't until the doctors cut him open to remove it that they realized the cyst had been Everton's fetal twin. Everton bragged around the hood about being a cannibal, said he was a Crip so down he'd killed his own twin brother over turf. Everton shaved his whole head, even his eyebrows, and he paid a tattoo artist on Sunset to put a full-size image of his own face on to the back of his head, like Janus. They said Everton would never get caught slippin' because he could see you coming up behind him through the eyes of his tattoo.

Ballard and Everton had first met after a Korean guy blasted Everton with a sawed-off gauge in a liquor store lick that went sideways. According to the Korean, Everton had ducked, reflexively raising his hand to ward off the shotgun blast, and wound up leaving two of his fingers behind on the linoleum floor of the liquor store. That was how Ballard caught him. He printed the fingers.

Ballard and his partner, Crowe, came loaded for bear to serve an arrest warrant for Everton in the infamous Blessed Chateau apartments, sometimes referred to as the Los Angeles County coroner's southern satellite office because of all the bullet-pocked corpses that turned up there every weekend. But Everton slipped out the window as soon as they tossed in their flashbangs. He managed to steal a black and white and he led Ballard and Crowe on what remained the best vehicle pursuit of their careers, bar none.

Everton led them all the way from South Central to Toluca Lake, where he crashed the stolen black and white through the front of a ranch house off Riverside. The carrion birds were already hovering when he crashed. Six choppers, all the local affiliates, plus two Spanish stations, carrying it live.

By the time Ballard and Crowe reached him, Everton had already wrenched the Remington 870 shotgun out of the rack in his black and white. And he was trying to jack a round into the chamber when Ballard gripped the black-faced lawn jockey by the shoulders, yanking it up from its rectangular plinth-impression in the grass, and swung the statue like a sledgehammer.

Everton dipped his shoulder and tucked his wing like a prizefighter absorbing a hook to the body. And the plaster jockey exploded laterally against Everton's side and for an instant both Everton and Ballard disappeared in a cloud of pulverized plaster. Everton stumbled sideways, stunned long enough for Ballard to get the handcuffs on him.

Everton took the whole lawn jockey thing the wrong way. Ballard swore he hadn't meant any kind of racial insult by it. He tried to explain to Everton that the lawn jockey was just something handy to hit him with. Christ, he could have shot him. He would have been in policy.

"I wish you would have," Everton said. "This was humiliating. Shit."

"Well, I'm sorry," Ballard said, meaning it. "Look, next time I promise to shoot you, okay?"

He and Crowe had Everton calmed down by the time they put him in the holding tank. Still, Crowe had warned Chauncey from Internal Affairs Division to give the gangster a few hours to cool off before Chauncey interviewed him. But Chauncey had insisted on debriefing Everton right away because CNN was already running footage of Ballard hitting Everton with the lawn jockey and Chauncey thought this was going to be big.

Detective III Chauncey Hampton had never solved a homicide, but he was the best-dressed dick in the unit, so they promoted him to Internal Affairs Division. People looked at his threads and assumed he was dirty, but Chauncey had an off-duty gig as a high-end bodyguard, watching the homes of wealthy celebrities after fans mailed their publicists dead kittens or Ziploc baggies full of semen. Chauncey claimed to be tight with Tiger Woods but said he really didn't like to talk about it. He told long stories in which he played Kevin Costner to Tiger's Whitney Houston, Chauncey teaching Tiger important life lessons while protecting Tiger from would-be assassins. Nobody came right out and called bullshit because they didn't have to. They were detectives. They just listened, asked Chauncey specific follow-up questions, and smirked when he stammered, trying to come up with answers that didn't contradict what he'd already told them.

After Ballard and Crowe tossed him in the tank that night, Everton squatted and shat into his own palm. Then when Crowe opened the door for Chauncey, Everton shotputted a handful of shit into Chauncey's face. Ballard still remembered the clay sound it made hitting Chauncey's mouth. Chauncey was spitting and gagging, but he had to have swallowed some of it. Still, nobody ever teased Chauncey about eating shit because he was black and litigious, even by LAPD standards.

Chauncey had a serious hate-on for Crowe after the whole turd thing because he had to be tested for hepatitis and HIV and he blamed Crowe for what happened. Chauncey called for an investigation. He swore that Crowe had somehow put Everton up to gassing him, which Crowe did. But Ballard didn't see how Chauncey could have known that.

"What can I do for you, Everton?" Ballard asked Everton now, digging some crust out of his eyes. He crept into Connor's weekend room, finding his way by nightlight. Connor was with his mom, but this was Ballard's habit whenever he woke up. He leaned over the bed, put his face into the boy's pillow, smelled his son's scalpy scent, and felt another stab of guilt over the death of the Red Ranger.

"I hit this place up in Angelino Heights," Everton told Ballard.

"Well, congratulations are in order, I guess," Ballard said. "Is that it?"

Ballard liked Everton. He was a gangster, yeah, but it was hard not to like a guy who'd caused Chauncey Hampton to eat shit. And Everton wasn't your typical turf bandit. He'd long since graduated from liquor stores and these days he only jacked dope dealers. His favorite targets were Sinaloa Cowboys, the midlevel traffickers who ponied cartel white up from Mexico to Los Angeles gangs. Everton was playing a dangerous game because the Sinaloa Cowboys were a hell of a lot better armed than any Korean liquor-store owner. But it had worked out so far because it wasn't like Everton's victims could call the cops on him.

He and his crew would come dressed as cops, kick down the door to the dope pad like they were serving a warrant, cord-cuff all the Cowboys inside, and clean the place out before anyone figured out they were just outlaws posing as lawmen. Then, like a trapdoor spider, Everton would return to the safety of the Boot Hill Mafia hood where the blocks were long and lookouts posted on every corner warned him of approaching strangers.

In truth, Ballard didn't mind Everton jacking dope dealers, as long as he didn't kill anybody. So Ballard looked the other way and Everton helped Ballard with some of his homicide cases. The department required officers to register all CRIs (confidential reliable informants) down at Central Narcotics, but Ballard never wanted any paper connecting him to Everton. He didn't even refer to him as his snitch. He called Everton his private investigator, which pleased Everton to no end.

"The place in Angelino Heights," Everton said. "My guy said it was packed floor to ceiling with cash and crop, so you know how we do. We just hit it."

"You already told me that part," Ballard said. "So what are you, turning yourself in here? You found Jesus or something?"

"Just listen," Everton said. "The cash was all there, just like I'd been told, but the place was weird."

"Weird how?"

"For one thing, the house was empty. No lookouts. No guards. Just these creepy-ass statues everywhere, you know, of that lady with the skull face?"

"Santa Muerte," Ballard said, rummaging in his closet for a clean shirt. He was down to one of the quitters now, an oxford with a fraying collar. He buttoned it in the bathroom mirror. Christ, but he looked old. Back when he and Crowe were first running with the gang unit, Crowe had taken to calling Ballard Captain America. But he was deep in his dirty thirties now and the old nickname felt like a paper cut. Ballard had begun to look like some cruel caricature of his former self, a *Mad* magazine send-up of the Marvel superhero.

They said LAPD detectives aged like dogs, seven years gone from your life for every one you spent shoveling shit in the Augean stables. These days it hurt when he smiled and it looked like something was trapped behind his eyes, gnawing its own limb, bent on escape.

"What else?"

"The place had a basement and, and I seen some foul-ass shit in my day, nig," Everton whispered. All bravado bled away from him now and his voice was thin and tight. "But when I found him down there . . ."

"Wait," Ballard said. "When you found *who* down there?"

"My homeboy." Everton hissed. "Dude who told me about the house in the first place. They had him down there. Man, I thought, you know, I always thought Menjivar was just some made-up shit."

Heading into Angelino Heights in their Crown Victoria about an hour later, Ballard and Crowe stopped for a pack of coyotes crossing Sunset, their eyes shining like abalone coins. And now an eerie procession of mule deer gamboled across the boulevard. It had taken Ballard years to get used to the way wild animals roamed all over LA. As a young patrol officer, Ballard had responded to a burglary call in the hills, checked the back of the house, and found a cougar drinking out of the pool. But this was different, like something was driving the animals out of Echo Park. "Maybe there's a fire somewhere," Crowe offered.

Ballard cracked his window. The air was sharp and he thought he could smell the river on it, but he didn't smell any smoke. "Don't think so," Ballard said.

"Maybe it's *him*," Crowe said, grinning like Shere Khan the tiger. Crowe had a huge, hexahedral head and teeth as big as fingernails. He looked like he could have fit Ballard's whole skull into his mouth. The gangsters called Crowe the Big Bad Wolf because they said Crowe could sniff you out of a perimeter faster than the K9s. Think you've made it home to Grandma's house, homie? That's when Crowe takes off his granny suit and eats you.

They had a saying in the LAPD. You might get three great loves in your lifetime, and you'll own two great dogs if you're lucky, but you only get one great partner. And Ballard's was Police Officer III Luke Crowe. They'd gone through the academy together back in the nasty nineties and they'd been kicking in doors and going over fences ever since.

Ballard parked up the block from the swaybacked craftsman Everton had described. Graffiti marred the house. The windows were covered in plywood and a yellowed city notice on the door slated it for demolition. The place looked empty and haunted.

"This is it," Crowe said. "This is the one." He drummed his fingers on the dash. And Ballard saw Crowe wearing that Toad-of-Toad-Hall look he always got when he thought they might be close to catching El Endriago, Diogenes Menjivar.

"You know you sound like one of those kooks on TV, right?" Ballard smiled. "The ones wasting their lives looking for Bigfoot? Even after all the footprints and shit turn out to be hoaxes, they just keep thinking 'this is the one.'"

"What?" Crowe said. "You think Everton's putting us on?"

"I believe Everton saw something in that house that scared him," Ballard said. "And if it turns out to be a homicide, I'll investigate it, but I don't think it has anything to do with Menjivar."

Diogenes Menjivar was a barrio ghost story about a bogeyman who stalked LA's shadow kingdom. The gangsters called him El Endriago, the fire-beathing dragon, because they said he would burn alive any baller who crossed him. They said Menjivar was the Mexican mafia's angel of death. They said he was an enforcer for the Carillo Fuentes cartel. Some said law enforcement couldn't touch Menjivar because he had old connections in the intelligence community. Most agreed he was Salvadoran. It was rumored he had graduated top of his class from the School of the Americas, and that back in the eighties he had done his postgraduate work under the tutelage of "Blowtorch Bob" of the Nationalist Republican Alliance. They said he was a one-man death squad and he had forgotten more about enhanced interrogation than most spooks would ever know. They said he was a black magician. They even said Menjivar was one of the CIA operatives who first brought crack to South Central.

No one ever bothered to separate truth from tripe and for Ballard that was the fun of it. It was LA *menudo*. You ate it all and waited to see what backed up on you. But Ballard would never have placed El Endriago within the verifiable taxonomy of Los Angeles' flesh-and-blood criminals. He'd have filed Menjivar somewhere between Black Peter and El Chupacabra.

Crowe believed in Menjivar unequivocally. Menjivar was Crowe's Moriarty and his grail. And Ballard mostly went along with it because he knew Menjivar meant something to Crowe. While other cops wrought their mediocre municipal destinies and pensioned into oblivion, Crowe could believe in an enemy beyond the city's senseless parade of sorrows, beyond the drive-bys and dead kids. Crowe knew Menjivar was out there and he believed it was his destiny to face him down. And Ballard mostly didn't mind playing Sancho Panza because it was never about finding him anyway.

"Well, let's do something dumb," Crowe said. That was the highest professional compliment Crowe would ever pay another copper: *He likes to do dumb things,* meaning he's in my circle of trust, my kind of cow-puncher.

The entire car yawed on its shocks as Crowe stepped out of it and pulled his shotgun out of the trunk. The weapon looked small in his hands. Crowe put up six big plates every year at the divisional bench-press competition and had biceps like footballs. Ballard knew for a fact Crowe had to have elastic panels sewn into the sleeves of his shirts so he wouldn't split them. Crowe could break a wooden baseball bat over his thigh and Ballard had once seen him shatter a full bottle of Pacifico just by squeezing his fist, the veins in Crowe's forearm bulging like roots. Ballard remembered Crowe smiling his tiger's smile as the white foam ran over his fist, turning pinkish because he'd badly sliced the heel of his palm.

Yeah, Ballard thought. *Let's do something dumb. Why not? We'll both be dead soon enough anyway.* Ballard drew his Glock and followed Crowe across the brittle, brown lawn around to the back of the house. Crowe kicked the back door open and the two of them swept into the darkness with their guns up.

It was like walking into one of those caves at Lascaux, the interior of the house covered with all kinds of graffiti. Ballard recognized the usual *mara* tags, but some of it looked more exotic, might have been Mixtec. They stepped quietly from room to room, moving through blades of dusty moonlight that came in through the gaps around the plywood over the windows. There was no furniture in the house. The air was still and strangely cool.

Ballard almost tripped over an orange extension cord and followed the cord to where it ran down into the basement. Ballard stood at the open door to the basement and shined his flashlight down the stairs. The sharp smell of disinfectant wafted up to him. Beneath it was the cloying reek of burnt flesh and the coppery scent of blood.

Ballard followed his flashlight down the stairs. Crowe was right behind him. The darkness was liquid and seemed to close around him as he moved. It was hard to breathe down here.

A fluorescent light fixture hung from the ceiling and Ballard reached up and pulled the chain. The tubes buzzed, filling the room with jagged light. And Ballard and Crowe both almost fired on the robed figures standing around the blackened thing on the stone table.

Then Ballard realized they were forty or fifty statues of Santa Muerte, Dona Sebastiana, or Most Holy Death, statues resembling the Virgin Mary, but with a skull for a face. Some of them were life-size, wearing real satin wedding gowns, golden crowns, and veils. Others were no more than twelve inches tall. Red and green votive candles had burned down around their bases.

"Fuck me," Crowe breathed. Ballard and Crowe approached the blackened body curled like a prawn in the center of a stone table. The victim been male, maybe five six, but that was all you could tell about him now. All of his hair was gone. His eyeballs had burst, silver fillings melted in his mouth. There had been an IV drip in his left arm. There were stainless-steel basins on the table, surgical tools, and other equipment.

"Bastards kept him alive for a while," Crowe whispered.

There were unlabeled specimen jars on the shelf next to him, their contents suspended in amber formaldehyde, magnified and somewhat distorted by the walleyed shape of the jars. His fingers. Ears. Nose. His penis.

"Guess Everton wasn't kidding," Ballard said. "I'm calling this in."

The floor above them groaned and the hanging fluorescent fixture wobbled. Shadows swung and the statues seemed to shudder. Crowe put his finger to his lips. Tiny streams of dust spilled from the beams directly above them. Someone was moving around upstairs.

Now the footsteps stopped.

BOOM! BOOM! Large-caliber rounds punched down through the floor, bands of moonlight slanting in through each bullet hole. Splinters rained down on them and the statues around Ballard broke apart. Ballard fired blindly up through the ceiling. Fluorescent tubes burst, throwing sparks, and now the only light in the room was the strobe of their muzzles flashing as Crowe angled his shotgun and fired up through the floor, tromboning the slide to fire again and again. And two of the shooters crashed down through the floor in a rain of timber like skaters falling through thin ice. One of them landed on Ballard. Ballard bashed his head against the stone table and knew he was going out when the sound of gunfire faded to watery silence.

Ballard didn't see his life flash before his eyes. All he could think about was the death of the Red Ranger. It happened after he and Crowe worked overtime last week. Ballard had come home late and forgotten to let the damn thing back in the house. Then he'd awakened to coyotes keening, their goblin laughter celebrating a kill. He'd felt a jolt of panic that carried him out into the night in his boxers with a flashlight and his Glock, but of course by then it had been too late. He'd managed to hose the blood and hair off the driveway, like a murderer hastily cleaning up a scene, before Gina brought Connor for his weekend visitation. He and Connor had actually made up fliers that weekend, making it their little father-son project. Ballard, lost in a fog of self-loathing, had even offered an extravagant reward for the Red Ranger's return. Parenthood was like police work in that way. Sometimes it was about protecting them from the truth, your integrity in the end worth about as much as a dead cat.

Ballard woke up inside a trunk to the sound of screeching tires and his body thrown forward against the bulkhead. He knew they'd hit something, he'd felt it flop heavily under the wheels. And the car lurched to a sudden stop, doors thrown open, the men stepping out to inspect the damage. Curses. Some talk in Spanish of blood and hair in the grill. Laughter when one of them had the bright idea of giving Ballard some company for the rest of the trip. The trunk yawned open. Ballard kept his eyes shut as they tossed the dead coyote in on top of him and slammed the trunk shut again.

When they pulled Ballard out of the trunk, they

were somewhere in the marina. He stayed limp, letting his feet drag behind him on the dock as they hauled him to the waiting trawler. Its big diesel was churning phosphorescence at the stern. The gurgling green light hit all their faces from below and the effect was like holding flashlights under their chins.

They headed out into open water and Ballard knew he would never set foot on land again. He hoped someone would find his body because would be harder on Connor if his daddy just disappeared. The water around the trawler was velvet black. Ballard thought it looked like Dracula's cape snapping in flight.

"Now," Menjivar said. "Where the fuck is my money?"

"Where the fuck is my partner?" Detective Ballard saw something flicker across Menjivar's eyes now and he knew they didn't have Crowe. "You know I'm a cop, right?"

"Of course," Menjivar said. "And I know it was police who stole from me."

"It was a bunch of gangsters dressed as cops, you dummy." Ballard laughed, looking around at the men holding him in the chair, placing the bleeder with the AK. "You know, you have this rep, right?" Ballard said to Menjivar. "Mention El Endriago and everybody's shitting their chonies, like you're fucking Lex Luthor.

"My partner would be so disappointed," Ballard said, winding the lamp's cord around his foot. "I'm not even going to tell him about this part. How it turns out you're just another dumb-ass crook."

Ballard jerked his foot and the room went black.

He twisted away from them in the dark and heard

them shouting as he grabbed the heavy bolt cutters and swung them, connecting with somebody's head. He dropped the cutters, launching himself at the bleeder. He bulled the guy against the wall of the cabin, head-butted him, got his cuffed hands around the AK's trigger housing, and Ballard was in business.

Or thought he was, but in the dark, he pulled the wrong trigger, and he was thrown backward, ears ringing as acrid chemical smoke filled the galley. The 40 mm grenade had punched a distended hole in the hull big enough to drive a compact car through. The ocean rushed in and someone was screaming now as a dorsal fin unzipped the leaden surface like a gray scalpel. The shark made a tight turn, banking inside the room, displaying a bulging throat and long belly the color of bone. It moved less like a fish than some kind of wraith.

Ballard pressed his back against the wall. Burbling orange light came in through the windows and he could smell the diesel fuel cooking off the surface around the boat. There were more screams. By the firelight, he saw other dorsal fins and tails whipping frothy patterns across the room, nothing somnolent or even graceful about them. They darted through the galley with their backs hunched like jackals. The gangsters pounded and kicked them, but they were overwhelmed. Ballard saw a dead gangster bobbing in the pink water, his tattooed face rubbery and beatific as a shark rooted the bowels from his belly.

Ballard felt something slam against his side, his ribs buckled under the force of a shark's shoveling snout. Then it had his shirt clamped in its jaws, snapping its head from side to side until a swath of fabric tore away. Ballard lunged into the hallway, slogging through chest-deep water.

Dead men and broken furniture sloshed up against the walls as the pink waterline rotated like a sundial and he glimpsed the AK rolling on the ceiling with the other debris. The weightless sensation was sickening and he knew the trawler was rolling onto its back. It wouldn't be long now. Ballard's feet touched the ceiling. He was scrambling through water up to his throat, the floor just above his head. He grabbed the AK the next time it came around. He'd wanted those bolt cutters, but there was no chance of finding them now.

All at once the sounds became muted and close and the entire vessel had just slipped beneath the surface, totally submerged. Ballard knew the boat was going down fast now because felt the pressure building in his ears, and pinched his nose to clear it. Maybe six inches of airspace left, he had to crane his head to breathe. If he was going to get out, it had to be now. Ballard pointed the AK back down the hallway and pulled the trigger, hoping to clear a path. Bullets fizzed through the water like torpedoes. He took one more deep breath and swam, but it wasn't easy with the cuffs. He could taste blood in the water and felt the pressure waves of sharks passing close as he levered himself out through the jagged fissure in the hull, wriggling into open water. He was conscious of the lower half of his body inside the galley, his legs exposed. He tried to pull his legs out after him, but he was too late.

He felt the impact of the bite against his right shin. He hugged his leg to his body and passed his hands quickly over his shin, feeling for pulpy flesh and jagged bone. But he was intact. He'd only gashed his shin when he'd dragged it across the torn hull in his haste to scramble out. He saw ribbons of black blood curling from the wound like thin smoke, but there was nothing for it.

He was grateful the surface was still on fire or he wouldn't have known which way was up. He saw globular continents of burning fuel spreading, then detaching, like replicating cells as the diesel burned off the water. He kicked like hell, pulling with his cuffed hands, his lungs burning by the time he broke the surface, with islands of fire all around him, which seemed to keep the sharks at bay.

Someone had seen the flames from the pier, and a Coast Guard cutter came for Ballard before the fire died. They transferred him to an RA unit that took him to Harbor UCLA. He asked them about Crowe, but nobody knew anything. Chauncey met Ballard at the hospital and told him Crowe was over at Cedars, undergoing surgery for multiple gunshot wounds. "He's very critical," Chauncey said. Even he didn't wish Crowe dead.

Crowe was still intubated when Ballard badged his way in to see him after he got out of surgery, but they said he was conscious. Crowe looked weak and old. It was like he'd shrunk somehow. His eyes were glazed, unfocused, even when Ballard took his hand.

Ballard leaned in close. "I saw Menjivar," Ballard whispered.

Crowe turned to him, lightly squeezing Ballard's hand. His eyes asking Ballard for more.

"All that shit they say about him is true. He was worse than we ever imagined," Ballard said. "He burned the shit out of my eyelid, see? I mean, I almost died, brother. And you're going to be pissed at me, but I let the bastard get away."

Crowe squeezed Ballard's hand. It hurt like hell and Ballard knew Crowe was going to be fine.

DEAD DRIFT

SPRING WARREN

1.

I'd just put my feet up to read the paper on Saturday night. My dog, B8, was gnawing dried pork ear into sopping chamois at my side when Sam called me. "Turn on channel three."

I pressed the button on the remote and the news anchor said, " . . . investigating the explosion." Sam filled in for me. "Richard Levin's dead. While we were getting skunked on the American River, that poor sonofabitch was getting blown to bits. Hey, I'll bet Oliver doesn't even know yet."

I had my cheaters on so I leaned forward to read the news band scrolling underneath the anchor: *Businessman killed in Davis, California.* "Do they know what caused the explosion, Sam?"

"All I know is that they're calling in the SPP and the CBP."

Both entities, Security and Prosperity Partnership and the Customs and Border Protections, are arms of Homeland Security. Levin ran a business providing calcium carbonate to pharmaceutical companies, dredging the layers of carpenter oyster shells out of San Francisco Bay and shipping them by barge to Petaluma for washing and processing. Hardly seemed worthy of Homeland Security involvement and I wondered what else Levin was into.

Sam asked, "Do you think I should try to get in touch with Oliver?"

"He said he wasn't so close to Richard."

"He came with him to the Flyrodders' meeting."

I generally let people find out their own news, but Sam was going to call Oliver, I knew that already. Sam feels being a busybody is a community service, which is why I even knew who Oliver Allen was in the first place. Sam brought him on our fishing trip. While I believe in the solitary nature of fishing, Sam believes in the restorative nature of fishing and brings his hardluckers along on our adventures.

That morning I was standing at the trailhead, B8 tugging at her leash, and Sam drove up with Oliver Allen in the seat beside him. Sam knew I wasn't too happy and explained Oliver had troubles: job in jeopardy, lost his wife a few years back, kid on the ropes, the whole shebang.

I pulled off my hat. "What the hell does that have to do with me, Sam?"

"C'mon, Jack. He likes fishing. He's a friend of Richard Levin's."

Being a friend of Levin's didn't impress me. Levin was the kind who threw linen napkins over mud puddles. Hosted the Golden Gate Troutsman last April; hired UC students so desperate for book cash they agreed to stand on the banks of the American River in white ice-cream suits with dishtowels slung over the left arm to pour scotch and hand out cigars. Sam told me I was jealous.

I like scotch and cigars likely more than the next guy, but you can't cast with impunity if you think you're going to snag a history major while you're at it.

I picked up my gear, grunted "howareya" at Oliver, who carried a cheap pole in one hand and a battered aluminum tackle box in the other. The three of us headed for my fishing spot at a good clip.

Allen was a good twenty years younger than Sam and me, breathed slow and easy while I was working a little harder than I found it comfortable to hide. Sam, for his part, goddamned me all three miles in. I found the sweet spot that I'd marked with a small boulder of rhyolite rolled against a tree. Sam and I each stuck a fly box and a spool of tippet in our pockets and we were ready to start. I waited to see what Allen was going to pull out of that big ol' tackle box, betting if he was a friend of Rick Levin's he was one of those technical fishermen who was going to rattle up and down the riverbank with miniature scales, thermometers, hatch charts, and about a hundred more pieces of shiny crap that caught his eye at Cabela's.

But Oliver leaned his rod against a valley oak, scraped his tackle box across the dirt with his foot, and settled himself on the bank to take in the view for a while. He said he might wander around and snap a few pictures.

No skin off my nose. I waded in with a March Brown on my single barb, tied with variegated silk floss I'd had to fight a couple of little old ladies for at Michael's. It was sure to provide an embarrassment of riches. I cast upstream about twenty feet, then as the nymph drifted down, I stripped in the line so there was no pull *whatsoever* across the current—a perfect dead drift. I waited for the fish to strike.

By lunchtime I'd conceded defeat and lay down on the bank for some shuteye. First, however, I had to listen to ten minutes of Sam chattering about Richard's fishing trip to Chitral, Pakistan. That was followed by Sam stumbling over Oliver's battered tackle box, which bounced loudly down the embankment and was then noisily retrieved. All was topped off by Sam crowing, "Sure, you can borrow a fly!" and the following confab about what was not working (March Browns) and what was, before I actually got some peace.

I wasn't getting much peace now either, as I sat on the couch and thought about Richard Levin. People are getting killed right and left in car crashes and industrial screw-ups, falling down stairs and swallowing fat pieces of frankfurter, but it makes you think when you know the person it happens to. Makes you think hard if it wasn't an accident but purposeful.

According to the news anchor, Richard Levin was drawing his last breaths just about the time I was wishing Sam would shut up about yaks in Pakistan.

2.

Sam and I met a couple of days later over a beer. I asked him how Oliver took the news about Richard Levin.

"Okay, kinda quiet. Hope Richard's kicking it doesn't mess up any more business for Oliver, he's a nice guy." Sam took a slurp of beer. "He sure takes shit pictures, though. We downloaded them at my place and most are a mess. He got a good one of B8 he said I should forward to you."

"Did they ever figure out what blew Richard up?"

Sam nodded. "Picric acid. They've put a recall on all LevinCal oyster shells until they figure if terrorists were lacing women's calcium supplements with the stuff, I guess."

"Killing the infidels by osteoporosis?"

"The other theory that seems to be rising is Levin was doing some dirty work himself. That 'fishing trip'"—Sam made air quotes—"Richard made to Pakistan makes the feds think our pal might be some sort of agent."

I thought about the guy, all boat shoes and manicure, and could hardly believe it. Sam continued. "They're looking high and low, that's for sure. I'm answering a few questions in half an hour." He quaffed his beer and gazed sadly at the diminished level of ale. "Guess I'd better hold myself to one."

I knew Sam was keeping sharp not so much to answer questions but to ask them. He was a researcher of the first degree. Not only did he know where to look for information, but his academic tweed jacket, lace-up walking shoes, and Sebastian Cabot beard on an earnest face put people at ease. Anyone would talk to him. I bet he'd ask the cops more questions than he answered.

"While you're making your statement, Sam, find out if there was any wool, feathers, or thread at the explosion site."

"Gotcha."

"I just don't see using picric as a weapon. I mean, it's around, sure. They use it in labs for staining slides and urine detection . . ."

Sam looked over his glasses at me. "That's the trouble with not knowing your history." Sam retired from the history department at UCD the same year I retired from chemistry. "They made grenades and bombs with picric in World War I, called it Lyddite for Lydd, England, where they tested it."

"That's the trouble with not knowing your science," I shot back. "Picric acid in suspension is not particularly dangerous. Dry it's more so, but even dry it usually needs a booster, like a primer to create the explosion. Find out if there was anything like that. And . . . ask if they found a bottle with a metal lid."

Sam checked his watch and asked, "You sticking around?"

I dryly assured him I had nothing better to do than wait around for him. The truth was, however, I didn't. The first year of retirement it was a fine thing to sit back and caterwaul eupeptic greetings to the faculty members rushing from meetings to classes to lunchtime lectures. Ah, the afternoons were long and warm, fishing a near daily indulgence. A few years in, however, I sensed a ghostliness about my life, as though I were becoming transparent. My fellow professors and students were likely to look right through me. Yelling, "Hey, what's your hurry?" my voice was reedy and hardly carried farther than the next table. At least Sam had his books to write.

The next thing I knew Sam was back, pulling up a chair, extricating the notebook from his jacket pocket. That was another thing I noticed since retirement: time folded in on itself with terrible lubricity. I sat up feeling unsettled.

Sam motioned for two more beers, fairly buzzing with information. There was no evidence of any sort of booster or primer to set the picric off, Sam informed me. "But they did find Icelandic wool, some pheasant feathers, and an ancient pair of hackle pliers."

"Rick Levin was tying flies?"

"One would think—using the picric to dye the feathers, or dubbing wool."

I waited for the other shoe to drop. Sam said, "Found his fingers, here and there—pink as roses. You know what they called the guys in the munitions factories who worked with the stuff? 'Canaries.' Picric turned them bright yellow."

"Gloves?"

"Not a flinder of latex."

"The bottle?"

"Bingo. An old one with a zinc cap."

"Picrate salts."

Sam looked at his notebook again. "They mentioned that. What's the difference?"

"The salts are formed by the reaction of picric acid with metals, and they are far more reactive than the acid itself. If the salts formed on the bottle between the cap and the glass, just the friction of taking the cap off . . ."

"Boom?"

I nodded, then nursed my beer for a while. What bothered me more than the unlikely event of Levin getting blown up while dying dubbing for a Royal Coachman was the unlikely event that Richard Levin was tying his own flies, period. He might own the Purple Lithuanian Bat fly, but only if he bought it. Levin was an American Express–type guy. "Did you ever see Rick Levin with something that wasn't brand spanking new, Sam?"

"Just that classic Corvette."

"Exactly. Even if Levin had decided to actually make something, he wouldn't have had an old bottle of picric in his kit. Police say anything else?"

"They're browbeating the gardener, I understand. He's Pakistani and seems to have stolen a pretty impressive bag of money. Fifty thousand dollars stowed under a planter."

I raised an eyebrow. "Bet he says he didn't do it." Then asked, "How's Levin's wife doing?"

"I'd guess she's broke up."

"You met her, right?" When he nodded, I said, "You should offer condolences."

Sam nodded slowly. "You think?"

"I think it would be rude not to."

We stopped off at Safeway and picked up a bouquet of day lilies wrapped in a cone of lime-colored acetate, then headed to the northwestern part of town, where the big houses had names on their gates. It was a relatively new development and looked like architectural schizophrenia. A Santa Fe hacienda sat next to a Swiss chalet, abutting a neoclassical colonial—all of them huge. Levin lived in the hacienda named Lariat.

Skeins of yellow DO NOT CROSS tape seamed the side yard of Lariat, where a blackened Belgium block foundation sat skewed on charred ground. Shards of drywall and wood, wire, pink insulation, glass, and nails littered the dirt. A chunk of roof and a few asphalt shingles clinging to the plywood were tangled in a tree forty feet away.

Lariat itself had not been spared effects of the explosion, with several windows blown out, curtains waving limply outside the sashes.

Sam said, "Poor Richard. I'll bet he never knew

what hit him." He sighed. "Not much consolation." He turned away from the explosion site and knocked on Lariat's door, using a bronzed knocker shaped like a saguaro cactus the size of a toddler's arm.

Mrs. Levin answered the door and showed us in. She was pale and looked shaken up, as I'd expected. But she was also much younger and considerably more beautiful than I would have guessed of Richard Levin's wife, even considering his fortune. I wondered if there had been a first Mrs. Levin, or even two before this one. There was something about her that was very familiar and I paged through my failing memory bank to try to figure out just where I'd seen her before.

Sam handed her the cheap flowers and got misty-eyed saying how sorry he was, and he'd sure enjoyed the pictures of Chitral. She must be glad to have the memories.

Mrs. Levin spoke firmly. I imagine she had said this to at least a dozen police officers and Homeland agents since Rick's death, "I wasn't there. Rick liked to fish alone."

Sam swiveled around and gave me a look that I pretended not to notice. I stuck out my hand. "Mrs. Levin. I'm Jack Hazel." She took my hand slowly and cleared up the mystery of where I'd seen her before. "Professor Hazel. I took your chemistry class. I mean it was ages ago."

It would have been about three years ago, which could be ages to a girl like her. In any case I now remembered her—there aren't too many model-caliber blondes in advanced chemistry.

"I was Cheryl Gage then."

"Of course. I'm sorry about Richard."

She nodded. "You want to sit down?" We followed her in and she commenced talking. "I had just found out he'd booked another one of those trips, Kamchatka, Russia, this time, and I was so mad, packed a bag, left a note, and went to a friend's. The police came the next day." She sat down and smoothed the crease of her slacks with her thumb. "I feel so bad we separated, I would have had another night with Rick at least."

Sam said, "Well, not to be insensitive, but all in all it's probably a good thing; you might have been killed as well."

I thought to myself it was probably an incredibly *coincidental* thing, unless, of course, she made a habit of flouncing off every third day. I asked, "Had you left before?"

"Once. Rick talked me into coming back. Said we'd go somewhere together on the next vacation and do what I wanted. I'm not saying it's murder or anything, but I don't like killing things."

I felt confused for a moment, then figured out she was talking about fish. "Did Rick tie flies, Cheryl?"

"I guess he did." She had a slight note of defensiveness in her voice.

I reminded myself she was in mourning and said, "Well, we should go." I couldn't resist one more question as I shook her hand. "Decided not to go into chemistry?"

She colored a little. "I wasn't all that good at it."

We walked to the door and Sam added, "Oliver Allen sends his condolences, Mrs. Levin."

"Quiet guy, worked with Rick?" She seemed embarrassed and explained, "That's how I found out about Kamchatka. Rick was bragging to that Oliver guy about it and I heard and pitched a fit. It was awkward. Oliver had come by the house with papers and a bamboo pole for Rick the night of that Chitral talk for the Flyrodders, and not only did Oliver witness my blowup, I could see the guy really didn't want to go to the presentation, either. Looked about as hangdog as someone could look heading out. But Rick was pushy." She took a trembly breath. "The pushiness irritated me last week. Now I miss it."

She opened the door and looked out on the scorched wreck. "It happened right there in Rick's lair. Where he kept all his 'boy' stuff." She smiled, then turned away from it and closed her eyes for a second. "He has to be cremated because he's in so many pieces. I keep being afraid I'll find a toe or something if I walk around."

"They're pretty thorough about cleanup."

She nodded. "I'll say. The crew found fifty thousand dollars in a box under the planter. They say the gardener had it stashed there to send to Al Qaeda or something. Sent his son to Pakistan for a family wedding that was apparently more like a training camp. With Rick having just been there . . ." Her voice trailed off, then she added, "That gardener told Rick he wanted help in starting his own business making green cleaning products. I thought it was such a nice idea."

3.

When we'd backed out of the drive, Sam said, "Green cleaning products. You think the gardener wanted money for the business, then when Rick wouldn't help him out, he stole it and bombed Rick?" Sam answered his own question. "Sounds thin."

I said, "It's the biodegradable polymer in oyster shells." Sam gave me a blank look and I elaborated. "The polymer of aspartic acid found in the shells is useful in making environmentally friendly detergents. I suppose the gardener was hoping to get some shells on the cheap." I mused for a moment before adding, "Cheryl would have known that. She was one sharp student. Seemed like she didn't want me to remember how sharp." I puzzled for a moment longer and tried out my thoughts on Sam. "Pretty lucky she just happened to be out at the time of the explosion, don't you think?"

Sam said, "You're thinking death by chemistry, she had something to do with it, and she's framing the eco-gardener?"

"Maybe. She would also know about picric, she took my Organic Reaction Mechanisms class as well as Methods of Analysis."

Sam muttered, "If she didn't sleep through the lecture anyway."

I ignored him. "To top it off, she and Rick were having troubles. Maybe she thought she'd rather be a widow than a divorcee. Especially if they had a prenup that didn't favor third wives."

Sam shook his head. "First wife. Neither he nor she had ever been married. No prenup." He thought for a moment. "She was pretty darn upset over that Pakistan trip, though. On the other hand, that's what wives are supposed to do—complain about the hubby spending too much time on fish, too little taking out the trash."

I stared at him. "What, are you stuck in the fifties? No wonder you're lonely." He glared at me and I said, "Maybe there's another woman involved and he was taking *her* fishing. Wish I'd seen the slide show."

"*PowerPoint,* Jack. Talk about being stuck in the fifties." He grinned, then said, "It's on my computer if you want to see it."

At Sam's we opened his laptop and sat through about two dozen slides of yaks, villagers playing polo, the Highfish Tours company jeep that drove them into Chitral, a table along the water set with silver and china, guys in hip waders casting into rills, the Hindu Kush glowing in the background. Not a hint of bad behavior anywhere. I rolled back in the chair, saying, "Ah, hell."

Sam was exasperated as well. "I'm thinking we have too much time on our hands, Professor." I agreed maybe that was the case. Sam said, "Tomorrow morning, you, me, and B8 on the river."

"Agreed. *Nobody else.*" Sam nodded and it occurred to me I hadn't seen the photos of the last trip. "You got Oliver's pictures?"

"Oh, sorry, I was supposed to forward the picture of B8." He clicked through his photo gallery, highlighted a folder, and brought up the images. Sure enough, one out of every two pictures was out of focus, Sam waving like a blur, the tree behind him sharp, or badly framed, the top of B8's head and the brush behind him. There were a few he managed to do a fine job on, though, including two pictures of B8 swimming and one of me, hat over my eyes, mouth gaped in midsnore. I tapped one of the pictures of B8 swimming and another where she was just a blur against the sharp scatter of leaves.

"Print those off for me, I kind of like them."

Sam clicked PRINT, and I asked, "Why'd Allen borrow a fly?"

"Didn't bring any, I guess."

"What kind of fisherman was he?"

"Decidedly . . . awkward. But he got better. Next time he'll smooth out."

4.

I headed home, fed B8, and made myself some pasta tossed with anchovies and garlic and a scratch of Romano. I was feeling a little down, thinking maybe I shouldn't have taken retirement. I was going stir-crazy. Next thing I'd be shouting down neighbors at block parties, showing up at faculty meetings for the hell of it, and taking shit pictures like Oliver Allen just to have something to do.

Maybe I needed to shake my life up, do something really adventurous. That fishing trip to Chitral looked pretty good, though pretty expensive too. Probably cost a year's worth of dog food. B8 whined beside me.

Still, after I ate and washed up, I got on Google and typed in Highfish Tours, then clicked the Pakistan tab. I was agog as I scrolled through the very familiar pictures: a Highfish Tour jeep, a table along the water, yaks, polo, guys in hip waders, the Hindu Kush glowing in the background. I was further taken aback when the photo credit went not to Richard Levin, but to Highfish employee Chip Merric.

I put my cheaters on and looked again. "Rick Levin, you bastard." I sat thinking for a while, then picked up the phone and got Oliver Allen's number from information. Maybe he had an inkling of what his business associate enjoyed more than fishing because I'd bet anything Rick didn't go to Pakistan at all.

A crepitant voice answered the phone, and when I asked for Oliver, he said his son wasn't in right then and though he'd like to, he couldn't guarantee he'd remember to pass on a message. "You'd be safer just calling back. Are you from work?"

"I'm . . . a fishing buddy."

He laughed, then said, "Olly doesn't fish. Made him go too often when he was a kid, all weather bad and worse, and he'd stand there glaring at me, hands jammed up his armpits. My fault. If I'd brought him along gentle, we might be out on the bay right now with my Pinky Gillum bamboo fly-rod."

I felt the sensation of ice riveling down my spine at the mention of the Pinky Gillum. I sighed and the old man asked, "What's your name again?"

I told him and he said, "Now, I'm not likely to remember. So if you want Oliver to know you called, you should call back. I'm not likely to remember."

I called Sam.

He was preparing for tomorrow's trip. "I'm banking on EZ nymphs, Jack. Going to catch every fish out there, some twice. Ten nymphs on number-ten hooks, ten on number fourteens, an assortment of yellow, olive, and hare's-ear dubbing, bead heads."

I interrupted him. "What do you know about Oliver Allen's company?"

"It's a PR firm, does promotional pamphlets, films, multimedia. Oliver says they're heading for bankruptcy. He's already looking for a replacement job. Like I told you, the guy's in dire straits. Kid's in some rehab program in Utah that you can't believe what it costs, sucks up a college fund in a couple of months.

Pisses me off they take advantage of someone's hard time like that." He caught himself mid-rant. "Why?"

"I think Oliver was hoping to get a job with Rick Levin; the papers Oliver showed up with were likely résumés. To sweeten the deal Oliver brought Levin . . ." —I paused for effect—"a Pinky Gillum fly-rod."

Sam groaned. "Tell me it didn't blow up in the explosion."

"He had to go buy a new rod to go fishing with us."

Sam maintained a respectful silence for a moment, then said, "A Wal-Mart special. What a comedown."

"Also—Oliver must have put together that Powerpoint show of Chitral for Rick, and the pictures weren't Levin's. They came off a Highfish Tours Web site."

Sam hooted. "I wondered why there wasn't a picture of Rick showing off his catch."

"Maybe if Oliver felt like he wasn't getting a job, he thought he might extort some money."

"I don't know—you extort money for big stuff like infidelity or siphoning funds. 'Give me a boatload of money or I'll tell your angling club that picture of that big ol' fish wasn't yours' doesn't seem to cut it, much less be a reason to blow him up afterward." Sam sniffed. "I'd kill him to get that Gillum rod back, though."

I agreed with Sam. He added, "The G-men are still hot on the Pakistani gardener as the culprit. They figured out your biodegradable polymer angle and think the gardener might have been planning to contaminate some oyster shell. What oyster shell can't be used after recall for food use can be gotten cheap for detergent, apparently. The Pakistani also has a teenage son who was arrested for spray-painting AMERICA SUCKS on the I-80 overpass."

"If we're answerable for our kids' behavior, the entire nation should be on parole."

Sam continued. "The gardener worked at Kaiser part time, sweeping up, had access to the Christmas tree dye that uses picric."

I shook my head. "He'd still need to know what it was, how it worked, what would happen if it didn't, where it came from, how to make it ignite."

Sam laughed. "Well now you're describing us." Then he got serious. "Come to think of it, you know that cop I talked to at first, who was so friendly? He was giving me the stink eye last time I went in."

"You did hold an all-night vigil with the Unitarians praying for social upheaval, Sam."

"I was lighting a candle for peace, Jack."

I nodded. "We'll let the authorities decide on that."

Sam huffed, "I don't know that I want to fish with you in the morning. Maybe I'll call Oliver instead."

"You hardly know him. Met him once before taking him fishing."

Sam said, "I'm telling you, Oliver's a nice guy. He's in a tight pinch is all. "

What I thought but didn't say is being in a tight pinch seldom engenders good behavior. I did say, "The thing that bugs me is, Sam, I can't figure why Oliver came fishing with us in the first place."

5.

I fell asleep on the couch. At about three in the morning Sam was on the phone again. "Let me in, you deaf sonofabitch!" He sounded drunk.

"Where are you?"

"Been pounding on your door for the last ten minutes. Your damn dog's so well trained, she won't even bark. If you don't bring me some cash, the taxi driver's going to shoot me, I swear to God!"

I got off the couch with the phone to my ear, and when I got into the foyer sure enough B8 was wagging at the door. When I opened the door Sam stumbled in, evidently having been leaning on it. I looked beyond the pool of light cast by my porch bulb to Tom Pederson, who ran the taxi service in Davis. He was wearing a bathrobe, and he wasn't packing heat. He seemed pretty bemused all in all. I handed him a twenty.

Inside, Sam had taken my place on the couch. "Oh, God, I'm not even sober yet and I can feel the hangover crawling up my spine."

"What have you done?"

He opened one eye. "Research. I wrote down everyone I knew of that knew Rick Levin at Flyrodders. Then everyone I knew of that knew Rick because of business, and everyone because of social stuff. One name was on all three lists—Fred Boscombe, and I happened to owe him a drink. I was clever, oh-so-clever. I didn't talk about Rick at all, just kept the drinks coming. Started out on fishing, then gravitated to business and marriage, 'cause that's how I found every goddamned nugget of historical import I ever found: researching *around* the subject.

"But next thing I know Fred's talking about karma and I think, when a guy like Fred starts talking about karma, I've let things slide too far, the archives were *closed*. But just as I'm pulling out my phone to dial the taxi, he says, 'Our friend Rick got hit with the karmic hammer.'" Sam straightened blearily up. "Fred told me Rick didn't have a nickel to rub together."

I thought about pointing out that Rick would be a more talented man than most if he could rub *a* nickel together, but Sam slapped his palm onto the side table and began mixing metaphors with a vengeance. "Used every penny to look like he was a hotshot. He was stretched like an O-ring around that big house and sports car, hoping for manna to fall from the skies, sweating every Cuban cigar he gave away."

"Showed his Pakistani PowerPoint to look like a big man."

"Yep, and when he was supposedly fishing from Chitral up the Hindu Kush he was actually begging loans from any bank, loan shark, uncle, or demented grandma he could think of."

But what about the fifty thousand dollars?"

"He squirreled money in the little house. If the notes came due, he was going to pick up the cache and run." Sam smiled. "Cache, cash, get it?" I winced and got him some water. He gulped out of the plastic bottle, then eased back onto the couch and spoke with grave disappointment. "I suppose Cheryl found out she was married to a pauper and got her revenge."

"Did he have a substantial life insurance policy?"

Sam grunted. "Apparently couldn't be big enough." He rolled onto his back and pretty soon his jaw dropped open and he commenced snoring. I thought of taking a picture, but remembered he had one of me and didn't like to think what he might do with it if I started something. So I sat back thinking about the mess people make of their lives, wanting more than they need, always more than they have, and how you can't guess what a person is by looking at them. I would have figured Richard Levin would die from a helicopter malfunction on the fly-in to Kamchatka, not sitting at a desk with an aniline dye bottle in his hand.

I scratched B8's ears as she stared fascinated at the tortured rabbit noise coming out of Sam's gullet. It still bugged me. Why was Levin, of all people, tying flies? Why did he have an old pair of hackle pliers? You could find the battle-worn items in my kit, or Sam's, or that of most of the old codgers in the Flyrodders Club, but I'd never expect Levin to have them.

I looked again at the blurry picture of B8, thinking about how Oliver Allen had pushed his tackle box with the side of his boot, what the dented red aluminum looked like, what the scrape looked like dug across the dirt. How his dad said he'd ruined Oliver for fishing.

I shook Sam awake. "When you kicked Oliver Allen's tackle box out at the river, it bounced down the bank."

"Like a rubber ball," Sam muttered.

"You said little house?"

"*Fred* said little house. He was talking in that unappealingly cute way he gets talking when he's drunk. Probably talks baby talk to his wife too."

I looked out the window. "Get up, it's almost light."

"I am *not* going fishing today."

"Suit yourself. You can go to bed after you print out those photographs Oliver took."

6.

Before we started driving toward the river, I called Oliver Allen's number again, and this time Oliver answered. I told him Sam and I were going fishing and Oliver was going to want to meet us. There was a long pause while I guessed Oliver was trying to figure why he'd want to meet us and just what it was I knew. Then he said, "I'll leave as soon as I get my dad sorted out. It'll take me a couple of hours to get there."

One of the things Oliver would soon find out I knew was that Oliver wasn't the photography hack I'd first judged him to be. Sam and I held up Oliver's photographs and by looking not at the blurry figure in the foreground, but by navigating by what was in sharp focus behind, it only took us an hour to find what we were looking for: fifty thousand dollars double-wrapped in Ziploc bags. Then we sat back to wait for Oliver Allen and watched the river roll by.

7.

When Oliver Allen found us, he looked like he hadn't even taken the time to brush his hair. He glanced at the Ziplocs and asked how we figured it out.

I told him when he showed up, his tackle box was heavy enough that when he scooted it across the ground with his foot, it left a gouge in the dirt, but by the time Sam tripped on it, the box was light enough to bounce down the bank. "There was something in there when you showed up, and it wasn't fishing gear 'cause you had to borrow a fly. I wondered what it could have been and why you'd left it behind."

I started explaining the rest and Sam broke in. "Why don't we let Oliver tell us? We already know how smart you are, Jack." I glared, then acquiesced.

Oliver sat down. "I went to see Levin about a job. I'd been the one to handle Richard Levin's account for my company, and since it was going bankrupt I hoped to get in on the growth Levin said *his* company was making—opening up an in-house PR division.

"I was, am, pretty desperate. I got my dad and my son depending on me, and my son's in rehab, and I need to keep him there. If I can get my kid through all this mess I think he'll be okay." He put up a dismissive hand. "Just so you know what my thinking was.

"I wanted to impress Levin. I knew he liked fishing, I helped him with that Chitral Powerpoint. So before I left Berkeley I went out into the garage and grabbed the bamboo rod and tackle box that was my dad's. I knew it was a good rod . . ."

I shuddered at this thin praise.

Oliver continued. "And Dad wasn't going to be using it anymore. Stick a nice hand-tied fly on it, and Levin'd think I was a good guy. Before I pulled up into Levin's drive, I opened the box to get a fly, but no-go. There was just old fly-tying stuff in there. I took the bare rod, knocked on Levin's door. We chatted, I gave him the rod. I told him I was looking for a job, and he blew me off, said he had one of the big boys in New York targeted. I knew then I'd been an idiot. People who hire big boys don't call them big boys. I should have known before. The pictures he used for his slide show were a scam as well.

"Levin then has the balls to tell me he's going to Russia to snag tarpon next month. His wife overhears and goes apoplectic. So there I was: having to brave it out like it's not happening, any of it, the blow off or the blowup, just keep smiling through the screaming, then follow Levin out to his den and look at his bass trophies he probably bought from a taxidermist. I even agreed to go to his fishing club, feeling compelled for some reason to be polite to this guy. All the time I'm thinking how I gave him my dad's fishing pole that frankly he didn't seem to realize the worth of.

"I sat with Rick while he drank and bragged and had a great old time. Then Rick went back to the big house for refills.

"Apparently his wife was waiting for him because I heard Rick and her picking up the argument again about Kamchatka. That's when I thought, maybe I could steal the rod back, toss it in the backseat of my car, which was parked about ten yards out the door, and he won't even notice. But when I stood up, I tripped on the rolling chair, which I knocked into his desk. It gouged a big dent into it. I knelt down by the dent, wondering how the chair could have done that to an oak desk.

"Turned out it was a thin plywood panel and I jig it up. Inside there was money. Bricks of hundred-dollar bills, enough to pay for another six months of rehab. I looked around for a bag or a box—nothing—then made a run for the tackle box in my car. I tried to fit the cash around the stuff inside, can't do it, so I take everything out of the tackle box, put it in Levin's trash can, and crumple a sheet of paper on top. Then I stuffed all the hundreds I could in the box. I just managed to get the panel put back in place when Levin returned.

"After another scotch, we headed over to the Fly-rodders' meeting. All the time I'm thinking, 'Christ, what am I doing? The only reasons people hide money like that are bad reasons. Levin's a drug lord or in the mafia, or a hit man. He's going to know what I did and he'll come after me, worse, come after my family.' I sat there in a fever during the Flyrodders' meeting, while Levin pretended those were his photos on Powerpoint, trying to figure out where I could hide the money. Then Sam came over and invited me to go fishing." Oliver made a beseeching gesture with his hands, then shrugged. "You know the rest."

Sam asked, "Did the police question you?"

Oliver nodded. "Next day. I hadn't even figured out my part in it. They were talking terrorists and what worried me for about ten minutes was the money I'd hid was blood money and Al Qaeda operatives were going to come looking for me. I did think about confessing right then and there, but not only did the whole terrorist thing ring kind of ridiculous, but I also wondered if the police would think *I* had ties to terrorists. I envisioned myself in Guantánamo, no money for a lawyer even if they'd let me see one.

"A few days passed before I heard the explosive was picric, that picric was a dye, and I got an inkling maybe Levin actually died because of the stuff I left in his garbage can. It was another day before I had the guts to ask my dad about the stuff in his fly-tying kit, did some research, and faced the truth."

Oliver looked pretty green around the gills, and the rims of his eyes were red from too little sleep or maybe tears. A guy stretched thin who'd made an impulsive move that locked him into jail time.

I thought of the old man Oliver had left at home. What would happen to him, or to his kid getting a second chance in rehab? Or maybe Oliver was playing us with his family stories to soften up the geezers and keep them from calling the cops.

I am all too cognizant of the fact that the older I get, the more likely I am to fall for sentiment—at this point I'm pretty sure to choke up at the damned *Sound of Music*. So I told Oliver to call his kid and to put it on speaker phone. I watched him dial the number, noted the Utah area code.

An operator answered, "Turnaround Treatment Center," and transferred him to a counselor who reminded Mr. Allen that patients were not allowed telephone access except on Sundays and in case of emergencies.

Oliver said, "I'm sorry. This is an emergency."

After a few minutes a kid came on the line. His voice at that awkward breakable stage the rest of an adolescent boy is in as well. "Dude, what's wrong?"

"Nothing, Chris. Everything's fine."

"You're good? Grandpa. Is Grandpa okay? What's the emergency?"

Oliver looked at us. "Grandpa had a hard night, a dream. He made me promise to check on you, tell you we love you."

The kid was silent. "They're not going to consider that an emergency."

Oliver said, "I know. I'll let you go."

The kid said, "See you. Tell Grandpa I'm fine and . . . love him too."

Oliver hung up.

Sam turned away to look back toward the river and blew his nose.

Oliver shook his head. "I've thought about how the picric could have gone off in the garage, killed Chris or my dad. It could have exploded while I was driving and killed dozens of people on the highway. If Levin hadn't noticed the stuff, the cleaning people might have been killed or Cheryl Levin."

I guessed we were all thinking how maybe if someone had to be killed, Richard Levin was not such a poor choice. I imagined Rick Levin sitting in his den the day Oliver, Sam, and I were fishing in the American River, frowning at the odd assortment of hide and bottles and monofilament he'd just noticed in his stainless-steel garbage can. Stirring through it, picking up the bottle, trying to read the corroded label, sniffing it, and then finally screwing open the zinc lid.

Oliver added, "I'm not meaning it isn't terrible it ended up being Richard. It is. But it was an accident. I didn't think it would change anything except make things a lot harder for my dad and kid if I were to turn myself in. I figured I'd just let the money rot and forget any of this ever happened." His voice changed, his face showing he hoped I'd tell him Homeland Security was conceding defeat. "But I heard they're blaming the gardener. That's crazy, right?"

Sam said, "They've got him in custody, Oliver."

The muscle in Oliver's jaw twitched, then he said, "Time to talk to the authorities."

Sam said, "You tell them the truth, it'll be okay."

I wasn't so sure about that. Once Oliver confessed that he'd left the picric in the garbage can *after* he discovered the money, it couldn't go well for him. And if the Homeland guys were sweet on the idea of espionage, Oliver could be in even more trouble than he'd guessed. I thought about the kid's panicked voice—"Dude, what's wrong?"—and Oliver's dad saying he should have brought his kid along easy.

I shut one eye and edged out. "Listen . . . don't tell them about the money. Just say you were bored and while you waited for the Levins to stop arguing, you decided to dump the old crap out of your dad's box in preparation for getting some new gear. Your dad's in good enough shape to tell them about the picric?"

Oliver twitched that jaw muscle a couple more times before he managed to say, "Yeah, he just won't remember he told them."

8.

Sam and I showed up at the Levin place with shovels and a potted palm tree. The yellow tape had been removed. Cheryl opened the door. "Professor Hazel, Sam."

I held out the palm. "We'd like to plant this for Rick, in memoriam, if it's okay with you."

She looked out to the newly raked soil where the little house once was. Her voice was flat, but she clenched her hands together when she spoke. "I'm going to have to sell the place. There's been bad financial news."

"I'm sorry, Cheryl." I looked out to the yard. "Might help the place sell, a little palm tree looks pretty."

She shrugged. "Can only help, we lost the gardener. I wasn't sure if he was more upset over being called a terrorist or a thief. Of course, who can blame him?"

She hesitated. "I have to admit, I was more than ready to pin it on him, myself. Made it so much easier to have someone to hate, to blame. A poor judge of character is what I am, Professor. I think I might return to chemistry."

Sam spoke up. "Studying *history* might deepen your understanding of people, however."

She gazed at him and Sam turned pink and muttered, "Can't go wrong with humanities."

Cheryl said, "There's a sprinkler system; try not to hit the lines, okay?"

Sam and I took turns digging. Sam groaned, "Isn't it deep enough?" I nodded and we each dumped a Ziploc bag into the hole.

We threw in some dirt, stepped around on it a while, then I plunged my shovel into the center of one bag for verisimilitude. We pulled both bags out, stuck the tree in, and returned to the front door.

We showed Cheryl the bags. Cheryl took them from us. "Buried? I don't understand why we keep finding money. Do you think I should tell the police?"

I told her, "I had an aunt who kept a coffee can of money in the yard, never felt secure unless she had that can. I suspect Rick had a little of that in him too. I'd just get it into a savings account."

She thanked us several times, after which we left. In the car Sam looked out to where the little palm tree stuck from the earth. "You said it was going to be a memorial, Jack. We should say a few words."

We rolled down the windows. Sam said, "Over ten

thousand people were injured or killed in 1917 when a shipload of picric and TNT exploded in Nova Scotia. Last week it killed Richard Levin."

I took off my hat and added, "Picric acid is named from the Greek word *pikros*—which means 'bitter.'"

GRANITE HAT

BRIAN M. WIPRUD

"So let me get this straight . . ." Sid swirled a glass of VO thoughtfully. "You want I should fit you for a hat?"

Leon stopped pacing at the far side of the cabin, an eyebrow raised at Sid. "Hat?"

"It's what you call an expression." Sid was perched on a red tartan sofa and was nursing an impish grin. "You want I should kill you, fit you for a granite hat, like a tombstone."

"Then it is true?" Leon ran a trembling hand over his thin blond hair. "What they say down at the diner is true, that you were a hit man?"

Sid stood and turned to the bar cart. *Were. Was. Had been.* No so much hit man as a soldier, an enforcer, though he guessed that sometimes that amounted to the same thing. Those days were behind him. He had retired after prison. Why else would he be living in Hellbender Eddy? Sid lifted out a bottle, popped the cork, and splashed some more vodka into Leon's glass. "Lemme ask you, Leo. Can I call you Leo?"

Leon gulped some vodka and pulled on his tie. "Leon."

"Why do you want to die so bad, Leo?"

"I have my reasons."

"That palace you have upriver makes this log cabin look like an outhouse. That's your Bentley sports car parked in my driveway. Those are thousand-dollar shoes on your feet." Sid cocked his head. "Looks to me like you've already died and gone to heaven."

Leon turned toward the wall, eye to eye with a mounted carp. "How much will it cost? It has to look like an accident."

"You like that fish? I caught that. Right here in Hellbender Eddy."

"In the Delaware River?" Leon blinked rapidly. "I didn't know there were big fish like that in the river. So will you do it?"

Sid rattled the ice in his glass. "You don't fish, do you, Leo?"

"If you won't kill me, then can you refer me to someone who will?"

"So let me guess." Sid couldn't help himself and chuckled. "You'd kill yourself only you're afraid you'll botch it. And because you don't have the nerve. That about the size of it?"

"I don't see the humor in my predicament." Leon wandered away from the fish, his eyes red and his lip trembling. "When you want something done right the first time, you don't do it yourself. You hire a professional. If you're not that professional I don't see any reason to torment me."

Sid put a hand on Leon's shoulder and gave it a squeeze. "I apologize. Here, siddown." He guided Leon onto the sofa next to the floor lamp, handing him the refilled glass of vodka.

"Leo, I only laugh because you're going to get arrested going around asking for referrals for a hitter. To tell you the truth, I should do you and your family a favor. I should put the cops on you and get you onto a shrink. Suicide means you're mental."

Leon buried his face in his hands. "This is a last resort. This is what's best for my family. This is what's best for me."

Sid splashed some more VO in his glass.

It wasn't hard for Sid to see what was troubling Leon. He needed his murder to look like it was an accident for the life insurance, and to save face. The reason he needed the money could be any number of things, but probably one of the usual reasons. Bankruptcy, financial ruin, gambling debts, investments zeroed out, business belly-up. There was a lot of that going around. And that Bentley in the driveway? It had dealer plates. Sid recognized Leon. He owned a string of dealerships. His flashy smile, blond eyebrows, and buttery tan were on billboards all over that part of Pennsylvania boasting zero percent financing for cars: *Leon's got your number: zero!*

Seeing the way cars weren't selling at that time, it was easy to see how Leon could have gotten in a jam. And the way he played with his wedding ring—sliding it on and off his finger—could have meant he had practice taking it off. Most devoted husbands had trouble getting their rings off.

It was enough to know the basics. The combinations of the usual details weren't important.

"You sure you want to die?" Sid swirled his VO.

Leon lifted his face from his hands and fixed eyes of resolve on Sid. "I've never been more sure of anything."

"Because once you're dead, there's no changing your mind."

"I'm positive."

"One-way ticket."

"I have no reservations about this—"

"That last second before you go, you may wish you were staying."

"No hesitation."

Sid squinted down at the broken man. Early in his career, an old hand once told him: *They all struggle and beg to keep from getting whacked, even the ones in bed half dead from cancer. Only old guys so old there's nothing new don't mind getting bumped off.*

"Where would the money come from to pay me?"

Leon's eyes were alight with the flicker of grim hope. "I can raise sixty thousand, cash. There are assets. Either you or the bank would get them."

Sid turned to the taxidermed carp on the wall, admiring its golden girth.

"One condition."

"Name it."

"You have to go fishing with me."

"What?"

Sid turned and pointed his glass at Leon.

"You have to go fishing with me three times."

"Fishing? But I don't see what—"

"Of course you don't see. That's why I'm the professional and you're hiring me, because you trust me to do it right, to know how to make this go down to your satisfaction."

Leon stood, his trembling hands making the ice in his glass chatter. "I understand that you used to kill people . . . quietly. I mean, no blood or shooting or . . ."

"Wouldn't look much like an accident if you were shot, would it? Unless we staged a hunting accident. But we're not going hunting. We're going fishing." Sid grinned. "Leave it to me. Be back at your palace day after tomorrow, five in the morning. Tell your family that you're going up to your river place alone to take up a new hobby, fishing. And bring the first twenty grand, and don't tell anybody, and I mean nobody, that we ever met. Otherwise, when you're dead, and they get back to me, the whole thing will come out that it was no accident."

"Yes, okay, perfect." Leon went to the bar cart, glugged more vodka into his glass, and drained it. He picked up his blazer and put out a hand to Sid. "Then it's a deal?"

"Never shake hands with death, Leo." Sid winked. "Punch him in the face, if you dare, but never shake his hand."

Two days later Sid drove the foggy, winding road to the turnoff for Leon's palace. The sign on the gate read RIVERVIEW MANOR.

The driveway curved gently down to the white columns of a Georgian mansion, the brick facade covered in ivy. He parked his late-model Mercury next to the Bentley sports car, and when he got out he found Leon approaching from the house, a cigarette in his hand. It looked like he'd had a shopping spree at L.L. Bean for the occasion, the outdoor clothes new, plaid shirt still with creases.

"I was afraid you might have changed your mind." Leon tried a smile.

"I was afraid you might have changed *your* mind. Money?"

Leon lifted a thick envelope from his vest pocket and handed it to Sid, who flipped through the contents. He knew how high twenty grand in twenties should be—about two inches, used. He tossed the envelope into the open window of his Mercury. "Ready to fish?"

"If I have to."

"You have to. Ever cast a fly-rod?"

"No."

"Spinning rod?" Sid opened his trunk, which looked to Leon like it contained an entire tackle shop. Sid held up a rod—in two pieces—and pointed to the reel. "This is a spinning reel."

Leon tried to contain his exasperation. It seemed pointless to learn anything new, much less fishing, just before dying. But as Sid said, Leon had hired a professional, so this exercise must have some purpose. "Maybe once when the kids were little, I dunno. Snoopy rod."

"Shoe size?"

"Ten. Why?"

"Me too. Here."

Leon took the waders Sid extracted from the trunk. "They look like rubber pants."

"Don't worry. I have rubber pants for me too."

A half hour later the two men in rubber pants descended the grassy embankment in front of Leon's palace to the stony shores of the Delaware River. The fog had lifted some, but still shrouded the tops of the pines and diffused the sun's early light. Sid had a tackle pack and a net. Leon held the spinning rod, a flashy metal lure dancing at the end as he tromped down the shore.

Sid began walking into the river.

Leon stopped. "You're not going to drown me, are you?"

Knee-deep, Sid looked back at his uncertain client. "We're going fishing *three* times. *Come on.*"

Leon gingerly followed Sid out to the middle of the river. The current wasn't fast and came only a little over Leon's knees. Sid stopped upstream of some large boulders. The guide waved his hand, asking for Leon to hand over the rod. Sid demonstrated how to cast, then Leon took the rod, and after only a few minutes' practice, found he was able to flip the silver lure almost as handily as his guide.

Leon grinned. "That's kind of fun all by itself."

Sid waved Leon to follow him downstream closer to the boulders. The guide put a hand on the client's shoulder and pointed at the rocks. Leon sent the silver lure sailing through the air, and it splashed down within a few feet of the boulders.

"Reel faster," Sid said, rolling a hand in the air.

"Maybe I should practice some more?"

"We're not *practicing*. Cast again."

Fifteen minutes and four boulders later, Leon was wondering what Sid expected to happen.

Then it stopped.

Halfway back to the rod tip from the boulder, the lure just stopped.

"Rod tip up!" Sid shouted. "Up!"

Leon lifted the rod and felt the line tighten, and then wobble. The water burst and a small brown fish leapt from the river.

"Reel!" Sid shouted.

The little brown fish sailed through the air again, and Leon laughed with surprise.

The fog parted upriver, and a ray of sun made the little fish look yellow when Sid netted it.

"I caught a fish." Leon was amazed. "I caught a fish."

Sid smiled. "You did. You caught a fish, Leo."

That day Leon caught twenty smallmouth bass, none much larger than a drumstick. But each astounded Leon as much as the first with the force of its resistance, its refusal to give up. Many escaped and were not caught at all. All those landed went back into the river. As Sid explained: *It doesn't seem right to kill these little guys when they want so badly to live, does it?*

When the sun arced over the river and went down over Little Hound Mountain, Leon invited Sid into his palace, where they drank expensive scotch and ate sandwiches. Leon wanted to know everything about fishing. After a few hours' discourse in front of a field-stone fireplace on the merits of various fish and techniques, Sid excused himself to drive home.

"Thanks for the cocktails. See you again tomorrow, at five thirty."

The next morning, Sid had Leon drive to a small lake, where under bluebird skies they waded the weedy shores, catching pickerel. The green barracuda-like fish attacked the twirling surface plug viciously.

"I've never heard of these fish before." Leon gaped at the prickly jaws of a pickerel in Sid's hand. "Why are they so, so . . ."

"Ballsy?"

"This fish must be starving to attack the lure so violently."

"Not starving. And the reason they're not starving is because they don't let opportunities escape." Sid let the fish slide into the lake, and it flashed off into some nearby lily pads.

The afternoon was spent in a cool mossy creek under a canopy of trees. It was such a small, sun-dappled trickle Leon had a hard time believing that it could contain a fish larger than a minnow. Sid had him cast with a tiny rod not much bigger than the Snoopy rod from all those years ago. At the end of the wispy line was a small gold lure with a spinning blade and a tail of feathers.

Sid pointed to a deeper pool under an overhanging pine.

Leon cast, and reeled.

As the lure came toward him, a bulge in the water did too.

"Keep reeling!" Sid rasped.

The creek surface boiled, and a foot-long trout shot out of the water, the lure on its lip.

The fish raced around Leon's feet when Sid tried to net it, and before the fish could be captured the lure spat out of the water.

The trout was gone. Escaped.

"Where'd he go?" Leon squinted at the water in disbelief. "We had him."

Sid sighed, patting Leon on the shoulder. "You don't have a fish until you *have* him."

"How could there even be a fish like that in such a small slip of water like this?"

"Just when you think you know where all the good fish are, *and aren't* . . ."—Sid winked—"the fish prove you wrong."

"Can we get him again?"

Sid was already headed to shore. "You get one shot at some fish."

That evening Leon made martinis and grilled steaks for Sid, who told stories of arctic red salmon, great silver tropic tarpon, and beefy Amazon bass the colors of the rainbow.

As Sid headed to his car by glow of the porch light, Leon followed. "So what are we going to catch tomorrow?"

"Tomorrow we fish the Big D."

"For what?"

"Big fish."

"What big fish?"

"*The* big fish. See you at five."

More than the martinis tingled Leon as the Mercury's taillights disappeared up the driveway, another twenty grand on the seat next to Sid.

It was drizzling the next morning, the skies roiled and dusky. They stood up to the waist in swirling current, where Sid had positioned them in front of a bend in the river where a jagged rock wall ascended hundreds of feet. The pool before them was deep and ominous as a smoky cave. A large, almost circular hook was at the end of a stout rod that seemed to Leon like it was made to catch whales. A few feet above the hook was a lead weight the size of his thumb.

Sid skewered a piece of garlicky liver onto the hook, and pointed at the pool.

Leon hesitated. "What's in there?"

"Let's find out."

"You mean you don't know?"

"All kinds of things might be in there. But we won't know exactly what until you chuck that in there. Maybe nothing. *Maybe.*"

Leon was afraid.

But he did as he was told, and the liver and the hook and the weight splashed down in the pool and vanished into the cave.

"Do I reel it in?"

Sid shook his head. "We wait."

The sound of the river swirling around his waist seemed to get louder and louder as Leon blinked at the dark recess of the unknown. The rain came down harder.

"Rod tip up!" Sid shouted.

Leon didn't see anything move, didn't feel anything, but the shout made him obey.

The line was tight. The line was unmoving. The line seemed stuck.

Then Leon looked at the rod tip. It began to bend.

"What is it?" Leon shouted.

Sid's hand shot out and grabbed Leon by the back of the collar.

Leon found himself underwater, but still holding on to the rod as he struggled to get free of Sid's grasp. Then he felt the rod yanked from his hands. Had the fish taken it? Or Sid?

Then Leon swallowed some water. His lungs felt like they were turned inside out, and he couldn't get a hand around behind him to free himself from Sid's grasp. Leon could hear himself squealing with panic under water.

His vision began to flicker.

Brightness. And air. Sid had yanked him back to his feet. Water vomited from Leon's mouth as Sid grabbed his arm to keep him from falling.

Then the rod was shoved back in his hands.

Leon couldn't speak, exhausted from having almost drowned. He could barely stand, though he found strength in his rage over what had happened and swatted Sid's supporting hands away.

And Leon found strength in that rod.

After a twenty-minute battle in the pouring rain, Leon was on his knees in the shallows at a gravel bar, wheezing. Before him, corralled into a shallow pool, was a muddy catfish the size of a small dog. Barbels splayed like slick worms from the fish's flat, gasping lips. The eyes were smaller than shirt buttons, black. Man and fish: subdued.

Sid waded ashore and picked up the fishing rod from the gravel bar. He thought about saying something but instead walked back up the embankment to his car and drove home through the storm. To his way of thinking, the sixty grand had come honestly. He had killed Leo. The Leo who had asked to die, who wanted to die, was gone.

Leon went bankrupt. Leon got divorced. Leon moved to Myrtle Beach where he managed his cousin's gift shop and sold driftwood sculptures he made in his apartment.

He never picked up a fishing rod again.

Only in his dreams.

MR. BRODY'S TROUT

WILLIAM G. TAPPLY

Stoney Calhoun was sitting in a wooden rocking chair on the front porch of the fly shop, sipping from a can of Hires root beer. Ralph Waldo Emerson, his Brittany spaniel, lay snoozing in a patch of sunshine on the rough pine-plank flooring at Calhoun's feet. It was the middle of the afternoon on a lazy early August day. Kate had left about an hour ago with clients—a middle-aged son from Augusta treating his elderly father to an afternoon of fly-fishing for striped bass with maybe the best—and surely the prettiest—saltwater fly-fishing guide in the state of Maine.

Leaving Calhoun and Ralph in charge of the shop. KATE'S BAIT, TACKLE, AND WOOLLY BUGGERS, it said on the sign. They hadn't had a customer all afternoon. It was always pretty slow in the summer.

So Calhoun was rocking and sipping root beer and remembering how good Kate had looked in her snug blue jeans and Grateful Dead T-shirt, with her long black braid poking out the back of her pink fishing cap, when a big shiny blue sedan eased into the shop's side lot. It stopped beside Calhoun's old Ford pickup, and a white-haired man slid out and came hobbling up the path to the front porch of the shop. He climbed the three wide wooden steps, then stopped when he saw Calhoun sitting there in the afternoon shadows.

The man looked to be in his seventies. He had thin, wispy hair, pure white, and papery pink skin. "Are you

Stonewall Jackson Calhoun?" he said. His voice was surprisingly strong and deep.

Calhoun nodded. "I'm Calhoun. This here"—he nudged the sleeping dog with his toe—"is Ralph. You looking for me?"

The man nodded. He had watery blue eyes, a hooked nose, and a strong jaw. A scrawny little man. He came over and held out his hand. "You, sir, are precisely who I'm looking for. My name's Brody. Arthur Brody."

Calhoun pushed himself to his feet and shook Arthur Brody's hand. The old guy's grip was firm and strong. "Me, huh?" Calhoun said.

Brody nodded. "May we sit?"

Calhoun gestured at the rocking chair beside his, and Brody sat in it with a sigh.

"How about a root beer?" said Calhoun.

Brody waved his hand. "I'm all set, thank you."

Calhoun sat down. "What can I do for you, then?"

"I know your reputation, Mr. Calhoun. I want to hire you to guide me on what I expect will be the final leg of my life-long quest. Before I go any further, may I ask you: Would you be willing, if the price was right, to devote the last two weeks of this August and the first two weeks of September to helping me to catch a ten-pound native Maine brook trout?"

Calhoun shook his head. "In the first place, I never guarantee anything. Fishing ain't like that, sir. That's why we call it fishing, not catching. And in the second place, hell, man, a ten-pound brookie is a certified trophy. It's the fish of a lifetime."

Mr. Brody smiled. "I know that, Mr. Calhoun. I've been a fly-fisherman all my life. I know how it works.

I'm not asking for any guarantees, and I know it would be the fish of a lifetime. Of my personal lifetime. My own Moby-Dick. I've caught my giant rainbow trout and brown trout and cutthroat trout. The wall in my den back in Arizona lacks only a trophy brook trout. I know how hard it is, Mr. Calhoun, how much perseverance and good luck it takes. I know all about failure. I'm not hiring you for results. I'm hiring you for the opportunity. I've done my research. I know that ten-pound brook trout do swim in some of your northern waters, and I know for a fact that you're the number one trout guide in the state of Maine. You're my best hope for getting a shot at one of those fish. So answer my question, Mr. Calhoun. Are you willing?"

Calhoun cocked his head and looked directly at Arthur Brody. "I might be," he said. "It depends."

"You name your price, sir," said Brody.

"It don't depend on the price," Calhoun said. "It depends on, do I think I can put up with you for a month."

Brody glared at Calhoun for a moment. And then it was as if a lightbulb clicked on inside the little man's head. His eyes lit up, and his whole face beamed a smile, and he slapped his thigh and roared out a laugh that echoed into the street. "Oh, that's perfect," he said. "Excellent. I like you, sir. Oh, I like you very much. We'll go fishing, and we'll see about the catching. We are going to get along wonderfully, Mr. Calhoun."

And then Calhoun laughed too. "So you understand," he said. "Wherever I go, Ralph goes."

"I like dogs," said Arthur Brody. "And they generally like me."

And so they shook hands, and it was a done deal.

O

"Daniel Webster caught his giant brook trout from the Carman's River on Long Island on a Sunday morning in the spring of 1827," Arthur Brody was telling Calhoun. They were eating pork chops and beans in the kitchen of their two-bedroom cabin, looking out the front window at the lake, its rippled water shimmering in the slanted late-afternoon sunshine. "The locals had spotted this trout a couple years earlier in the milldam pool. It kept showing up, and everyone tried to catch it. They thought it would weigh twenty pounds. One of Webster's friends owned a slave, and his job was to keep an eye on the pool, so when he opened the church door and stuck his head in during the sermon that morning, Webster and his friend snuck out. The fish was in the pool, and Webster caught it on a wet fly. It weighed fourteen and a half pounds, and they ate it that night."

"Fourteen and a half pounds," Calhoun said, trying to imagine such a fish.

"Your brown trout," Brody said, "and your rainbow, oh, the really big ones might go thirty pounds or more. Those on my wall, my fish of a lifetime, are over twenty. Even cutthroats run bigger than brook trout. Nobody has ever caught a brookie bigger than Mr. Webster's trout."

"It's the record, then?"

Brody sopped up some bean juice with a hunk of bread. "The official record belongs to Dr. William Cook," he said. "His brook trout also weighed fourteen and a half pounds. He caught it from the Nipgon River in Ontario in 1916. He used a live sculpin." He pointed with his fork at the lake. "Do you suppose there's a fourteen-and-a-half-pounder waiting out there for me, Stoney?"

The local game warden was an old-timer named Edwin Coffin, who had grown up in the northwestern corner of Maine hard by the Canadian border, where there's not much except pine woods and water. Edwin was on a first-name basis with every whitetail deer and black bear in the whole region, and he knew every pool and riffle in every brook and stream, and every point and drop-off on every lake. Calhoun figured if there was anybody who could help them locate a ten-pound brook trout, it was Edwin Coffin, so when he agreed to join Arthur Brody on his quest, Calhoun called the old warden.

Coffin hadn't seemed shocked at the audacity of it. "Sure, we got ten-pounders up here, Stoney," he said. "Hell, we got brookies biggern that, and I can show you where they live. Catching 'em is another story altogether."

When Edwin showed Calhoun and Brody where the ten-pound brook trout lived, he waved his hand vaguely at Peewumptick Lake and apologized for being unable to be more specific. "They're out there," he said. "I seen 'em. The big ones move around. This time of year, I'd concentrate at the head of the lake where the river comes in. Fish get hungry, knowin' winter's coming, and you're likely to find 'em cruising the shallows toward evening, looking for minners and crayfish and anything else that might come washing down the river."

Edwin Coffin's cousin owned a nice two-bedroom peeled-log cabin on the lake, which he was willing to rent out by the week. It featured a two-hole privy out back, hand-pumped lake water in the kitchen, a cast-iron wood cooking stove, two cord of cut and split ash stacked in the woodshed, half a dozen kerosene lanterns hanging on wooden pegs, and a cribbage board. A twenty-foot Grand Lake canoe with a four-horse Johnson motor went with the place.

Arthur Brody gave the man a full month's rent. "If we can't do it in a month," he said to Calhoun, "I guess we can't do it."

They'd been living in the cabin on Peewumptick Lake for about a week. It was easy to lose track of the passage of time when there was no radio, no television, no newspapers. Calhoun and Brody loaded their fly-fishing gear and Ralph Waldo Emerson and their two selves into the canoe every evening after an early supper, and they motored up to the head of the lake. Then Calhoun shut off the motor and poled them around the area where the stream's current pushed into the lake, with Brody standing up in the bow with his fly-rod ready, and they looked for cruising fish in the failing twilight.

They saw large fish every time, and Arthur Brody was able to cast to several of them. He caught two of them, both on the same evening when they spotted the fish gorging on some grasshoppers that got blown into the stream and washed into the lake. One of those trout weighed four and a half pounds, and one was a hair over five. Arthur said both fish were bigger than any brook trout he'd ever caught.

But he was holding out for a fish twice that size. Two or three times they'd spotted what looked like such a fish, but it had disappeared before Arthur could make a good cast to it.

Just knowing that such a fish was there kept their adrenaline flowing and their attention focused.

When it got dark, if it was a moonless night, they'd beach the canoe and wade out so Arthur Brody could cast to where the ledge dropped off. Calhoun hovered by the old guy's left side to catch him if he misstepped, to help him decide what fly to tie on and where to cast, and to land any fish he might hook. Brody was a good angler. He cast effortlessly and patiently, and he didn't complain when nothing happened for long stretches of time.

On nights when the moon shone on the water, Calhoun knew there was no sense in bothering, so they piled back into the canoe and motored downlake to the cabin and played a few games of cribbage, a nickel a point, before bed.

Calhoun got up a couple hours before sunup each day. He started the fire in the stove, loaded up the coffeepot, and got some bacon going in the skillet. The aroma always brought Arthur Brody out from his bedroom. They had eggs and bacon and bread and coffee and were in the canoe headed uplake while the stars still glittered overhead in the big Maine sky.

They fished until midmorning when the sun was bright in the sky. If the day dawned cloudy, they stayed out there till lunchtime.

Most days they caught some trout. Twelve-, fourteen-, even sixteen-inchers, really nice brook trout, and rolled in cornmeal and browned in bacon grease with fried potatoes and canned beans, they made a good supper. But they weren't what Arthur Brody was after.

Sometimes in the afternoons Edwin Coffin dropped by the cabin to see how the fishing had been that morning and to make sure the arrangement was working out. He always stayed for an hour or two. Sometimes the three of them had a cribbage tournament, sometimes they just sat around sipping coffee and watching the lake. Calhoun figured the warden needed the company of somebody other than the same old local folks once in a while. Calhoun from the big city of Portland, and Arthur Brody, from Arizona, were downright exotic by comparison.

Other days after lunch they piled into Calhoun's truck, with Ralph perched up between the two men in the front seat, and they bounced over the twelve dirt-road miles that followed alongside the Peewumptick River, which emptied the lake, to the crossroads that marked the little village of Peewumptick Crossing to pick up supplies.

The folks they ran into were unfailingly friendly, as if they were hungry for human connections—or new connections, at least. After a few visits to town, Calhoun believed he'd met just about everybody and knew more about them than they knew about him.

The general store was the social hub of the village. Local folks gathered on the porch to drink coffee and exchange complaints, and they considered it rude not to sit a spell with them. The store was owned by Tiny Cartwright and managed by his live-in girlfriend, Nellie. Tiny went about 350 pounds. Nellie was a skinny little thing. They were both somewhere in their forties, missing several teeth, skin all leathery and wrinkled, eking out a living by being the only source of supplies in a radius of about seventy-five miles in all directions.

The garage across the street, with the river flowing right behind it, was owned and operated by Pierre Boucher, who everyone said was the richest man in town. The service station had two gas pumps and one bay. Boucher had a thick black beard and a bald head. He could repair anything, from an outboard motor to a chain saw to a bulldozer. He owned a tow truck, which he mounted with a plow in the winter. He was Peewumptick Crossing's closest thing to an indispensable man, and he insisted everybody pay him in cash.

Edwin Coffin lived alone in a double-wide trailer a half mile from the intersection, though his territory was so vast that he was away from home more often than he was there, especially during deer season. The warden's cousin, Norman Smith, from whom they were renting the cabin, had his own trailer just up the road from Edwin's, which he shared with his wife, Julia, and their four children, who ranged in age from seven to thirteen.

There were a couple dozen houses and trailers scattered along the paved north-south road, with the river flowing along behind them. Sheets and underwear flapped on the clotheslines. Rusted-out truck bodies sat in the side yards. Geraniums and petunias bloomed in window boxes, and tomato vines and pole beans grew in rocky gardens out back. Along the roadways there were apple orchards, blueberry burns, dairy pastures, potato fields, and woodlots. Hardy Maine folk, scraping by the way their folks had scraped by. Barely.

They all hunted and fished, though not for sport, and Edwin Coffin confessed to Calhoun that he didn't pay too much attention to the fish and game his neighbors harvested or whether they happened to take it during the open season. People had to eat, and there was more than enough wild bounty to go around.

Halfway through their second week at Peewumptick Lake, in the total darkness of a misty moonless evening, Arthur Brody, standing knee-deep in the water and casting out into the tongue of current where it spread into the lake, grunted and then said, "This is a heavy fish, Stoney."

Calhoun, who was standing at Arthur's left side, found himself nodding. Over their time fishing together, he'd come to respect the old fellow's experience. Arthur Brody never seemed to be bragging, but the man had fished all over the world for just about every species a person could expect to take a fly. He'd caught a lot of fish on the fly-rod, including the certifiable trophies that hung on his wall back in Arizona.

"Don't baby him," Calhoun said. "You've got a stout leader. Turn his head. Don't let him go where he wants to go. The longer he's out there on the end of your line, the better chance he has of getting off."

"That's good advice, Stoney," Arthur said.

Calhoun couldn't see much. Arthur, standing right beside him in the water, was a shape just a slightly different shade of dark from the darkness of the night. Calhoun wore a headlamp so that he'd be able to use both hands if he needed them, but didn't want to turn it on for fear it might spook the fish.

After a short time—it was hard to know how long—it seemed like about half an hour, but Calhoun knew how the passage to time could be distorted in the darkness—Arthur said, "He's close. I think maybe he's close enough to net."

Calhoun flicked on his headlamp. He'd brought the long-handled boat net with him, even though he believed that carrying a net around pretty much guaranteed that you wouldn't catch anything worth netting. Arthur insisted he bring it, called Calhoun's reservations a stupid superstition. Calhoun agreed that it was stupid, but he still felt uncomfortable with the net. One way or the other, he felt in his bones that the damn thing would bring them bad luck.

"Oh my goodness," murmured Arthur Brody when Calhoun's light shined on the fish. It was barely ten feet from them, lolling, exhausted, on her side near the surface of the water, barely moving her broad tail. A big fat female brook trout, a true native, a descendant of the trout that had swum in this watershed since the glaciers disappeared ten thousand years ago.

Calhoun slid the net under the fish and scooped her up. "Got her," he said.

He turned and headed for shore, following the light of his headlamp. Arthur Brody sloshed along behind him.

They knelt side by side on the rock-cobbled shore and slid the big fish out of the net. "A fat hen fish," said Calhoun. "Full of roe. Ready to make babies. Big enough for your wall?"

"The fish of a lifetime," whispered Brody.

"Look here," said Calhoun. He pointed to a round white scar on the big trout's back alongside her dorsal fin.

"What caused that?" said Arthur.

"Great blue heron," said Calhoun. "Nailed her with his beak. She survived it, though."

"Good thing she did," said Arthur. He took a little digital camera from his shirt pocket and snapped a couple of flash pictures of the trout lying there in the net. Then Calhoun took a few shots of Arthur Brody cradling his fish, holding her chin in one hand and the base of her tail in his other.

"I bet she's as big as Daniel Webster's trout," said Arthur.

Calhoun took out his tape measure. He laid it along the trout's side, from the tip of her nose to the fork of her tail. "Twenty-eight and a quarter inches," he said. He measured her girth. "Twenty and a half." He took the measurements again, then tucked the tape into his pocket. "I can't do the math in my head," he said. "But she's heavy. We'll call the warden when we get back, find some official scales, the post office, maybe, and weigh her, and then we'll get her to your taxidermist as fast as we can. We'll wrap her in a wet cloth and—"

"No," said Arthur.

"No? Huh?"

"Let's put her back, Stoney."

"Wait a minute," said Calhoun. "This whole thing, this quest of yours, it was to get a trophy brook trout for your wall. Here you've got it. A trophy if I've ever seen one."

"I can't explain it," said Arthur, "but we've got to put her back. Come on." He plucked the hook from the great fish's jaw, lifted her in his arms, and waded out into the water. Calhoun followed along behind him with his headlamp lighting the way.

Arthur Brody bent over and held the fish in the water. He moved her back and forth, and Calhoun thought he heard the old guy singing to his trout, murmuring a quiet lullaby in the misty darkness.

Pretty soon the big trout's gills began to pulse. "She's ready to go," Calhoun said.

Arthur took his hands away. The fish hovered there in the water beside the two men for a minute. Then she gave a flick of her tail, and she was gone.

They didn't talk during the long ride back to the cabin, and even after they were sitting at the table by the window sipping from cups of hot tea, neither Calhoun nor Arthur Brody seemed to want to say anything about the giant trout that they'd just let go.

After a while, Calhoun found a pad of paper and a pencil and did some calculations. Then he looked across the table at Arthur. "Fourteen point eight pounds," he said. "A new world record."

"You think she weighed that much?"

"The formula's pretty dependable," Calhoun said. "The square of the girth times the length, divided by eight hundred." He shoved the pad of paper across the table. "Check my math."

Arthur looked at it, then looked up at Calhoun and shrugged. "Would've been good to weigh her officially," he said. "Just to know for sure."

"Too late now," Calhoun said. "You set her free."

"I got no regrets," said Arthur Brody.

The next morning instead of going fishing, the three of them, Stoney Calhoun, Arthur Brody, and Ralph, piled into the pickup and drove into town where they could get cell phone service. Calhoun called the shop and talked with Kate for a while, and then regretted it, because it made him miss her. Then he called Edwin Coffin's cell phone. The warden said he was patrolling in his truck but not far from town. "Why ain't you out fishing?" he said.

"I got some pictures I want to show you," Calhoun said.

Arthur Brody made his calls while leaning against the front fender of the truck, which was parked in the street. Calhoun figured the old man was bragging to his friends about his big trout.

Twenty minutes later Calhoun and Arthur Brody were on the porch of the general store, sipping from mugs of Tiny Cartwright's murky coffee when the warden's dark green SUV pulled up in front. Edwin Coffin in his khaki uniform came striding up the front steps. He took the rocker beside Calhoun and said, "Let's see what you got."

Arthur Brody took his digital camera out of his pocket and handed it to the warden. "Click on that button there," he said, "and you can run through all the shots."

Coffin held the little camera up in front of his face and pressed the button several times. Then he looked at Arthur Brody. "Oh, my," he said. "Did you weigh her?"

Brody shook his head. "Stoney took measurements, though."

"Fourteen point eight pounds, according to the formula," Calhoun said.

By now several people had gathered on the porch, and Edwin Coffin handed the camera to them so they could see for themselves. Tiny Cartwright was there, and so was Nellie, wiping her hands on the apron she usually wore, and Pierre Boucher had wandered over from his garage across the street to see what the fuss was all about, and a little while later the warden's cousin, Norman Smith, showed up, along with two of his sons. There were several others whose names Calhoun wasn't sure of. He wondered how the word spread through the little town so fast.

They passed the camera around. These were folks who knew a big brook trout when they saw one, and after they'd all had a look at the photos, they moved down the other end of the porch and commenced murmuring and whispering among themselves in a way that made it clear they didn't want Calhoun or Arthur Brody to hear them.

Finally Calhoun touched Edwin Coffin's sleeve. "What's their problem?"

"One of them observed how a world-record brook trout from Lake Peewumptick would've likely brung a lot of attention to our town," the warden said with a shrug. "There'd be news stories and articles in the angling magazines. Fishermen would come here from all over the world, hoping to catch themselves a giant trout. Local folks, for once, might've made themselves some real money. Restaurants, housekeeping cabins, motels, fishing tackle shops, handmade canoes. Every man who grew up around here thinks he'd make a good fishin' guide. They're kinda pissed you let that trout go."

"Well," Calhoun said, "this way that fish is still swimming in the lake, so anybody's got a chance to catch the world record."

"You got a point," said the warden, "but these folks don't see it that way. A certified world record would've put Peewumptick Crossing on the map. Plus, they think your photos kinda suck. Too blurry and poorly exposed to reproduce, use for advertising. Far as they're concerned, Mr. Brody's trout ain't worth more than a rumor."

"Well," said Calhoun, "I'm sorry they feel that way."

"I'm not," said Arthur Brody. "The hell with them."

Even though their mission was accomplished, Arthur Brody said he wanted to finish out their month in the cabin on the lake, which he'd already paid for, and he hoped Calhoun, whom he'd also paid for the whole month, wouldn't mind staying with him.

"You don't need to guide me or cook for me, Stoney," said Arthur. "Hell, I can paddle a canoe. I'll take you fishing for a change. I can fry a steak and heat up a can of beans as well as the next man, for that matter. I can bear my share of the load. Anyway, I got a lot of reading to catch up on, and I want to hike through the woods, get in some solitary time. I got things on my mind I need to straighten out, and I never get much time alone back in Arizona."

"Sounds okay to me," Calhoun said.

Edwin Coffin came by the next afternoon. It was a rainy, windy, nasty cold day, and Calhoun and Arthur Brody had stayed in. They were reading and sipping coffee and enjoying the patter of rain on the cabin's roof, and when they asked the warden if he'd like to stay for supper, he said he wouldn't mind. Arthur fried some chicken that they'd bought that morning at Tiny Cartwright's store, and he boiled some potatoes and steamed half a dozen ears of corn, and Edwin proclaimed it the best meal he'd had since he visited his mother down in Bangor back in July.

They were in the middle of their second three-handed cribbage game when Coffin's two-way radio squawked. He got up from the table and took his phone out to the porch to talk in private.

When he came back in, he looked at the two of them and said, "You boys might want to come with me."

"What's up?" Calhoun said.

"Something I think you'll want to see."

So the four of them, including Ralph, piled into the warden's green SUV and drove into town.

Coffin pulled up in front of Pierre Boucher's garage. Calhoun told Ralph he'd better wait in the car, and he and Arthur Brody followed the warden around to the back door. The warden rapped on it with his knuckle, and a minute later Boucher opened up.

They all trooped into the kitchen, which had yellow linoleum on the floor and soot-smudged green paint on the walls. It smelled of fried onions and propane.

Boucher pointed into the sink. "There it is," he said. "Milly opened the post office for me so I could weighed it on her scales. She'll vouch for those scales. Fourteen pounds, fifteen ounces."

The three men stood side by side and looked. It was a very large brook trout, a female fat with roe.

"If that weight's accurate," Coffin said, "you got yourself a new world record. You aware of that, Pete?"

Pierre Boucher nodded. "Yes, sir."

Calhoun bent closer to the fish in the sink. Then he

turned to Arthur Brody. "Look." He pointed at the round white scar on the fish's back.

Arthur took a look. Then he turned to Boucher and said, "That's my fish."

"I guess it ain't," said Boucher. "It's my fish. I caught it."

"Where?" said Coffin.

Boucher jerked his head in the direction of his back door. "From the river."

"What'd she eat?"

"Big old nightcrawler. She was hanging alongside that log in the pool below the stone bridge."

"That right?" said Coffin. "Stoney, take a look at this." He lifted the fish from the sink and pointed under its chin. There were three symmetrical red gashes right below the fish's gills. "What's that look like to you?"

"Looks to me like this fish was snagged by a big grappling hook," Calhoun said. "It don't look to me like this fish was caught fair and square."

"Them marks was there when I caught that fish," said Pierre Boucher. "It ate a nightcrawler. I told you that."

"This fish lived up in the lake," said Arthur Brody. "You didn't catch her from the river here. That's a good twelve or fifteen miles from where she lived." He looked at Calhoun. "Remember, we thought we heard a motor out on the lake this morning?"

Calhoun nodded. "I reckon that was you, Mr. Boucher. You went up to the lake and you spotted Mr. Brody's trout, and you heaved out your grappling hooks and you snagged her under the chin and hauled her in, and unless I'm wrong about that, this fish don't qualify for any rod-and-reel record. Fact is—and you can correct me if I'm wrong, Warden—you broke the law catchin' and keepin' a fish you snagged this way."

Coffin nodded. "That's a fact, Stoney. Damn thing is, though, we got this here fish, which is surely a world record, and we got no witness to say how she was caught."

"I'm innocent if you can't prove me guilty," said Pierre Boucher. "Hell, I'm innocent anyway. Caught it fair and square on a nightcrawler with my old spinning rod."

"So now what?" said Calhoun to Edwin Coffin.

The warden shrugged. "I'm gonna have to do some research, see how issues like this are resolved. I got a feeling it'll end up being my judgment call."

"This man snagged my fish," said Arthur Brody. "He's lying. I caught her fair and square at the head of the lake two days ago on a Mickey Finn bucktail, and Stoney and I measured her and photographed her and revived her and let her go, and then we showed our pictures around, and next thing we know, this sono-fabitch goes up there and snags this precious fish by ramming a gang of hooks into her, and he kills her and dumps her in his kitchen sink, and that's against the law. This man should go to jail, if you ask me."

"Nobody asked you," said Boucher. "You can't prove nothing. That there is my world record trout, and I expect you to certify it for me, Edwin. That's your job."

"We'll see," said the warden.

The next day dawned cloudy, misty, warm, and still, the kind of conditions that, when they all came together, made what Calhoun called a "soft day," which he believed was ideal for fishing.

Arthur Brody said, "You go ahead, Stoney, you and Ralph. My heart's not in fishing just now."

"You sure?" Calhoun said.

Arthur smiled. "Yep. Have yourself a good day. I'll take care of dinner."

So Calhoun and Ralph piled into their Grand Lake canoe and motored up to the head of the lake, where they found some trout feeding off the surface. Calhoun lost count of the number of brook trout he caught on dry flies, but he guessed it was a couple dozen at least. The big males with their hooked jaws were all decked out in their crimson spawning colors, as bright as the leaves on the maples that grew along the shores of the lake, and the females were bursting with roe. None of Calhoun's trout came close to matching the size of Arthur Brody's giant fish, but among those he landed were three that would've gone over five pounds if he'd been able to weigh them. He put every one of them back into the lake so they could reproduce and grow bigger.

He and Ralph didn't get back to the cabin until about five o'clock in the afternoon. Arthur Brody had a vat of beef stew bubbling on the stove along with a fresh pot of coffee, and they sat out on the porch with their mugs while Calhoun recounted his day of fishing.

"You should've been there," he said.

"We'll go tomorrow," said Arthur. "It'll be fun to fish without goals. No need to catch a big fish. No need to catch anything. Just go and be there and do it with you. I've wasted too much precious fishing time in my life going after trophies. No more goals, Stoney.

I've learned that these past few weeks with you."

"Sounds like you've had yourself some kind of epiphany today," observed Calhoun.

"I guess I did," said Arthur. He nodded and smiled. "I surely did."

They were sitting there on the porch watching the sun sink behind the trees across the lake when the warden's green SUV came skidding to a stop on the gravel beside the cabin. Edwin Coffin hopped out and came over. "You two boys," he said, "I want you to come with me."

"Come sit for a while, Warden," said Arthur. "Have a mug of coffee, stay for supper. We got a nice pot of stew on the stove."

"None of that," said Coffin. "I got something to show you."

"Another damn record trout?" said Calhoun.

But the warden just turned and got back behind the wheel of his vehicle, leaving Calhoun and Arthur Brody no choice. Calhoun got in front beside Coffin. Arthur and Ralph got in back.

"What's up, Edwin?" said Calhoun. "You seem kinda pissed off, if you don't mind me saying so."

"I don't mind," said Coffin, "because it's true. You'll see."

He drove into town, took a right at the intersection, and pulled to a stop at the bottom of the hill where the Peewumptick River flowed under the stone bridge. "Follow me," he said, and he got out and started along the path that followed the river to where the big pool opened up. This was the pool, Calhoun figured, where Pierre Boucher claimed he caught Mr. Brody's trout.

Around the bend on the other side of a screen of alders they came upon half a dozen local men. Calhoun had seen each of them at the store at one time or another. They were all standing there with their hands in the pockets of their overalls as if they'd been waiting for the warden to bring Calhoun and Arthur Brody along.

Edwin Coffin walked up to the river's edge and pointed. "Take a look," he said to Calhoun and Arthur Brody.

Calhoun looked where the warden was pointing, and he saw Pierre Boucher lying belly-up like a bald, black-bearded dead fish on the bottom of the river alongside an old sunken log. A big three-pronged gang hook was jammed into the side of Boucher's neck, and a tangle of nylon fishing line was wrapped tight around his throat. A few yards downstream from Boucher's body, attached to the other end of the fishing line, was Arthur Brody's world record brook trout, also belly-up in the water.

Edwin Coffin looked from Calhoun to Brody. "What've you boys got to say for yourselves?"

"I'd say he looks dead," said Calhoun.

"Yep," said Arthur Brody. "I agree with Stoney. Drowned, it appears. Though those gang hooks in his neck could've punctured his carotid artery."

"Or maybe that line around his throat strangled him," said Calhoun.

"I can see he's dead," said Edwin Coffin, "and the police will figure out how, if they ever get here and take this business off my hands. What I'm wondering about ain't how. It's who."

"Stoney didn't do this," said Arthur, with a glance at Calhoun, "if that's what you're wondering about.

He was with me all day."

"I was actually wondering about you, sir," said the warden to Arthur Brody.

"Why would I want to murder this man?" said Arthur.

"Because he snagged your trout."

"You think I'd kill a man over a fish?"

The warden shrugged.

"Arthur was with me," Calhoun said, "just like he said. We were fishing up the lake. Had ourselves a helluva good day too, though we didn't catch any more world records."

Coffin shrugged. "Well," he said, "somebody did this, and if it wasn't one of you two . . ."

"Pierre was porkin' Gus Fleming's wife," offered one of the men in the crowd. "Everybody 'cept Gus knows it too."

"He fixed the engine on Charley Burley's tractor," somebody else said, "charged him nine hundred dollars, and when the damn thing seized up two days later, he charged Charley another eleven hundred to repair it all over again."

"Pierre Boucher has been pretty unpopular among local folks for a long time," said the warden, looking directly at Calhoun, "but up until today, nobody killed him."

"You ever read *Moby-Dick,* Edwin?" said Calhoun.

"I skimmed it," the warden said. "Long time ago, at the university. I found it kind of boring, to tell you the truth."

"Did you get to the end?"

Coffin shrugged. "If I did, it didn't stick."

"Captain Ahab has been hunting Moby-Dick, the great white whale, for a long time," Calhoun said. "Ever since he lost his leg in an encounter with the beast. Getting revenge on the whale is an obsession with him. It's all he can think about. To Ahab, the white whale is the embodiment of evil. Finding it and killing it is his whole purpose in life. It's made him crazy and cruel, and he's brought a lot of misery down on a lot of people in pursuit of his quest. In the end, Ahab tracks down Moby-Dick and harpoons him, but the harpoon rope tangles around him, and the whale drags Ahab to his death in the sea."

"Sounds like Ahab got what he deserved, then." The warden nodded slowly. "You figure that big trout did this to Pierre? Tangled him in his own line and drug him to his death, like Ahab?"

Calhoun looked down at Pierre Boucher's submerged body, with the gang hooks stuck deep in his neck and the fishing line wrapped tight around his throat, and shrugged. "Looks like a fishing accident to me."

LUCK

T. JEFFERSON PARKER

Paxton watches the river through a lodge window. Late spring, the water high and fast. He is thirty years old, the only son of a roaming father and a mother who doted, drank, and sobbed. Thus Paxton understands opportunity and need. He is handsome and often referred to as charming. When instructing skiers and seducing neglected Aspen trophy wives grew dicey, Paxton stole off to Sun Valley and taught himself to fly-fish, and when the fishing bored him he took up guiding fly-anglers, and when guiding bored him he took over management of Rolling Thunder Lodge on the East Walker in Nevada. Rolling Thunder is of, by, and for the rich. Paxton sees it as a land of milk and honey and himself as a pretender trying to find a way in, but he presents as the man in charge. He perceives in himself the need for putting down roots.

He watches more of the new guests arrive, collected at the Reno airport by Don in one of the Rolling Thunder Escalades. Paxton has asked Don to make this run for him, paid him nicely for the favor. Now Don swings out a rear passenger door and offers his hand, which goes untaken for a long beat.

Then Paxton sees her hand appear in Don's, then the flash of her blouse and the unfurling of denim and the black bounce of her hair as she steps out and lands with a light little hop and of course she's smiling. Lourdes. Lourdes of Austin. Married since their Aspen days, new last name. From around the vehicle comes the husband—hawk-faced, silver-haired, no taller than she is. He surveys her with pride of ownership. A Denver entrepreneur, Paxton knows—private security, fat on Iraq contracts. And a onetime regular at the Jerome Hotel where Lourdes once tended bar.

Paxton takes a deep breath and strides through the door to meet his new guests.

"Welcome to Rolling Thunder, Lourdes."

"John? Johnny! Honey, John Paxton, the best ski coach in all Aspen! John, this is my husband, Cole Trainer."

"Cole."

"I remember you," says Trainer.

She waits for the men to shake hands before offering her own, checking over Paxton with that generous smile. "It's good to see you again."

At cocktail hour in the dining room Paxton rises and pings a knife against his beer bottle to quiet down the spirited conversation. Elk-horn chandeliers high in the beam ceiling cast their glow over the redwood walls and redwood bar and redwood floor, all taken, according to Rolling Thunder lore, from a single Coast Redwood downed by a storm on Cape Mendocino a century ago.

"I just want to say welcome to all of you. Some of you know each other and some have just met. What we've got here is twenty great people, twenty fine anglers . . ." At this, words of protest rise toward the chandeliers, mostly a few of the women demurring, though Paxton hears Cole Trainer crack something about being lucky to catch one damned fish . . . "And of course, that means ten good teams who have paid up some good money to see who can land the biggest fish on a fly. Trout, that is. The carp in the pools don't count. Now, before we get to all the measuring and photographing and release rules, let's get the dollars straight: the teams are already good on the ante for the first five days—that's ten grand per team per day. Then it's going to double to twenty thousand per team per day for the last two days, kinda like the flip in hold 'em, which will give us a pot of nine hundred thousand dollars. You wanted winner take all so that's what you've got. It's a nice pot if everyone stays in for the whole week. It's not going to make or break anybody in this room, but it certainly ramps up the fun level on the river!"

Laughter. Paxton thinks that nine hundred grand would go a long way toward making *him* but he has spent a lifetime masking such thoughts. People like these, he knows, will hardly notice that their wagers would be his fortune. Paxton has learned that their own hale and hearty voices are all these people really hear or have ever heard. The common man is just that. Privilege has its privileges.

Paxton smiles and lifts his beer, then runs down more of the rules: ten beats on five miles of river, beats assigned by random drawing each night after dinner, beats may be traded or sold between consenting teams; barbless artificial flies fished no more than two at a time, no scents or additives of any kind; all fish to be digitally photographed while hung upon IGA-certified Boga grips that will be issued tomorrow, the scale and the fish must *both* be in the picture and the poundage clearly visible; each grip will be marked with unique designs and numbers to discourage scale substitution and other trickery; all fish caught dawn to dusk; all fish revived and released.

"But basically it's an honor system," says Paxton. "It's either that or an auditor watching over every shoulder. We're not the IRS!"

The first morning Paxton watches the Trainers on beat one, just west of the lodge. Breakfast is done, the beats have been drawn by lottery the night before, the Boga grips have been issued.

The morning is cool and breezeless and jays bicker in the stand of lodgepole pines that line this part of the river. The water is high and fast with runoff, near-record snow pack in the Eastern Sierras last season, the East Walker rushing at eight hundred cubic feet per second, the tremendous volume disguised by a smooth surface and straight runs. Where the river bends, the pools are trenched deep by time and water, and in the pools and in the heads of pools and in the tailouts lie the big fish.

The Trainers move slowly along the bank, close to each other, and Paxton, back in the trees, catches bits of their conversation. They stop at the first pool and rig up dry-droppers. Wrong choice, Paxton knows. Their voices have the eager tone of anglers getting ready. Cole holds up his terminal fly to Lourdes and she looks at it and nods and of course smiles. She pulls a dispenser of split shot from her vest and tips out some weight and drops it into his outstretched hand. Until now he had no idea she fished. In Aspen she was one of the best beginning adult skiers he'd ever taught, a tall, raven-haired, fair-skinned beauty who had glided her way into his heart with the same effortlessness with which she had learned to ski. She was single then and Paxton had used every trick in his book to interest her, but she'd seen him for what he was and found him wanting.

Cole Trainer kisses her lightly then heads upstream. He picks his way along, arms out for balance, the metal studs of his boots chirping against the rocks. He's short but wiry and athletic, and a beginner at this, Paxton sees. There is something endearing about them, he thinks: the way they can kiss eye to eye, the way he's willing to take up her sport, their expensive matching waders and boots, rods and reels. Something puzzling, too: he's twice her age, not much to look at, exhibits only moderate personality. Money? Maybe not. Paxton remembers Lourdes in Aspen tending bar at the Jerome, working hard for the tips and not wasting them on anything he could see. Guys stacked up five deep with offers for her of everything on God's earth. One of them Cole Trainer, of course. She rented a little condo year-round down in Basalt. She cooked at home most meals, drove an aging Subaru, bought her skis and boots one-year-used from a local outfitter. She was maddeningly sensible. He couldn't shake her loose with fine wines, expensive restaurants, or good blow. She'd just smile them off and turn in early so she could hit the mountain when the lifts started up the next morning.

Trainer sizes up the next pool. One of the best on the whole five miles, Paxton thinks. You can fish up through the tail-out, then about midway there's a string of big boulders that reach halfway across. Only the first three are visible from shore now, with the runoff raging down the Sierras in this unseasonably hot spring. The last rock is just underwater, a great, de-clined, moss-greased tabletop nicknamed Monster Rock and the saying here at Rolling Thunder is that there are only two kinds of anglers, those who have fallen off Monster Rock and those who are about to. Further guidelines: don't even try this pool without good studded boots and a staff and a wading belt worn tight; the bottom is stacked with boulders and sharp branches so if you go in, keep your feet in front of you and use your arms and hands to protect your head; let the current take you down and across; you'll hit the tail-out eventually; stay out of the big tangle of boulders and root balls along the west bank because it's superdeep and fast; Bill Overby got caught in there two years back, no belt, waders filled and he drowned. Nice guy, a good man.

Trainer wobbles out onto the first boulder, then the second, then he makes the third. He pokes his wading staff into the East Walker and it nearly rips it from his hand. He's only ankle deep on the rock but Paxton watches his balance come and go. He's surrounded by depth. Trainer has his arms out again for stability. His knees are bent and his weight is forward like a new skier and Paxton knows that just a little surge in the current or a little slip on the mossy rocks is all it will take to dunk the man.

Somewhat surprisingly, Trainer makes it to Monster Rock. He collapses the staff and worries it back into the sheath on his belt. Then he slowly stands up straight and brings the rod closer and unhooks the terminal fly from the line guide. He sways. Paxton thinks that he looks like a child's toy, one of those bottom-weighted dummies that always springs back upright after being kicked or hit. Trainer casts upstream but with far too much power and the flies and split-shot bolo into a gruesome tangle that lands on the swift water and streaks downriver past him.

Then, with a sharp yelp, he falls.

Paxton makes the bank and times the current and wades into the same murderous flow. He's in sandals and shorts and a light windbreaker and years ago he lifeguarded down at the Wedge in Newport and even the mighty East Walker can't touch the Wedge. Can't touch it. It is very damned cold though. He intercepts and steers Trainer downstream and sees the fear in his eyes, but he eases the little man to the bank and drags him up on the smaller boulders of the tail-out. Trainer climbs over the rocks on all fours, breathing fast and whinnying quietly. Paxton turns to see Lourdes crunching across the rocks toward them.

"Where's my rod? I lost my fuckin' rod."

After dinner Trainer finds Paxton at the bonfire. The flames throw shadows on the private security man's face, sharply divided by a curt mustache. He wears a golf shirt with his company logo on it. He has a tumbler of ice and booze of some kind. Paxton hears the boom and trill of laughter on the other side of the big fire. It's been a good day for the Swedes—Lars and Ursula Lagervist, owners of a commercial fishing fleet plying the Baltic Sea—who landed a five-pound, seven-ounce brown trout on beat nine, besting Sean and Cassy Robertson of Jackson, Wyoming. Lars's laughter booms again.

"I owe you thanks," says Trainer. "So, thanks. And I do mean it."

"You bet. I've seen it happen there before. Monster Rock. I'm glad I was close by."

"Took me an hour to thaw out."

"Water was fifty degrees this morning."

Trainer eyes the lodge manager. "Just happened by at the right time, didn't you?"

"Good luck for both of us, for sure."

"You've had some practice, happening by at the right time."

"What do you mean by that?"

"I remember you from Aspen. One of the gigolos."

Paxton and Trainer lock stares as men do.

"Every other man's a gigolo when you hit fifty," says Paxton.

"There was Jan Firestone and Deb Morse and Jennifer Donovan."

"Yes, there were. Good people. I didn't realize you were keeping such a close eye on me. Or was it on them?"

"Security. It's what I do. I know their husbands. You wouldn't last a half hour in my world."

"You barely made it five minutes in mine."

"I never make the same mistake twice."

"Good luck in the contest."

"I've got luck. But I caught squat. And Lourdes's little two-pounders won't cut it."

"You had enough luck to get the best beat today, Trainer. That's where the biggest fish are. If you draw it again in the lottery, you better make it pay. If you don't draw it, you can always buy it from a willing seller. Shitcan that stimulator fly. Put a size-sixteen Green Copper John on top and an eighteen Red Tiger Midge on bottom. Get some of those articulating midge flies made by that guide over in Mammoth makes. We sell 'em here in the shop. If you don't get grabs, switch colors. Go deep, sink-tip line, three-X fluorocarbon tippet. You've got six more days to fish."

Trainer clinks his ice and drinks. "Why the advice?"

Paxton isn't entirely sure why. Something to do with a genuine desire to offer a thing of value, something of his father's notions of romance and his mother's need to please her husband against all odds. "A wedding present to you and Lourdes."

"I know about you and her."

"There isn't much to know about me and Lourdes."

"Keep it that way."

"Take care of your wife," said Paxton. "And I'll take care of the lodge."

Trainer drinks and clinks and studies Paxton. "Thanks again. For the tips."

"Nymphs don't always work on the East Walker. Sometimes the only way to get the big pigs is with a streamer—low light, mornings and evenings when the sun is off the water. If you're not in the lead by Friday, it's time to switch out. Tell Don in the shop we talked."

"I've never fished a streamer," said Trainer.

"It can get technical," said Paxton, thinking: any idiot can fish a streamer.

"Hey, gigolo, if I win this contest on your setup, we'll split the money."

"Deal."

"You just keep the good advice coming in. And keep it between us."

Early the next morning Paxton stands before one of the lodge windows and watches the Trainer cabin.

Their matching waders hang side by side from the lacquered log wall, their matching boots wait below them, their matching rods and reels are slotted into the rod holders. Only their vests are different—olive for Lourdes and tan for Cole.

Paxton views this tableau, this outdoorsy fantasy of doing what you love with a person you love, and he knows it's partially a marketing illusion but he buys into it anyway. Completely. It just takes money and a person you love, he thinks. He would buy in if he could. He sips his coffee and indulges ideas of what he could do with his half of the Trainers' $900,000. Big Sky, maybe—not the high-end stuff but something small and warm, maybe an acre or two. He could find a woman to love in Bozeman. Or Mammoth, maybe—neat little condo, slopes to ski. Women all over. Or screw the cold altogether—rent back in Newport Beach again, out on the peninsula, lifeguard part time, no worries, man, and wall-to-wall women.

He watches Lourdes and Cole come out to the cabin deck and gear up. Of course their coffee mugs match. They sit in big rough-hewn rockers to yank on their boots. They talk unhurriedly, like old friends, though Paxton can't hear the words. Cole hands Lourdes two small boxes and a small opaque tub that Paxton recognizes as the fly containers used by the lodge shop. Lourdes cocks her head in interest. So, Paxton thinks: sometime between last night and now Trainer has prevailed on Don to supply him with sink-tip line, backing, Copper Johns, and articulating midge flies. Trainer is serious about this. From his vest he produces a spare spool and hands it to Lourdes. She begins to tie on the backing.

After the Trainers set off for beat eight Paxton waits a few minutes and follows. Again he watches them unseen, Lourdes landing small fish and Cole landing nothing, hooking nothing, his small body emanating an almost visible frustration. He shouts profanities. He sets the hook on an already vanished trout, or perhaps a twig or rock, and the line jumps into the air above him in a hurricane of tangles. More profanities. The private security man has around him an aura of razor wire.

In the early afternoon housecleaning is in the Trainer cabin. The front door is propped open by a wheeled red bucket from which a mop leans against the doorjamb. Under the guise of keeping an eye on the help Paxton enters the cabin and gives the woman a nod. He sees the still-unmade bed. He imagines the smooth beauty of Lourdes and the gristly reality of Cole and wonders that they share the same bed. This is a mystery he tries to solve but cannot. It strikes him that he will never have enough for Lourdes or any woman like Lourdes, enough of anything they need, and the money is just the beginning of what he'll never have enough of. On his way out he sees the rustic hat rack in the corner, Trainer's big Stetson on an upper stump and Lourdes's lavender lace nightie hanging by a thin strap, off center and somehow occupied.

The Swedes best their own record with a six-pound, five-ounce rainbow measuring twenty-four inches. They gloat through cocktail hour and dinner, big-toothed and blue-eyed and clearly addled by the Maker's Mark. The Robertsons of Jackson have managed a five-pound brown; the Keelers of San Diego landed one slightly heavier; a father-son team out of Michigan landed a four-pound, nine-ounce fish. But none of them matter. Lars and Ursula Lagervist pour bourbons all around and Lars tells a long joke about the agonizing humorlessness of Norwegians.

Late that night Paxton walks to the river and watches the moonlight wobble upon the currents of beat two. He senses something nearby, then he sees a shape in the darkness. A bear, he thinks. He watches and backs off a few steps, but the shape becomes Lourdes sliding down from a boulder.

"I'm glad you're not a bear," he says.

"So am I."

"Cole here?"

"Sleeping. He told me about your deal—the winning strategy for half the money."

"Is that okay with you?"

"Why wouldn't it be?"

"It's your money too."

"I'd love to see us all win. It's all in good fun."

Nine hundred thousand dollars is not good fun, thinks Paxton. He says nothing as his awareness of their present differences cascade down on him. He feels like a tiny man staring up at a towering cliff whereupon giants enact great scripts.

"Why'd you offer to help him?" she asks.

"Looked like he could use some help."

"You wouldn't believe how lucky he is."

"I might, Lourdes."

"At things he has no talent for."

"He'll need more than luck to catch some fish on this water. Spring is the toughest when the runoff is like this. You should have done the contest in November."

A moment goes by.

"How do you like running the lodge here, as opposed to giving ski lessons?"

"Steadier work. You know."

"Haven't met anyone yet?"

"Just playing. Thirty's the new twenty."

"It's not anysuch. You'd jump at the right one and you know it."

"You were the right one. I told you so."

"Not like you meant it!"

"I was quietly planning some self-improvement on your behalf."

"Maybe you shouldn't have been so darned quiet about it."

"Why him?" asked Paxton, genuinely interested and genuinely perplexed.

"It's all in the heart, Johnny. He was the last one I would have predicted, really. He's got good morals. Stubborn as a goat. He's the toughest softie there is. Never had an advantage and made himself into what he wanted to be. He'd do anything on earth for me. I don't seem to be doing him justice by talking about him. It's hard to explain. I don't really have to, do I?"

"You don't."

Paxton looks at Lourdes in the moonlight and he feels all his old affections and desires. There was a time when *he* would have done anything on earth for her, and that time had submerged years ago then breached into the present, but what was the point of doing anything on earth for someone if they didn't know you would? Why had he been so darned quiet about it? Why had he believed that she might be more drawn to his athletic grace, his charm, his looks, his fine wine and fun drugs, than to the larger fact that he loved her with all of his imperfect heart and really *would* do anything in the world for her? Except tell her.

"I always liked you, Johnny."

"I didn't know that. I liked you so much I missed it."

"I was pretty darned quiet about it myself. People like us, we hold out, you know? We wait. See, with Cole, it's a whole different thing, he forces you to react to him, one way or another. Just barges right in. He does that to the whole world. But we're okay, you and me. We're good. It's never too late to make a friend, is it?"

"It's a good thing to make a friend, Lourdes."

On the sixth day of competition, Paxton watches again through the lodge window as Lourdes and Cole emerge from their cottage with a lantern and cups of coffee, pull on their waders and boots, and fiddle with their leaders and flies. The weather has turned cold overnight and smoke faintly issues from the cabin chimney. The Trainers have a rosy glow that angers Paxton.

After they leave he wends his way to beat seven, stopping to watch and talk with the teams along the way. At beat five he watches Ursula Lagervist land and, with the help of her husband, weigh, photograph, and measure a seven-pound, eight-ounce, twenty-five-inch rainbow.

"This fish cannot be defeated," Lars insists. "We have won the competition."

"Two more days, Lars," notes Paxton.

"We will catch one still bigger," says Ursula.

"You crafty Swedes will be tough to beat!" says Paxton.

At beat seven he kneels unseen amidst the boulders behind Cole and watches the man flail away with his casts, tangle his line, curse, hook nothing. Even from this distance Paxton can see that Cole will not fool a single fish with his drifts. The line is tight, the drag pronounced, the East Walker fish far too wary to fall for a fly that bullets downstream then slows to a wake-inducing crawl for another twenty feet while it angles sharply across the current. Cole may as well be grabbing at the fish with his hands. Paxton intuits that his $450,000 has all but slipped away.

Downstream Paxton finds Lourdes and again he crouches among the rocks at the tree line and observes. She fishes like she skied—without strain. He watches her high-stick the hole, ride out the drift and lower the rod tip, let the flies rise up through the water column as the line tightens, and pop the flies once in case a trout likes a rising bug. Then she water-hauls, letting the river load the rod before she arches a roll cast that morphs into a reach cast that nicely turns over the flies and weight upstream. And again, and again, each cast finding a new slice of river.

At dusk Paxton is down in the lodge basement, working on the drag system of a failing reel. He likes this semi-hidden lair, likes the workbench and the tools and the scent of pine pitch and earth, likes the whiskey he's already had two of, likes this time of evening. It is hot outside again but cool down here in the eternal half-light.

He stands at the workbench and looks out one of the ground-level windows. And he sees first Cole, then Lourdes Trainer loping up the trail from the river toward the lodge. They are running hard and purposefully and Lourdes is smiling, of course she's smiling, and she's so beautiful it hurts. They're whooping and yipping like war party braves. Cole stumbles and rights himself and now he's smiling too.

Out on the lodge veranda the Trainers present the pictures of their fish and of the certified grip from which the fish hangs, and one nonrequired photo of the fish laid out on the bank beside a tape measure held taut in Lourdes's lovely hands.

A brown trout, deep black and honey yellow and fired through with red dots. Bulky, kype-jawed, magnificent.

Nine pounds, seven ounces.

Twenty-eight inches long.

Paxton takes his turn on the camera. His first reaction is he respects this fish. His second reaction is that he respects the person who caught it. His third reaction is that he's just made $450,000 and this slab of cold muscle has changed his life.

"It was pure luck," says Cole. "It just happened about half hour ago. I was reeling in the line for another cast and I was cussing my fool head off because I hadn't even had a grab all day and then the damned lure gets caught on a rock and I cuss even louder and yank the damned pole and guess what? The rock swims away! It goddamned swims away! And you'll like this, Johnny—I caught him on my own setup. I got sick of all that sinking fly-line and put my floatin' stuff back on. And I got rid of all those hooks and weights you had me on, and I tied on my lucky fly, it's a Royal Coachwhip or something like that, and guess what? It gets the job done. It nails that fish. What do you think of that, Gigolo John?"

Later that night around the bonfire Cole Trainer cuts Paxton off from the herd and states his case: "I thank you for all your help, Paxton. I do. But I caught that fish on my own stuff with my own methods and therefore I will not split the money with you. Doesn't mean a nice tip won't be in order. If I end up winning, I mean."

"I understand, Cole."

"I won it fair and square. On my own."

"Yes, you did. But it's not over. The Robertsons have beat one tomorrow and there are bigger fish than yours in that hole. I've seen them. I've caught them."

"Don't worry about beat one. I already bought it off the Robertsons. Cost me twenty grand but it was worth it."

"You're cagey, Cole. But let me tell you something. Don't call me what you called me tonight in front of the other guests. Do not do that again."

Trainer pauses a beat. "Naw, I won't. I'm sorry. I shouldn't have said that. Nobody likes the truth thrown in their face at cocktail hour."

But for Paxton it's too late for apologies. By midnight he's downed the rest of the whiskey and opened a new bottle. He walks to the river. He walks through the woods. He stands in the now empty dining room with the tables already set for the predawn anglers' breakfast. He feels clear, heightened, acutely sober. It isn't the money that makes his fury. It isn't that Cole Trainer has luck. It isn't that Paxton had had a grab from Lourdes in Aspen but was too busy trying to impress her to even know it and so had failed to act, opening the way for Cole Trainer to deploy his blunt forces upon her. No. What makes his fury is Trainer's rudeness, his enormous rudeness. In front of Paxton. In front of his guests. In front of Lourdes.

He takes another swallow. He can see their cabin from here, still in the night. *I always liked you, Johnny.* Paxton hears the sudden roaring in his ears, the sound of the Wedge waves breaking around him on a September south swell, the sound of dashed hope, the sound of continuing fury. It is growing. He drinks again. He can bear the thousand injuries of Cole Trainer, but his insults? These must be avenged. He must act now, for the past and present and the future, for Lourdes and for himself.

Half an hour later he stands at the basement workbench, one of Cole Trainer's wading boots clamped firmly in the vise before him, sole up, studs twinkling in minor moonlight coming through the ground-level windows. Paxton tests the firmness of the boot in the vise. The boot is firm. It moves very little as he vees the blades of the bolt cutter up against the tiny carbide cleat and clips it off. He hears it ping to the floor behind him. Then the next, and the next. Then the second boot, then the steel file and some elbow grease, get those stumps smooth, get them ready for Monster Rock. He stalks back to the Trainers' cabin under cover of the night, drunk as a pirate but quiet as a cat as he holds his breath and sets the boots back where they belong.

Paxton dreams terrible dreams, rises well before the sun, breakfasts with his guests, and later watches the Trainers head off for beat one. They walk side by side down the trail on this last day, Cole with one arm around Lourdes's waist. He angles his head toward hers to hear her better. He looks every inch the man to beat, a man with a nine-plus-pound, kype-jawed, nine-hundred-thousand-dollar fish to his credit. A man with luck. Luck enough for Monster Rock in late spring. Strands of Lourdes's black hair wobble free from her hat and catch the first unfettered sunlight coming through the trees.

Paxton fusses around the dining room, watches the cable news turned down low. A slaughter of tourists in a luxury hotel. More nuclear exhibitions by a rogue state. A deadly flu pandemic brewing. Drought and flood. War and famine. Genocide and celebrity babies.

At evening Paxton sits and waits in the shade of the veranda. He feels like a man awaiting a verdict. He can see the East Walker rolling silently by, its great tonnage disguised by its glassy surface. He leans his head back against the logs of the lodge and falls into a dream in which Lourdes sits beside him, right here on the Rolling Thunder deck, and the years have grayed her hair but her beauty is still intact. In the dream Paxton has aged too, and there is an understanding in their silence, a knowing complicity in all it has taken to get them here. They hold hands. From within the dream he hears Cole Trainer cry out and Paxton awakens.

A minute later Trainer comes slowly walking up the trail through the trees. In his arms is Lourdes, dripping river water, her legs jack-knifed over one of his forearms, her shoulders supported by the crook of his other arm, her arms dangling and her hair swaying in rhythm with his steps. Cole stumbles but catches himself. He stops amidst the trees and rears back his head and roars.

They lay Lourdes out on one of the veranda picnic tables and Paxton prepares to begin CPR, but Cole Trainer throws him against the lodge wall. "Don't touch her. I did that. I did that already."

"I'll do it again."

"You won't touch her."

"She can come back."

"Go to hell, John. Don't touch her."

Then some of the early-returned anglers are there, and one of them is a doctor from Santa Fe, and he takes over in a bluster of activity: he orders a call to 911, orders Don to fetch blankets; he checks her eyes and pulse and commences chest compressions and orders Cole to do the interval breathing for Lourdes and this goes on for five minutes and then ten. But Lourdes is utterly without sign of life. Paxton stands and watches in dull horror. The Rolling Thunder housekeeper appears at the far end of the big deck, big-eyed, crossing herself. After another five minutes the doctor stops his compressions and sets a hand on Lourdes Trainer's forehead.

"It's okay, Cole," he says softly. "We've done what we can."

Cole Trainer rises from her mouth and roars again. Paxton leans over the table, looking into Lourdes's face, one hand placed on her arm as if trying to awaken her and the other brushing across the sole of her wading boot, feeling for the studs but finding only the smooth stumps on which he had staked the beginning of his new life.

CONTRIBUTORS

Will Beall is the author of *L.A. Rex* and currently is working on its film adaptation as well as his second novel, *The Lionhunters*. He recently retired after more than ten years as a Los Angeles police officer.

C. J. Box is the best-selling author of eleven novels and he has won numerous awards, including the Edgar, the Anthony, and the Prix Calibre 38 (France). His novels have been translated into twenty-two languages. Box lives and fly-fishes in Wyoming.

Michael Connelly is the author of many best-selling books including, most recently, *The Scarecrow*. He lives in Florida.

James W. Hall is the author of sixteen novels, four books of poetry, a collection of short stories, and a collection of essays. His latest novel, *Silencer,* will be published in 2010. He lives in Boone, North Carolina.

Victoria Houston lives, writes, and fishes in northern Wisconsin. Mostly recently she published *Dead Renegade,* the tenth title in the Loon Lake Fishing Mysteries. This series is set in the Northwoods of Wisconsin against a background of fly-fishing as well as fishing for muskie, walleye, bass, and bluegill. Houston has been featured on the front page of the *Wall Street Journal* and on NPR's *Talk of the Nation.*

Melodie Johnson Howe's latest book is *The Diana Poole Stories,* about a working actress in Hollywood.

Howe says, "The short stories are about the desperate search for fame and love, which are often confused in Hollywood, and murder." She lives in Montecito, California.

John Lescroart is the creator of the Dismas Hardy/Abe Glitsky series of crime books and is a *New York Times* best-selling author of twenty novels, including, most recently, *Betrayal* and *A Plague of Secrets*. He's never had a day of fishing he didn't like. Lescroart lives in Davis, California.

T. Jefferson Parker was born in Los Angeles and has lived all his life in Southern California. He is the author of seventeen crime novels and is a three-time Edgar Award winner. When not working he enjoys fishing, hunting, and tennis. His latest book is *Iron River*.

Ridley Pearson is the nationally best-selling author of more than thirty crime and young adult novels. In 1991 he was awarded the Raymond Chandler Fulbright Fellowship in Detective Fiction at Wadham College, Oxford. He also plays bass guitar in an all-author garage band with Mitch Albom, Dave Barry, Amy Tan, and Scott Turow. Pearson lives in St. Louis, Missouri.

Dana Stabenow was born in Anchorage and raised on a seventy-five-foot fish tender in the Gulf of Alaska. She knew there was a warmer, drier job out there somewhere and found it in writing. Her first science fiction novel, *Second Star,* sank without a trace; her first crime fiction novel, *A Cold Day for Murder,* won an Edgar Award; her first thriller, *Blindfold Game*, hit the *New York Times* bestseller list; and her twenty-sixth novel and seventeenth Kate Shugak novel, *A Night Too Dark*, will be published in 2010. Stabenow lives in Homer, Alaska.

Mark T. Sullivan, formerly an investigative reporter, is the author of seven mystery and suspense novels. His novel *The Purification Ceremony* was a finalist for an Edgar Award, won the WH Smith Literary Award, was named one of the best books of the year by the *Los Angeles Times*, and has been translated into fourteen languages. An avid angler, skier, and martial artist, Sullivan is also an entrepreneur; his startup builds eco-friendly roads as an alternative to asphalt. Sullivan lives in Montana with his family and is at work on a new novel, tentatively entitled *The Eighteenth Rule*.

William G. Tapply passed away during the summer of 2009, shortly after submitting the story in this volume. During his career he wrote thirty mystery/suspense novels and a dozen books on outdoor sports, mainly fly-fishing. He was a contributing editor for *Field & Stream* and a columnist for *American Angler*. He lived with his wife and dogs on Chickadee Farm in Hancock, New Hampshire.

Spring Warren wrote *Turpentine*, winner of a Barnes & Noble Discover Great New Writers Award. She grew up in Wyoming, where she learned not only how to fish but how to tie a mean fly and stretch a fish skin over a styrofoam form.

Andrew Winer's novels are *The Color Midnight Made* and, forthcoming in 2010, *The Marriage Artist*. A recovered Hollywood scribe, Winer received his MFA in creative writing from UC Irvine and currently teaches fiction at UC Riverside. He recently received a grant from the National Endowment for the Arts.

Don Winslow is the author of thirteen novels, several short stories, and one nonfiction book. His principal claim to fame is failing to catch a single fish on four continents in a single calendar year. Winslow lives in San Diego.

Brian M. Wiprud is the award-winning author of six books, most recently *Feelers* in 2009 and *Buy Back* in 2010. He lives in sunny Brooklyn, New York, and his home waters are in the Poconos. Wiprud has written extensively for fly-fishing magazines; his Web site is www.wiprud.com.